DARK MEMORIES

Liliana undid the few buttons on the back of her dress and let the blue linen slide down her naked body.

Before her stood the off-white coffin that her parents had selected for her. She opened the lid and the smell of earth hit her nostrils. The yellowed satin had begun to gray and fray. The threadbare pillow lay crooked. The pretty lace dress her mother had selected for her lay to the side of the coffin. Bits and pieces of the convoluted lace spiked out from the dress. The light layer of dirt scattered across the bottom of the coffin clumped where her fingers had dug into the soil.

That first feeding frenzy had gripped her tightly in its spell. Sade had allowed her body to be underground too long. She had awakened famished, clawing at the satin surrounding her. At first she had thought that she still lived, that she had to reach the surface or die. After two days lying conscious in the coffin, she realized she couldn't be alive. No gasping for air. Sleep did not come to reprieve her from the insanity of being enclosed in a small space. She had to be dead, and this was possibly her eternity.

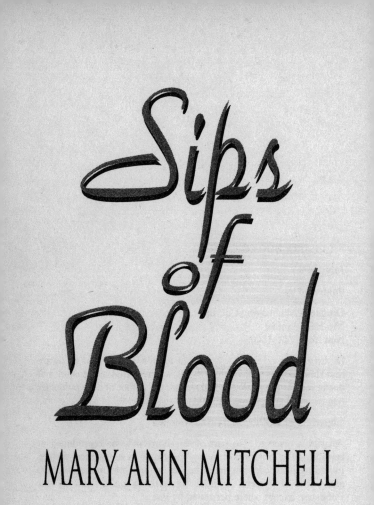

Sips of Blood

MARY ANN MITCHELL

LEISURE BOOKS NEW YORK CITY

A LEISURE BOOK®

July 1999

Published by

Dorchester Publishing Co., Inc.
276 Fifth Avenue
New York, NY 10001

ISBN 0-8439-4555-9

Printed in the United States of America.

Yes, John, there are vampires. And thank you for loving me in spite of it. Some historical facts have been altered to suit the needs of the Marquis de Sade.

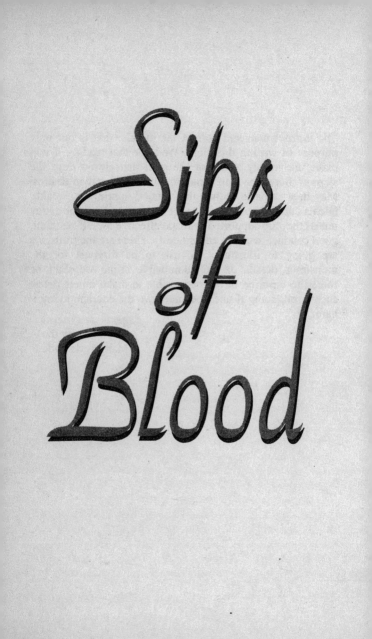

"To instruct man and correct his morals: that is our only purpose in writing this story. We hope that reading it will make one keenly aware of the peril that always dogs the steps of those who stop at nothing in satisfying their desires. May they come to realize that a good upbringing, wealth, talents and gifts of nature are likely only to lead one astray unless they are supported or made effective by self-restraint, good conduct, wisdom and modesty. These are the truths we are going to illustrate. We ask to be forgiven for the monstrous details of the abominable crime we shall be forced to describe: it is not possible to make others detest such wrongdoing if one does not have the courage to lay it bare."

Eugenie de Franval
by the
Marquis de Sade

Prologue

Nineteenth Century

The silk material tickled her flesh as she tossed the robe off her shoulders. She shivered, smiling while savoring the pleasant sensation. The paisley robe was now wide open and was draped across the crooks of her arms.

Liliana looked at her neck in the mirror and saw how pale it seemed beneath her made-up face. The milky whiteness of her neck spilled down across her shoulders and continued down her bare chest until it was shaded between her tender breasts. The points of each mound swirled into a pink sweet waiting to be plucked to attention.

Liliana hissed and bared her elongated incisors. Maybe tomorrow she would try again, but tonight she couldn't do it. He was so young—barely nineteen. His innocence gave her comfort. How could she steal it away from him and herself?

She slipped off the robe and rose from the chair. When she walked, she was aware of the suppleness and tone of her body. Each taut leg stepped before her with absolute straightness. Her abdomen lay flat, with only a hint of the dome covering her female organs. Her breasts bobbed proudly. Her upper arms showed the outlines of solid, slender biceps.

As each foot touched the earth inside the coffin, she felt her breathing become easier. The nostrils flared, the throat cleared, and the lungs softened. The years swept through her body. How long? Forty, fifty years? She did not remember how much time had passed since this quasi-life had begun. Barely seventeen, Liliana had tossed back her head playfully in front of her uncle Donatien. He took the opportunity without thinking and swallowed her young life in a passionate embrace. Now she, too, was being lured by a spirited adolescent.

Liliana bent her knees and lowered her body into the box. Upon contact with the earth, her skin crinkled as it accepted its age. The skeleton protruded slightly where joints linked. Muscles went limp.

The enticement of this lethal sleep that she sought each day settled softly throughout her body. She raised her arm, and her hand touched the yellowed satin of the coffin's lid. While pulling the lid toward her, she closed her eyes. Liliana heard the coffin snap shut. She dug her hands into the dry dirt and sighed, inhaling the sulfurous odor within the casket. Other worlds merged here. She remembered the innumerable lives she had passed in quest of her hedonistic cravings. The memories lullabied her soul. Eventually she succumbed to an ebony dream.

The next evening Stuart arrived at Liliana's home earlier than even he had planned. She waited in the living room, dressed in a pale sheer gown with a high waist that lifted her breasts brazenly above the deeply scooped neckline. Meanwhile, her caretaker and confidante invited the youth into their home.

When Stuart walked into the room, Liliana had to consciously prevent herself from rushing toward him. She wished her cheeks could flush pink as they had many years ago. There was nothing like a blush on a young girl's cheeks to seduce a male. But that gift was gone forever.

The blond curls danced around his face with each step he took. The faint hint of a mustache suggested a pretension to maturity. Across his right cheek was a purple scar caused by a wound he had received during the battle against Napoleon's forces at Waterloo. But this mark did not mar his appearance; instead it added a boldness to his features. He stopped just inside the doorway, giving her time to assess the mold of his body beneath the fitted uniform. Her eyes followed the outline of his pectorals pressed against his military jacket. In her mind she imagined the solidness of that chest, with perhaps some wisps of pale hair barely visible. His waist and hips squared off his form. The blue material of his pants flirtatiously sloped down between his thighs. She saw his right thigh tense as he resumed his step.

"I hope this is not an inconvenience, but I couldn't bear the wait. You don't know how distressing it is to be away from you."

"I know. I feel the same when I cannot be with you, Stuart."

He kissed her hand, and when he raised his head she could see his blue eyes shimmer with the delight he felt as the meaning of her words stoked his passion.

"I am looking forward to meeting your guardian this weekend. I have a special request to make of him," he said. His cheeks swelled, and his thin lips spread into a smile.

There was no guardian. Ashamed of her deceit, Liliana released her gaze from Stuart's and shyly peered down at the floor. The Persian carpet swirled into myriad colors beneath her feet. She knew each color was made up of many fine knots that no one could see unless one bothered to search under the surface. How like herself, she thought. Her fair, wrinkle-free skin and thick black hair belied the fact that she was well into her middle years. Never before had she been so conscious of her charade.

Stuart scooped her chin upward in the palm of his hand. He leaned into her body, lowered his face to hers, and kissed each of her cheeks softly. She wanted to ravage him, but she was not ready to rip away her facade as yet. Internally she burned; on the surface she melted onto a side chair.

A shiver shook Stuart's shoulders, and he moved to the fireplace. He knelt in front of the fire and used a poker to stoke the embers beneath a charred log. The fire, frenzied by his touch, soon raped the surface bark from the log. And the log yielded with a sideways jerk to the flames. He began to speak of his home in Scotland and his family. His past was hers, his dreams were memories of a life she had wished for, once. He laughed at his childhood pranks, and she giggled conspiratorially.

Suddenly, her mood changed.

"What about death?" she asked.

"Death?"

"Yes. Wasn't there ever a death? Perhaps a sister or a cousin who died young?"

"I don't want to talk about death tonight. We are both young, Lil, and should be thinking about bringing life into our world."

He stood and moved toward Liliana. Taking her hands in his, he knelt before her.

"I love you, Lil. I—"

"Are you taking me to your friend's dinner? If we don't leave now, we will be forced to remain here, and I must admit that all our cupboards are bare, so we would suffer from hunger the rest of the night."

"I already suffer a hunger, and it will not be sated by a fancy dinner," he said.

Liliana bowed her head to hide the wetness of her eyes.

She ate little at his friend's house, since food no longer nourished her body. The heavy port at the end of the meal produced a thirst within her that could not be quenched in the crowded dining room.

"It is too warm here," she said to Stuart. "May we go outside, perhaps take a walk by the lake?"

After being informed that they were leaving, the friend slapped Stuart on the back, kissed Liliana's knuckles, and scurried back to his guests. The curtness of his friend embarrassed Stuart, but Liliana's chuckle caused them both to break out in laughter.

Instead of riding in the carriage that had brought them, they walked down the hill to the lake. The path was illuminated by a full moon. In her delicately brocaded heels Liliana found her gait unsteady and therefore clung closely to Stuart's arm. She tripped, and Stuart instinctively threw his arm

13

about her waist. He withdrew it a second later when she regained her footing.

He is so afraid of offending, she thought. *It would be easier if he would seek to gain an advantage over me.*

Lilac, honeysuckle, and primrose teased their senses. The fragrances made the pair giddy. Liliana savored the youthfulness of her companion. These were years that had passed quickly for her and had abruptly ended in a delirium of blood lust. But Stuart saw her, touched her and loved her as the seventeen-year-old she had always wanted to be.

She encircled his arm with her own and pressed her shoulder against his biceps. She could feel his muscle tense through the jacket. Her bare arm reacted involuntarily and duplicated the action. At this point, Stuart took hold of her hand, which had been gripping his forearm. He held it in his until they reached the lake. Liliana settled herself down on the grass. He sat next to her, and they talked of his past.

"Why do I always tell you of my life when I really want to talk about our lives together?" said Stuart.

"Because I want to know everything about you," she responded. "I want to live your past and present with you."

"And what about the future?" he asked. "Shall we live out our futures together?"

She looked at him. Her mind jumped from the present into his future, rupturing the tenderness of his words.

"Ah! But I know so little about you," he said, confused by her silence. "The brief sketches you have given me only whet my desire to experience more of you."

Liliana yearned to possess this youth and his simplicity. But she knew that once taken, his innocence would flee. He would learn, as she had, to feign emotions. He, too, would be driven to corrupt others. She clasped her hands together tightly.

"What is this?" he said as he tried to pull apart her fingers.

"Stop it," she shouted and jumped to her feet, flinging her arms out for balance.

Liliana's beaded bag flew off her wrist and sunk into the water of the lake. She leaned forward and could see the bag lying a short distance from land but out of her reach.

"Here, let me get it," Stuart said.

Stuart undid his brass buttons and stripped off his jacket. Liliana received his jacket across her outstretched arms and pulled the cloth against the cleavage of her breasts. The moon glittered against his flesh as he stretched out his hand to reach the purse. His skin was shaded only by the outline of his ribs. His broad back flexed several times before his hand could touch the purse. It was then that she saw the swollen veins running down the inside of his forearm. The juicy fullness of these vessels seduced her, and she moved toward him. The water drenching her feet and the bottom of her dress did not distract her. She inched forward, her mouth opened wide, and a drop of saliva fell from one incisor.

"Damn," shouted Stuart as he toppled into the lake.

Liliana's body jolted as the water swallowed her treasure.

Stuart lifted himself up and stood dripping wet while holding the golden beaded bag indecorously in his right hand.

"Don't look so serious, Lil. The bag and I shall dry out soon enough." He laughed.

Her jaw ached as she closed her mouth and attempted to spread her lips into a smile.

Stuart waded onto the land and built a small fire with the dry pieces of wood, twigs, and leaves that lay abundantly around them. Liliana watched, sweeping her long nails across her lips. Eventually she sucked the middle finger of her right hand and winced when she realized she had drawn her own blood.

Stuart sat in front of the fire and placed her purse at his feet. Gently he pulled Liliana down beside him. His jacket fell from her arms onto his knees. She looked into his face and saw his irises dance with life before the flames. The whites of his eyes nestled this life in their cloudy softness. His mouth met her lips for the first time. She spread apart her lips, and he pulled away. The jacket was in his hands, and he was nervously grabbing for something in his pocket. A black velvet box appeared in the palm of his hand. He presented it to her. She opened the box. Inside was a ring whose colors under the fire's light rivaled any rainbow she had seen. However, the reflection of the diamond against her tears caused a stabbing pain inside her head.

He embraced her. The warmth of him against her cold flesh made her tremble. He held her tight against his chest. His heart pumped hard; she could feel the steady throb. The sounds of the liquid passing through its chambers roared in her ears. Liliana could even smell the succulent red corpuscles flushing to his skin's surface. She pressed her face deep into the crook of his neck, then drew her tongue across his shoulder. Suddenly she bit hard into his flesh, not to steal his blood but to stem her own

16

passion for him. She pulled her mouth away from his shoulder. The skin was bruised but not broken.

She loved him. Not simply with a physical passion in which she had taken so many other lives, but with an almost forgotten purity, gentleness, and empathy.

Liliana swept her hand across his cheek and refused the ring with a slow shake of her head.

"I absolutely forbid that my body be opened upon any pretext whatsoever. I urgently insist that it be kept a full forty-eight hours in the chamber where I shall have died, placed in a wooden coffin which shall not be nailed shut until the prescribed forty-eight hours have elapsed, at the end of which period the said coffin shall be nailed shut; during this interval a message shall be sent express to M. Le Normand, wood seller in Versailles, living at number 101, boulevard de l'Egalité, requesting him to come in his own person with a cart, to fetch my body away . . ."

Last Will and Testament,
D. A. F. Sade

Chapter One

Early Twenty-first Century

The house stood on a corner lot. A busy thorough-fare passed by on the right of the house; the other side faced a decrepit old cottage that was probably held together by chains of termites. The entrance faced a quiet street, not a dead end but near to it in the amount of traffic passing through.

A Victorian charm made the house look inviting. Curlicues and gingerbread decorations swept across the exterior. Lacy gauze curtains covered each window, except for the dormer window. Red-wine velvet curtains hung from that one. No hint of light ever shined from the top window, no flowery vase as appeared in the living-room window. But once a week, if neighbors bothered to look they would see the velvet curtains parted. Two hands would lift the window, and a third hand would quickly dispose of a blessed liquid offering that fell onto the abundant spring and summer flowers growing below. In winter the liquid would soften the layer of snow covering the ground. Year round the goddess accepted the offering.

On this night a full moon backdropped the black cat-shaped weather vane. Louis Sade had noted the sight before approaching the sage and pine wreath hanging on the front door. A thirtyish earth mother, Heloise, had brought him here to experience the old religion.

Now Louis stood in that dormer room, part of a human circle. They held hands. The earth mother's hand felt rough and strong. The woman on his other side had a softer, gentler grasp. He could hear her swallow in giant gulps as the others measured their breathing to the events of the evening. Undoubtably she was a new convert and a very young one, from what he could see. The girl appeared tender, unused, and highly susceptible. He would correct the cursory introduction that had been made by engaging her in a lengthy chat after the ritual had ended.

"Let us call the quarters," a meaty woman across from him said. "Zaira, would you perform the task?"

A spindly matronly-looking woman stepped from the circle and drew a black-handled knife from a scabbard lying low on her hip. Her green velvet robe dragged along the floor as she walked to the East. With the knife in her right hand she raised her right arm and spoke.

"Greetings unto the spirits of the East, Rulers of the Air, Gwydion, Master of Phantasy and Illusion. We call upon thee to guard our rites and protect our circle."

The lit candle before her flickered and died. Silence.

Louis smirked. If these women were really witches they would be unable to work their magic tonight, he knew. The young woman next to him seemed to stop breathing, while an octogenarian female used an altar taper to try and relight the Eastern candle.

"Zaira, please move on to the South," said the meaty woman, who was high priestess.

Holding her knife high, Zaira faced the South, and the flame on that candle immediately died. Zaira cleared her throat and spoke, while the octogenarian rushed to light the South's candle.

"Greetings unto the Guardians of the South, Rulers of Fire. Bridgit . . ."

The elderly woman had no luck in lighting the candle. She turned and shrugged in the direction of the high priestess.

"There must be a draft in here," Heloise whispered. She gripped his hand tighter.

"No draft," pronounced the high priestess. She shivered when she made eye contact with Louis.

"Does this happen often?" Louis innocently asked.

"It has never happened before," pronounced the high priestess.

"Once," Heloise interrupted. "When Penelope's cat was in the room."

The matronly-looking woman's back stiffened. She sniffed her indignation.

"Perhaps you should scabbard the knife, Penelope," Louis suggested as he saw her hand tighten around the handle.

"Zaira," Penelope answered.

"We have magic names," Heloise explained. "I

21

misspoke by using her mundane name. I'm Chris-yllis. Our high priestess is Bride, and then there's Amaranth," she said, nodding at the elderly woman, who continued trying to light the candle.

"And you, my dear?" Louis asked, turning to the young girl. Her eyes were wide, and she seemed speechless.

"She doesn't have a magic name yet. She's not initiated," said Heloise.

"So even in this room you're still called Lora." His eyes fixed on the girl's, and he rubbed the back of her hand with his thumb. She didn't pull away, but she looked frozen and incapable of moving. Wisps of short brown hair framed Lora's face, emphasizing the arched brows, the round blue eyes, the short pert nose, and the succulently thick lips, parted just enough for him to glimpse the straight white teeth. His mouth watered, and the swelling in his loins forced him to change position. He noted that Lora's nipples had hardened against the thin knitted cotton of her blouse.

"Louis." Heloise rested a hand on his arm. "The candles are relit. We're going to try again." She tugged at his sleeve until he turned to face the center of the circle.

The high priestess glared at him, and he amiably smiled back.

Gwydion was called again and the East went dark.

His smile grew broader as the high priestess' expression grew darker.

She's got me pegged, he thought.

"Why don't you call the guardians, Mr. Sade," said the high priestess.

Louis reached out for Zaira's knife and all the candles blew out.

22

"Don't give your athame to *him*." Zaira followed the high priestess's instructions and slid the knife back into its scabbard.

"Children, drunks, criminals, and the insane should never be trusted with sharp instruments. You are a sage woman." He sensed that the other women were confused, and each turned in a circle, checking each of the nonburning candles.

Finally Amaranth scurried over to the altar and took up one of the side candles.

"It will not be necessary to light the candles."

"But, Bride, shouldn't we try at least once more?"

"Amaranth, give the candle to Heloise's guest. Please light the candles, Mr. Sade."

For some reason unfathomable to Louis, the high priestess wanted a confrontation between him and the spirits. He knew she expected him to back down. Instead he took the altar candle and turned to the East.

In the East, South, and West, each candle's wick refused the flame's kiss; however, there were no other repercussions. He would complete the charade and then shrug innocently at his audience, he thought.

One last candle, in the North. Where the powers of the earth resided. He moved quickly in that direction, but found himself falling back a step, a heaviness building in his chest. He moved forward again and felt the suffocating weight of the earth pushing him down under its layers. He could not get within arm's length of the northern candle. Fear, an emotion that he had almost forgotten, tensed his body. He belonged under the earth, not above it. He should be decaying into the loam.

Bride now chanted in a Celtic tongue. He could not absorb the words; they seemed purposefully to rush by him. *To whom is that exécrable femme call-ing?* No one else said a word. The flame of the altar candle flickered. Hot wax fell onto the knuckles of his right hand. He gripped the candle too close to the flame. His hand was colder than it had ever been. The dripping wax caused practically no pain, since the hand was almost numb from frost. But he knew the room was warm. There was no chill, only the iciness of his death, which was coming for him again to recapture his condemned soul. Something hit the outside of the window, and the curtains be-hind the Northern candle shivered.

The smell of burning incense turned his stomach, but soon the fragrance was overcome by the odors of moss and clay. The earth wanted him back.

"No!" He tossed the altar candle at the window. "You can't have me!"

Bride was still chanting. He turned and saw that the other women were stunned. Amaranth sud-denly reached out a hand. He followed the direction in which she pointed and turned to see the bottom of the velvet curtains smoldering. Jagged swirls of smoke ascended, followed by the lick of flames. But no one else moved.

Louis reached out and pulled the curtain from its rod. The windowpane shattered, allowing a fireball to enter and light the North's candle.

Screams were rising behind him, but he stood his ground as a ribbon of fire circled the room.

"You *imbécile!*" he yelled at the high priestess.

And still she chanted in the Celtic tongue while the other women clustered together in the center of the room.

The black smoke from the carpet emitted a foul odor, a sickly, deathly odor of rotted souls sizzling in the depths of hell.

He would never succumb. He would survive and replicate as he always had done. The fire had cut off the exit. Black smoke clouded his vision. But he knew where the door was and rushed through the sooty fog.

"All universal moral principles are idle fantasies."

The 120 Days of Sodom,
by the
Marquis de Sade

Chapter Two

Sour, salty sweat dripped from the tip of his nose onto his protruding lips. His tongue licked the chapped and swollen flesh. The handcuffs scraped his wrists as his body jerked in fear. She dragged the flat end of the straight-edge razor down his erect penis. The dribble of his semen frightened him. His Maîtresse had forbade him to have an orgasm. But the cold steel of the blade caused a shiver of pleasure. La Maîtresse used the flat side of the blade to swat the tip of his organ. A warning!

He wanted to close his legs, protect his privates, but the bar separating his manacled ankles prevented that. Maîtresse la Présidente smoothed on more soapy suds across his loin and continued to shave his pubic hair. The delicate slide of the blade across his skin made his breath quicken.

The mirror to his right revealed the slow movements of his Maîtresse's hands. Her small white hand would set the edge of the blade against his organ and then glide the blade downward, removing foam and hair. The black votive candles burning on either side of the reflection gave the scene a surreal look. Was that Garrett Winter's penis bobbing and waving to the rhythm of La Présidente's hand? Garrett Norwell Winter III, power-hungry entrepreneur, feared by the titans of industry?

La Présidente reached for one of the black candles. She smiled up at him as she brought the candle closer to his penis. His loin, now naked of hair, looked vulnerable in the mirror. Even more so when she rubbed the side of the candle against his penis. She lifted his organ and poised the bottom of the candle atop its tip. Involuntarily he cried out as he watched the hot wax slide down the side of the candle. The wax stung the sides of his cock. The skin was unbearably stretched to the point of aching.

"Please, Maîtresse, may I now come?"

Her brown eyes glared into his own eyes, and she shook her head, denying him his release.

The safe word.

"Hyacinth," he shouted. La Présidente freed his cock and his semen spurted out, hitting the tops of her high leather boots. He would be made to lick the boots clean before he left the dungeon.

Chapter Three

The Celtic chant droned on for several minutes before silence replaced Bride's voice. And along with the chant the fire died.

Louis moved back to the doorway of the room. Smoke was settling its ash on the bodies of the five women. Bride lay before the altar, arms outstretched. The others had fallen in a pile on the center of the carpet. The searing stench of the synthetic carpet had used up the oxygen in the room, replacing it with an acrid gas. He had no doubt that the women were unconscious and perhaps close to death owing to the carpet's poisonous fumes. He should really drag each from the room and attempt to get help.

Louis sniffed. The fumes had no effect on him. He sniffed again and remembered the shattered window. Fresh air would eventually replace the repugnant odor. As he sniffed he caught the odor of something else. Coppery, ruby, young. Lora's body caught his eye. Heloise's dagger had slipped from its scabbard and Lora had, "unfortunately," fallen on it. Her wound was not deep, merely a slender cut on her right forearm. Next to her Heloise lay, slivers of glass from the windowpane embedded in her face. Blood trickled in slender rivulets down her cheeks. Louis licked his lips.

Perhaps they were already dead. Not Bride, he thought, when he heard a moan come from her corner of the room. And not Lora, whose plump breasts rose and fell in a weak but steady breath.

Could he now reenter the room without bringing down the wrath of the Northern guardians upon himself? He sniffed again. Lora's blood was rich, healthy, inviting; it was worth the chance. Louis crossed the threshold and nothing happened. The oppressive suffocating feeling was gone. He reached to his right and turned on the ceiling light. His eyesight was good in the dark, but he hadn't noticed the wall hangings: a unicorn, naked lovers entwined in each other's arms, a needlepoint pentacle surrounded by intricate needlepoints of various herbs.

Standing at least three feet high was a golden statue of Puck, looking very impish and singed. The velvet drapes lay on the floor, no longer red. Arterial red, he recalled. No. Now instead the drapes were blackened and tattered.

His blood hunger spiked and his fear withering, Louis moved closer to the cluster of women. The elderly Amaranth was still. Very still. Either she had died quickly from the fumes, or she may have suffered a heart attack in all the excitement, he thought. He felt Heloise's pulse at the neck. Her heart still pounded, and so did Zaira's. But Zaira probably had bitter blood, and Heloise's would lack the sensual thrill.

Ah! But Lora . . . Louis raised Lora's right forearm to his lips. His tongue drew a trail upward across her wound. Heady, slightly sweet, but not too. The taste full-bodied with the freshness of youth. However, in his experience he had found that the little bite of blood could vary from one part of the body to another.

Louis gently rested her arm across her abdomen. Using his hands, he worked her knit top up over her breasts. No bra. The *impétuosité* and *frivolité* of youth. The round, bulging mounds reminded him of the casks that had been kept in the cellars of his friend, Joseph de Fumel, the *propriétaire* of Chateau Haut-Brion. The wine had been beyond heavenly, even if it did need a long time in bottle to further its heavenly scent, he thought as he closed his eyes, savoring the memory and anticipating the delight he held in his hands. He leaned forward and with his tongue ringed her breasts with his spit. Finally he settled his lips on the hard nipple of her right breast and bit down. The blood flowed out in rivulets. Each suck brought a new stream. The smell of her flesh added to the delectable flavor of her blood. But the unhurried fluid motion didn't satisfy. He wanted more.

Louis raised his head and peered at Lora's face, tracing her features with two of his fingers. *"Quelle belle femme!"* His fingers roamed down her neck, then paused. A smile shaped his lips, and he bent forward. Again he smelled the odor of her flesh mixed with her blood, and it increased the closer he came to her artery. Quickly he took her, the gush of her blood causing his own breath to momentarily halt. His cock ached for fulfillment; adroitly he satisfied that urge, easing himself smoothly into her body.

By the time he left, Lora and Heloise had been drained dry. Dear Heloise, who had tried earnestly to satisfy his curiosities and who happened to be the only woman in the room able to identify and locate him.

Chapter Four

Marie stood in front of her Federalist-era stone house. It wasn't the kind of home she was used to, but she did find it charming, and she appreciated the isolation it afforded. The nearest house was two miles away and inhabited by a disgruntled old man who left her alone as long as she did the same for him. Once she had made the mistake of knocking on his door. After several seconds, a flabby man of about seventy-five had appeared.

What little white hair he had on his head stood straight up like stalgamites. What he lacked on his head was abundant on his eyebrows. Murky grayish-green eyes squinted at her. His nose was bulbous and pocked, the lips thin and heavily lined. But what shocked her was the fact that he had answered the door in a yellowish-white T-shirt and blue boxers that retained a water spot near his genitals.

"Hi. I'm Marie Masson. I've moved into the Rathbone house just—"

"Two miles away." His voice was gravelly, hoarse from disuse.

"But you do seem to be my closest neighbor." She smiled. She had dressed for visiting, with her white silk blouse and navy linen suit.

"So?"

"Well, I thought we should meet. You know, in case of an emergency."

"In an emergency it's every man *and* woman for him or herself."

Her shoes pinched a bit, but she had not expected to be standing for long. After all, a neighbor would certainly invite her in for perhaps a cup of tea or a taste of sherry.

"At least we should exchange names and telephone numbers, since we are quite cut off from other people."

"Listen, you decided to move into that old Rathbone house. Now suddenly you decide it's too lonely for you. That's your problem, not mine."

"I rather like the isolation," she indignantly replied. "But if there were any kind of emergency, it would be useful to have at least a casual acquaintanceship with—"

"Name's Keith Bridgewater. I'm not telling you my telephone number, and I ain't listed." He slammed the door, leaving Marie furiously pissed off.

Since then she had driven by the old man's house. Occasionally he sat on his front porch smoking a cob pipe and reading thick hardbacks. The temptation to stop was strong, but somehow his indelicate attire, which seemed to be the usual for him, put her off.

Just as well, she thought. *Wouldn't want to have an old man running after me.* Marie gave her age as sixty-two, but she probably could pass for ten or fifteen years younger. In her business, age seemed to give her clients more faith in her. Her bleached spun-gold hair was cut short to emphasize her delicate features. Her brown eyes were dark and penetrating with the sense that she was always in control. And her body was in pretty good shape. Not the same as when she was in her twenties and thirties, but still more zaftig than obese. The past century and a half had been good to her.

Marie tossed her foam kneel cushion on the ground. Her Blanc Double de Coubert and Frau Dagmar Hastrup roses needed trimming, while the Hansa roses needed trimming *and* love. She missed the purplish-red color of her Hansas. The buds just never bloomed completely. She had made a careful examination for aphids but found only a few. During the winter she had built mounds around the bushes and laid straw atop the mounds. The white and pink roses were doing fine; the Hansas were being disobedient.

"None of that," she said out loud. Marie knelt down and began her work.

An hour later she heard a car coming up the driveway. *Must be Louis,* she thought, *wanting to use the basement again.* The car door slammed.

"I really wish you would set up your own place. Some of the equipment is in need of replacement, and I expect you to pay half the cost."

Silence. No rants. No raves. No hissing at her purposeful derogatory statement.

Marie turned her head to view Louis. Only it wasn't Louis; instead Keith Bridgewater stood by the oak tree—dressed. Legs covered in old-man polyester pants. T-shirt hidden under a cotton earth-toned plaid shirt.

She stood.

"Mr. Bridgewater, or may I call you Keith? Certainly you should call me Marie."

"Plain Bridgewater is fine."

"And what will you call me?"

"Damn if I know. There don't seem to be any man living here. At least I never saw you drive by with any man in your car. So I don't know if you're a Miss or a Mrs. I don't like Ms."

"Oh, I'm tickled to know that you noticed me drive by your house. I kept meaning to stop, but our first encounter wasn't—"

"That's fine, keep going. Ain't asking you to stop."

"I wouldn't mind stopping, especially if you were wearing those trousers that you have on."

"I dress as is most comfortable for me on my property." He seemed to stand taller.

I could break you before you even knew I was trying, she said silently to Keith.

"Come in. I made fresh eclairs this morning, and I have some lovely imported hot chocolate." Marie moved toward the front door of the house, then stopped and looked over her shoulder. "Unless you'd prefer an expensive French cognac."

"Don't drink hard liquor. Have a beer once in a while."

How sophisticated. "Out of beer, Mr. Bridgewater."

"That's okay. I'm here to let you know my son's coming to visit me."

"How wonderful for you!"

"No it ain't. He's a pest. Wants to check up on how I'm doing."

"That is considerate."

36

"Wants to put me in some old-age home and sell the land."

"He said that?"

"I've known him all his twenty-seven years. I can read his mind."

"Your wife?"

"Dead. Died giving birth to the shit."

"I'm certainly glad you dropped by to tell me the latest news. If there's anything I can do—"

"There is."

Marie's gut knotted.

"See, he thinks I have friends."

"And you and I . . ."

He nodded.

"I'd be delighted to be your friend. However, since we are such old buddies, I must insist you come in for some hot chocolate, *dear*."

She saw Keith wince. *I dare you to correct me*. He didn't. She threw open the antique oak door and invited him in with a crook of her finger.

"If the eclairs are too rich for you, I have some angel food cake."

"Nothing wrong with my stomach."

"Good."

Chapter Five .

Louis had stopped at a pet shop, where he had selected a beautiful white rabbit. The animal was plump and healthy.

"I'll take it," he had said.

"I have to warn you, sir, he has a nasty temper and has nipped several people."

No problem, Louis thought, *Liliana can be far nastier when hungry.*

His niece, Liliana, had sworn off human blood ever since she had fallen for the British *espèce de crétin* Stuart. Melodramatic, he thought. He couldn't understand her constant whining about lost youth, when she would forever look seventeen. And she would never have babies. She would never have brats that would keep her locked away in an insane asylum, as he had had.

Suddenly the Jaguar was filled with an offensive odor.

"*Alors!* You were too well-fed. You'll have to sit in it until we get home, Monsieur Lapin de Garenne."

In answer there was a steady beating against the walls of the animal carrier.

"Ah, Liliana, obviously I would do anything to see you happy again. However, mortality cannot be my gift to you. Instead I gave you eternal life and received tears from you in return.

"*Lapin*, is that fair? If I were to give you eternal life . . ."

A loud fart came from the carrier.

"*Jamais!* Never! If Liliana does not suck you dry, I shall make a stew of you."

The cup slipped from her fingers and crashed into pieces against the porcelain of the sink. Liliana's hands shook. She needed fresh blood. The blood extracted from cadavers kept her going for only a short while.

Three years before, she had gotten a job near the city at an embalming company that serviced several funeral homes. She would position a dead body on the embalming table so that the blood would flow into the gutters that ringed the table. From there the blood would drip into pails. Most times she worked alone, but when another worker was present she would have to take great care to save the blood before someone could dispose of it. The blood was not rich in the nutrients she needed but did afford some assistance in staving off starvation.

Slowly she picked up the jagged pieces of china. Lennox. Relatively new and simple. Too simple for her uncle Donatien, who preferred the ornate and antique.

She dropped the pieces of china into the garbage.

"Ma petite!"

"In the kitchen, Uncle Donatien!"

"My precious pet," said Louis as he entered the room with arms outstretched.

Liliana tolerated the hug and the un-uncle-like kiss Louis persisted in giving.

He sniffed the air.

"Blood. Sour, bitter blood. Have you been drinking that horrid filth again?"

"I brought some home from work and just had a cup of it."

"Yech! Did you store that garbage in our cooler?"

"Yes, I put the leftovers in the refrigerator. I don't want to argue over it, Uncle."

"Dead blood in our home, among our vittles."

"Uncle, we're dead."

"Mais non. Dead is when you putrefy and disappear into dust. We, child, thrive in the arms of immortality."

"We can be destroyed."

"Ah, a sin."

"A reality check, Uncle."

"And here I have brought home a gift for you. Something at least better than that awful stuff you steal from work. Work!"

"I work to feed myself. I can't manage to get enough animal blood to satisfy my appetite."

"Of course not, animal blood is thin. It lacks the richness of warm fresh human blood."

"No, Uncle, I'm not returning to feed on others like ourselves."

"You compare us to these mortal wimps that cross our paths?"

Liliana started for the doorway.

"Wait! I've brought you something alive."

"And probably small and cuddly."

"You get pleasure drinking from those horrid rats?"

Liliana shrugged and faced her uncle. "What did you bring home?"

"It needs to be cleaned up a bit. I was going to bathe him before delivering him to you."

"You caught something in the wild?"

"No, it has the . . . la *chiasse*."

"Dysentery! It must be ill. Where is it?"

"Not *malade*, more like ill-tempered. He's in the animal carrier in my car."

Liliana hurried out to retrieve the animal and was delighted and left breathless when she opened the carrier.

While being washed in the bathtub, the rabbit managed to take more than a nibble from one of Liliana's fingers. Her cry brought the sound of her uncle's French curses to her ears. Eventually the rabbit was cleaned and bundled in a natural Egyptian cotton towel and taken to be reacquainted with Louis.

"He is adorable. There's no way I can take his life."

"If you don't, I'll throw him live into a stew pot."

"You wouldn't dare!"

Donatien Alphonse François de Sade rose nobly from the feather cushion of the couch and walked over to where his niece stood.

"Please, child, you refuse the charming men I have brought home for you. At least accept this small token of my love.

"Your skin was once so soft. Now it is papery thin, and blotched from the many years of famine." He touched her cheek and slid the back of his fingers across her lips. "My favorite little girl."

During these awkward moments Liliana was glad

that she looked wasted to her uncle. She believed it was the only thing that saved her from his incestuous desire.

"Did you see Grandmother today?"

Her uncle shook his head and stepped closer. She was sure he would have taken her in his arms, except that the rabbit let out a loud and smelly fart.

"Mais non!" Louis quickly backed away. "I have not seen her in a couple of days, but she is fine. She always gets her way, why shouldn't she be fine?"

"Grandmother deals in a very dangerous business."

"Dangerous only for her customers. She is Maîtresse la Présidente. The finest dominatrix on the East Coast of the United States. Now, on the West Coast—"

"Please, I worry about her. After all, she is my grandmother and your mother-in-law. What if someone realizes what she is? Don't you feel any responsibility? You're the one who made her a vampire."

"She demanded to be made what she is. As for me, I had no choice. If I had refused, she would have left me in the Bastille for the rabble to tear apart.

"Ah, but you, my child, I made out of love."

Lust, Liliana silently corrected.

"I'm putting François in the hutch in the backyard with some food, and then I'm going to rest for a while."

"But it is night."

"I didn't have a chance to rest during the day. There was a lot of work to do. I had several autopsied bodies to work on and had to use the six-point injection. It's always more time-consuming for me when I have to drain the blood into the body cavity and then use a trocar to drain the chest of blood, making sure I don't lose any for my personal use."

"If you were not speaking of cadavers, you would be making me hungry."

"No kind of sensation is keener and more active than that of pain; its impressions are unmistakable."

The 120 Days of Sodom,
by the
Marquis de Sade

Chapter Six

Garrett swooned in the ecstasy of the bloodletting. That La Maîtresse deigned to feed from him elevated the thrill. His own orgasms did not have the power of her bloodsucking kisses.

Softly he felt her delicate breaths on his neck, felt the sting of the punctures and the moist exquisite movement of her lips.

He raised his body up into La Maîtresse's kiss, and she responded by tightening the clamp on his right nipple. The dark pink gag muffled his cry. Her long black fingernails traced a path down to his loin, and he found himself spreading his legs wider, praying for her touch to caress his manhood. Her fingernails danced circles around his cock, causing a pleasurable ache.

Garrett moaned and rubbed his tongue against the muslin material of the gag. His parched mouth, his neck wet with blood and spit, and his cock damp from the dribble of urgency combined to persuade him that the ecstasy must never end. Never cease to satisfy Maîtresse la Présidente, he told himself, for her pleasure increased his own fourfold.

He was fighting the end, resisting the inevitable release that he yearned for.

The nylon rope tying his hands behind his back limited his freedom, reminded him that he must hold back, allow the pleasure to go on and on. He fought himself and the rope.

Suddenly the knot on the rope gave way and his arms swung out from behind his back, laying out La Maîtresse in a bloody, disheveled heap.

Chapter Seven

Liliana hurried up the stone steps into her grandmother's arms.

"You are so pretty today, my little one."

"Grandmother, why are you tying and untying that rope around the rail?" As Liliana spoke she picked up the book her grandmother had been reading. *The Ashley Book of Knots*. She looked down on the stone porch floor and saw *The Klutz Book of Knots* and *The Boy Scout Fieldbook*. "Homework?"

"Thank heavens we vampires heal quickly."

"Grandmother, are you all right? What happened?"

"An accident caught me in the jaw, but my slave paid dearly for the mishap."

"I wish you would give up this brutal way of obtaining blood."

"There is no way to avoid brutality when we feed. You, my child, have chosen to limit your hunger to

47

small animals, but is it any less brutal than what I do? My victims simply have slightly higher intelligence quotients." She paused. "Sometimes. However, what about the dead that you feed upon? It is disgusting and unhealthy, child. Do I proselytize to you about that?"

"You try, Grandmother."

"Yes, but damn it, it hasn't taken hold. My business is blooming. You could assist me. No sex. Simply tie up, beat, and drain a few of my customers. It would allow me more time for my favorites."

Attempting to change the topic, Liliana asked about the T-shaped bench at the far end of the porch.

"It's an Eton bench that your uncle brought over. He wants to store it in my dungeon. I left it here out on the porch because I have no idea where it's been nor who has been enjoying their pleasures on it. Knowing your uncle Donatien, probably some cheap strumpets."

Liliana turned away from her grandmother to smile. Her grandmother was intolerant of most things Uncle Donatien did. *Perhaps with good reason*, she thought, remembering her childhood and the stories she had heard about her uncle, the Marquis de Sade.

A dusty gold Cadillac of 1960s vintage pulled into the driveway. Liliana did not recognize the man behind the wheel and feared that she had interrupted her grandmother's workday. A sloppy man in his seventies got out of the car.

"My dear, I didn't expect a visit from you today," her grandmother called.

"He's here," the man gruffly pronounced.

"Ah, your son. Liliana, this is Keith Bridgewater, *a close friend*."

The man grunted.

"And this is my granddaughter, Liliana. Keith's son has come to spend some time with his father. And we're both very excited about it." Marie flashed a smile at the man, who grudgingly nodded.

"How long is your son going to be staying, Mr. Bridgewater?" asked Liliana.

"Too long, probably."

"Keith has a wonderful sense of humor. Come up on the porch and sit for a while."

Slowly he climbed the steps. Reluctant to look at the women, he studied the ground instead. Once he was on the porch, his interest seemed piqued.

"What are you doing, studying about knots?"

"Oh, I wish I could share my interest with you, Keith." Marie reached out a hand to touch his face, and he backed away.

"I need to take a leak. Mind if I use your bathroom?" he asked.

"You know where it is, *dear*."

He sighed and twisted around, almost knocking Liliana over, but she quickly got out of the way.

Once he was inside the house, Liliana turned to her grandmother.

"You must know him well to let him go into your house alone."

"If I hadn't let him use the bathroom immediately, I'm sure he would have pulled it out and pissed from the porch."

"Grandmother, is he a beau?"

"Him! Child, he is in his mid-seventies, and not terribly well-kept at that."

"A client, then."

"No. Although I do have fun working my wiles on him. It's so different to be able to torture a man with kindness. Come in, let's have a little fun."

Liliana opened her mouth to say she couldn't stay, but her grandmother pulled her into the house.

The entry hall did not reflect her grandmother's taste. Black-and-white earthenware tiles covered the floor. Marie believed only in marble. The walls were covered with tiresome still lifes, some done by famous artists, but her grandmother favored portraits of nobility, especially those she had personally known. To the right was an American Revolutionary-era side table. Antique to most, considered contemporary by her grandmother, and not very well made at that.

Liliana wondered why her grandmother had never bothered to redecorate the entry; after all, she had lived there for the past five years. She knew that for her grandmother the house was temporary, to be lived in only briefly while Paris had time to forget the *madame* with the penchant for blood.

The salon had been altered. A portrait of Marie Antoinette stood above the fireplace mantel. Grandmother had met the queen only once, but she spoke of her as an old friend. The furnishings were Louis XVI, from the jewel casket that had been designed for the Dauphine to the writing desk covered with Sèvres porcelain. When she was fleeing Paris, she could not leave these objects behind, even though the French police had begun to take an interest in her activities. Grandmother had delayed her departure several weeks while she supervised the packing and removal of her favorite furnishings.

"Sit down, child, while I go fetch Keith a beer."

"A beer?"

"His favorite: a Schlitz."

"Oh." Liliana sat down on the green velvet sofa and waited for the show.

Bridgewater came into the room while still zipping up. When he saw Liliana, he immediately dropped his hands to his sides and rubbed his thighs.

"Fancy home your grandma has here."

"Yes, she's collected the furniture over many years."

"I bet. They real or reproductions?"

"Real."

Marie swept into the room holding a can of Schlitz in one hand and a beer mug in the other. She handed both to Keith.

"Don't need the mug." He snatched the beer from her hand.

"I should have known."

"I hope I'm not intruding on your visit, Mr. Bridgewater," said Liliana.

"Hell, no. Makes no difference to me." He plopped down in a chair once owned by Charles VI. Liliana noted how inappropriate he looked.

Marie seated herself next to her granddaughter.

"Aren't you two going to have beers?"

"Our tastes are a bit more refined, Keith."

"Nothing like a good beer. My dad loved the stuff so much, he used to joke about wanting to be fed beer up until the last, even if it was intravenously."

Marie screwed up her face. "Glad I never ran into your father."

He charged into the reason for his visit. "I'd like to bring my son over for a visit. Prove I've got a friend. He's a little peculiar. Lives in Greenwich Village in the city." He lowered his voice. "Into leather and piercings, that kind of thing."

"Really." Liliana noted how her grandmother's voice had brightened up.

"But don't mention the earring. He's also got

51

rings stuck in his nipples. God, I don't want to know where else he may have them."

"I would."

"Huh?"

"Grandmother said that she would never bring it up in conversation." Liliana noticed that her grandmother had kicked off her shoes and was rubbing the sole of her right foot against the base of the table separating them from Bridgewater.

"So when can he come over?" Marie asked eagerly.

Chapter Eight

De Sade's housekeeper, Matilda, had a daughter. A very pretty—no, beautiful—daughter, with blond ringlets floating down upon her shoulders and blue almond-shaped eyes. Long lashes naturally darker than her hair. A nose slender and pert. Full lips tinged a tomato red and teeth even, straight, and bright. Skin fair, clear, and he'd be willing to bet her flesh was soft and smooth. A body curved with luscious baby fat invited his touch. A student of dancing, she stood tall, although she was only five-six.

"Has Mom invited you to the recital?"

"Not yet. When will it be?"

"In two weeks. I'll be sure to get an invitation out to you."

"And I'll be sure I'm there, *ma petite*."

Matilda did not live on the premises, and she was limited to the public areas of the house. She kept the ground floor clean and ran errands during the day. The sun did not prevent Louis from leaving the house, but sometimes the languor that set in during the daylight hours slowed him down. Certainly he didn't want to waste energy on the mundane when the lower classes were eager for work.

Infrequently the housekeeper would bring her daughter.

"Cecilia, we'd better go now. Your father will be home soon."

Matilda never allowed her daughter more than a few words with Louis, explaining that she didn't want Cecilia to be an annoyance. But Louis knew better than that. She simply didn't trust Sade. On the other hand, Sade did everything in his power to spend time with the seventeen-year-old.

"Perhaps you could have a role in one of my plays," Sade offered the wide-eyed girl.

"You write plays?"

"*Oui,* and quite a few have been produced."

"Where? In New York City?"

"In France."

"Paris?" she breathlessly asked.

He neglected to tell the girl that the plays had been produced at the Charenton insane asylum.

"At the Comédie-Francaise." He had submitted there twice, and only their lack of perspicaciousness had prevented them from producing the plays.

"I'm sorry, sir. Cecelia, didn't I ask you to come along five minutes ago?"

"Obey your mother and run along." He almost reached out a hand to touch the girl's cheek, but he was aware of the mother's intent observation.

He watched the girl leave. Her high, tight, round bottom quickly slipped away from his view. He was tempted to see her to the car, except the mother might become too suspicious. He meant to have the girl and wanted to be sure to keep his channel of communication open to her.

His full head of hair was almost white. At least he had hair, unlike her father, who had but a fringe. Louis Sade was sophisticated. He could talk about anything, and she'd even bet he'd been everywhere. He used his slender body to magnetize a room. His speech had only a slight accent. Oh, but she loved the occasional French word he would drop into a sentence. His features were noble and warm. The few lines his face possessed instilled confidence in her that he had and could still wield terrific powers. His eyes seemed to contain a chuckle, especially when he looked at her.

Cecelia turned her head to look at her mother, who was driving the old Ford home. He had a Jaguar and even a Rolls Royce and a Harley motorcycle. Once she had seen him riding the Harley. He was returning from a vacation in the city. If only her mother hadn't rushed her off before she could ask him where he had stayed, what he had seen, to whom he had spoken, what and where he had eaten. *Shit!*

"What's the scowl for?"

The sound of her mother's voice made Cecelia's body jolt.

"You lost in your own world again?"

Cecelia shrugged.

"I wish you wouldn't talk to Mr. Sade."

"He likes me."

"He's much too old to like you."

"What does that mean? I can only talk to nerds like seventeen-year-old Joey?"

"You used to like Joey before you met Mr. Sade."

"Joey's okay for a movie and a pizza."

"Mr. Sade is old enough to be your father. You and he could have nothing in common."

"He writes plays and has had them produced in Paris at the . . ." *The French what?* "At a big playhouse. And he said . . ." Cecelia decided not to share his offer of putting her into one of his plays. "That they were very well accepted. Matter of fact, he was a sensation in all of France."

"He said that?"

"Yup." Cecelia rested her back against the seat and smiled.

They'd walk arm and arm down the Champs Élysées, the paparazzi sneaking shots for the world newspapers and magazines, the starstruck begging for autographs. She sighed.

Joey and she had had sex a handful of times, and they were getting good at it. When one would learn of a new position they would try it together. She was supple. Maybe she could surprise Louis Sade with the knowledge and ability she had.

"Uncertain of the torture, he pictures it in a thousand forms, one more frightful than the other; the least noise he hears may be that of his approaching assassins . . ."

Justine,
by the
Marquis de Sade

Chapter Nine

La Maîtresse had torn a piece of cloth from his white oxford shirt to use as a blindfold. He remembered the viciousness in her eyes and the strength in her hands. She had already chained his nude body to the gray cement wall, preventing him from stopping her.

Now he felt the coldness of the wall, the bite of the manacles, the heaviness of the chains, and the smell of freshly oiled leather. Blindfolded, he could not see but heard and experienced the breeze caused by the whip's sharp crack as it passed near him. Which whip had she chosen?

There were the bullwhips and blacksnake whips, but he had never seen her use one of those. Her favorite had always been the signal whip, used in the vanilla world to command dogsled teams. She had frequently whipped him into following her commands.

He felt the splash of the whip across the tops of his feet.

Silence. Stillness. Was he alone? Had she only meant to tease him? The passage of time continued. No breath except his own, which seemed more ragged. No gusts hinting at movement. Silence. Stillness.

Would she leave him in the dungeon alone, and if so, for how long? Would he be able to count the time in minutes, hours, days?

"Maîtresse," he called.

Silence. No answering lash for crying out. Silence.

The minutes passed. Did he smell something in the air? His own sweat heavy with fear. The drops of salty sweat languidly moved down his features, occasionally settling into a furrow where it would build until the sweat overflowed and continued its progress down to his chin.

Sweat gliding down his chest, matting his hair, tickling the flesh covering his ribs.

"Maîtresse!" This time he screamed.

Silence.

"Give me a taste of the whip, but don't leave me alone," he shouted.

Silence.

He pulled on the chains. He attempted to slip his hands and feet out of the manacles. Useless effort.

What was the time? He had to get home to his family by nine. He was expected to have dinner with his wife and teenage children.

"Maîtresse."

He was disoriented. Did he face the door? Was he even in the dungeon or in the midst of a nightmare?

Silence. Stillness.

His skin tingled. Prickly nerves searching, desiring the touch of leather, the kiss of pain.

Silence.

His arms and legs spasmed, jerked in the enforced tension of the confinement.

"Maîtresse!"

Quiet. His fingers touched the palms of his hands, grabbing for something solid. He threw his back against the wall. He was sobbing. His right foot slipped in sweat, but he couldn't fall, he couldn't move; fixed to the darkness of his world.

He breathed furiously fast. Too shallow. Not enough time to take in air. Not enough oxygen to feed his lungs.

A smell. A sound. The crackling of burning paper; the ash of paper. Something more. Cloth. His clothes! No, no, she wouldn't do that. The ripping of cloth to fuel the flames.

"Maîtresse!"

A rod fell to the floor. Metal, heavy.

Oh my God! Don't brand me, please.

They had discussed branding. Ornate letters marking him as hers. She had shown him the branding iron. It had looked used.

Heat singed the hair on his chest but never touched the flesh. The odor of burnt hair, his hair. Then the heat was gone.

Where would she choose to brand him? He heard the rattle of metal against metal. The iron being reheated.

A hiss and a spit.

A gloved hand touched his cock. The sting of alcohol from damp cotton.

"No!" he screamed.

The release of the whip bit his flesh.

"More!"

Chapter Ten

Marie looked forward to meeting Keith's son, Wilbur. Not a very promising name, but that decision had been in the hands of his father.

Another fifteen minutes and they would arrive. She had made her love cocktail, complete with rose leaves, white sugar, Grand Marnier, white wine, and rosé champagne. And for Dad there was the Schlitz.

Her dress was cut low, her heels high, and her jewelry came from the safe. Designed by the jewelers Böhmer and Bassenge, the necklace contained five hundred and forty diamonds. So expensive that Marie Antoinette had refused it when her husband offered to purchase the necklace for her. But Marie-Madeleine Masson de Plissay hadn't had to pay for it. Instead she offered Bassenge his life in return for the gift of the necklace. Later she would suck his life to seek revenge for a copy that he was making.

She heard Keith's dusty car pull up in front of the house. Early, but she was ready. The car doors slammed. She counted the seconds. The doorbell rang.

Slowly she walked to the hall, sucked in her belly, and threw the door open.

Stunned either by her necklace or the amount of cleavage, Keith said nothing. Behind him stood a tall young man, six-two, six-three, she judged. His black hair brushed the shoulders of his meticulously made charcoal suit. Stylish, natural fiber. A good sign. His features were strong: well-defined cheekbones, eyes the color of coal, nose pronounced, and lips filled out with a smile. *Charming*.

"Wil Bridgewater." The young man nodded and switched a decorative cane to his left hand so that he could extend his right hand. She felt the heat of his hand in hers. The flesh was softer than she had expected, unused to manual labor.

"My father likes to call me Willful." His teeth brightened his knavish face.

"I love willful men," she replied, waving the two men into her house.

"I never had that impression," Keith grunted and moved to the salon, where he seated himself in his favorite Charles VI chair.

The son allowed her to lead the way. The heat of his body made her dead flesh sizzle.

"Sit down on the sofa, Wil. I'll go get some refreshments."

"We can't stay long," Dad interrupted.

"You've just arrived." She heard the edge in her own voice.

"And we have nowhere else to be," Wil said,

crossing the room to the velvet sofa. He twirled his cane once before setting it down against the sofa's bulky rounded arm. His lissome body filled the room with the scent of salty-sweet blood.

Could he be pliant enough to earn a trip to the dungeon?

"Damn, can't you ever keep your mouth shut, boy?"

Marie had almost forgotten Keith.

"I have lots of Schlitz . . ." She glanced at the son. Certainly the father had done nothing to deserve endearments. "Keith."

"At least that's better than that deary stuff."

"Oh, is there something you forgot to tell me, Dad?" He winked at his father and turned a crooked smile on Marie.

"God forbid. I'll be back in a minute."

Marie's mouth salivated while she poured the love cocktail into two champagne glasses. Her fangs ached and her hand shook while lifting the Schlitz. Keith would not prevent her from having his son.

Wil had already seated himself on the sofa when she returned. First she brought the Schlitz to Keith. The stench of the old man's blood turned her stomach. But a fresh kill might ease Liliana back into the fold, if Liliana believed the death was accidental. She placed the tray on a side table and approached Wil with the glasses. The old man was brittle, an easy kill, a twist to the neck and . . . But with the father gone, would the son stay?

"Did you grow up in this town, Wil?" she asked as she passed one of the glasses to him.

"Yes. Hated it. Couldn't wait to leave. Even ran away a few times before I turned eighteen. On my eighteenth birthday I was out the door."

"Pimping. I found him in Greenwich Village pimping other young boys. At eighteen he moved in with a queen, and I'm not talking royalty. Disgusted, I let him be." Keith swallowed a gulp of the beer.

"I apologize for my father. He doesn't understand how to act in polite company."

"Don't apologize." Cautiously she reached out and touched Wil's arm. Solid muscle. "Your father and I are . . ." There was a moment's hesitation. "Old friends."

"I take it that you'd never move back here." Her fingers still pressed against his arm, she allowed herself the joy of tightening her hold.

Wil winced and turned his head to face her. Immediately she withdrew her hand.

"No, never."

She saw the hint of a bruise on his neck. A human bite, it had not drawn any of his precious blood. A faded scar on his left jaw fascinated Marie. She ran her thumb across the whiteness of the scar.

"How did you get this?"

"Sex play gone awry," he answered truthfully.

"A true professional would leave only desired scarification. Never a mark left in error."

"I was young."

"And now you are old?" She laughed, and caressed his cheek in the palm of her hand.

"You're a dirty old lady," Keith spit out.

Marie did not remove her hand from Wil's cheek.

"We all have a calling and are driven to sate our secret desires whenever we can. Some like the lick of the whip; others like to apply the taste of leather."

"I'm getting the hell out of here. Wilbur," Keith called.

Marie easily held the son with her eyes. Her fingers slid down to undo his tie. As the tie came free, she grabbed each end of the material and drew it tightly around Wil's neck. His breath caught. She loosened the hold and removed the tie from his shoulders. Using two fingers, she flicked the buttons open on the oxford shirt. Fine thin cuts crisscrossed his chest. He had recently made love. She yanked the shirt out of his pants to reveal the jagged loops that pierced his nipples. Not smooth rings, but crenulate gold pierced his skin. She slid her pinkies into the loops and pulled gently at first, then more forcefully, watching his eyes take on a glassy look of desire. His tongue wet his lips. Her pinkies left the loops to wonder down to the zipper of his pants.

"Christ! What are the two of you doing?" screamed Keith, who reached over to separate them.

A burning fire of anger rushed up her chest and she lashed out, knocking Keith to the floor. He fell short of the stone fireplace, hitting his head instead on the cushiony softness of the Aubusson rug.

"Dad!" Wil yelled. He stood and then dropped to his knees beside his father.

"Wil?" Marie softly said.

"Dad, take it easy. Try to catch your breath."

Ignoring the panting old man on the floor, Marie stood and put a firm hand on Wil's ebony hair. She clutched a handful of hair and drew his head back so that he was looking up at her.

"Come back without the old fart."

"What does one want when one is engaged in the sexual act? That everything around you give you its utter attention, think only of you, care only for you . . . every man wants to be a tyrant when he fornicates."

Philosophy in the Bedroom,
by the
Marquis de Sade

Chapter Eleven

La Maîtresse beat him long enough to draw blood. Her tongue caught the rivulets in strong lapping motions. Garrett had never seen La Maîtresse so impatient, so out of control. Her hands shook with the intensity of her emotion. Her glazed eyes looked beyond him. Could she even hear him?

A wail issued from her throat as she beat him with a strength far beyond her size. Garrett's eyes watered, not from pain, no, he knew there was someone else in her mind. A vision of another slave. Someone had managed to take control of La Maîtresse.

"Stop!" he shouted.

Not the safe word, but Maîtresse dropped the whip and slowly backed away from him. Her eyes focused, a hiss came out in a spray of saliva, and the blood on her lower lip hardened into a brown stain. The black corset she wore suddenly seemed too tight for her body, too confining for the energy that pumped her breasts into a spillage of flesh.

"Shut up, you piece of shit!" Her voice cracked.

He watched her grasp for control, but it kept slipping away.

"You are not worthy to speak to me, not even in a whisper. You're just shit that I wipe from my shoe. You're a turd from the bowels of the devil."

Maîtresse reached up and ripped away the material covering her breasts. Balanced on spiked heels, she slowly walked toward him. The shower of spit that hit his face caused him to close his eyes. Roughly she blindfolded him with the material in her hands. Edged in black lace, the material felt scratchy. But not warm. Not body temperature as he had expected. Indeed, her touch never heated his skin. Cold, chilling, icy, and yet the cool hand that caressed his face drove his body into desire. He could feel the erection. She withdrew her hand.

"Tell me a story. Tell me your secrets. When you're in the midst of fucking your mate, what drives you? Certainly not the insipid stench of her pussy. Nor the angular shape of her body. What is it you see, hear, and feel inside your head? Tell me, you weak ass!"

"The touch of leather splitting my skin. The whistling of the whip as it seethes through the air before striking me. I see you training me, guiding me, helping me to find my true pleasure in serving you. Please don't be angry because I envied another."

"Another?" she asked.

"God, I'm so sorry," he shouted. "I coveted your touch and attention, and I'm not worthy of either."

The whip cracked in the air, and he felt the strands cross his flesh. But the power no longer fed the sting. The pain paled in comparison to the earlier blows.

I must win her back. I must prove my worth as a total slave.

Chapter Twelve

Exhausted, she rolled onto her back. Cecelia always slept deeply after masturbating. *The deep, dark sleep of sinners*. She smiled. "Dirty old man," she muttered, remembering the fantasy she had had of her mother's employer.

The top sheet and blanket had been kicked to the floor, but she was too sated to retrieve them. She'd be cold later on when the sexual glow wore off.

Cecelia rolled onto her left side onto a puddle of her own juices and stared at the sheet and blanket. Languidly she reached out her hand. Useless, she knew. She would have to get out of bed to collect the linen.

She sighed and resigned herself to a frigid wake-up call.

*   *   *

Sade hungered for blood. The need to feed gnawed at his body, causing him to move along the street with a predator's gait.

Je meurs de faim!

Even the stale odor of the refrigerated dead blood had spiked his appetite. He had driven into Manhattan to feed. Here he could be sure of a wide selection any time of night, especially in Greenwich Village, where something always seemed to be happening.

On the corner of Sixth Avenue and Fourth Street at two A.M. a variety of blood passed by: the tourists, eager to experience it all; the youths, lost and vulnerable; the transients, some crazy, some on drugs and/or alcohol; lonely people unable to sleep in empty apartments; the elderly, unable to sleep, period; and the immoral, trying to find an easy mark.

Of course, Sade knew he did not fit into any of these categories. Yes, he was there to steal, perhaps even kill, but he was no different from anyone else who needed to hunt down food. Healthy survival was everyone's right. If there were a central blood bank he could use, would he feed from it? No, not fresh enough; besides, the violence added to the ambience of a good meal. And oh, the cold chill of refrigerated blood would burn his throat. How did Liliana stand it? Sade shook his head.

"Can you spare some change? I have to get back to Jersey City." The tall girl stood before him with hand extended. Her long straight black hair contrasted with the white makeup layered on her face. The black eye makeup did also. The bright red lipstick looked cracked and badly in need of a touch-up. Her black dress reached down to her ankles and covered the upper part of her military boots. The purple and black shawl matched her attire and purple fingernails.

A Goth, he thought. He loved Goths, they were so willing.

"*Mon enfant*, I'm going back to New Jersey and can drop you off. My car is but a block or two away."

"I'd rather take the PATH train." She still extended her hand.

Sade laughed. "*Il n'y a pas moyen d'échapper au fait que . . .*"

"There's no escaping the fact that I need the fare for the PATH train."

"You speak French, *mon enfant*."

"I'm a French major at Rutgers, and I'm not your child."

"*Mais non*, if you were my child you'd be severely disciplined for being out alone so late. I give you money and you travel alone on a train. With all the perverts in the world I could not allow that. Let me take you safely home."

The girl tilted her head but kept her hand extended. "How do I know you're not a pervert?"

"This is called mutual trust, *ma . . .*"

"Lucy. The name's Lucy."

"Louis," he answered. "See, we already know each other on a first-name basis. I know a coffeehouse that stays open late. Why don't we go there and share some more secrets."

"No." She finally pulled back her hand. "I'll take my chances on the street."

"Oh! Mighty Zeus, send down your terrible thunderbolt on these fools that have forgotten you." A wiry man with a sandy-colored beard and several missing teeth walked by the girl and Sade. He stopped a short distance away to wring his hands

71

and cry out again to the Greek gods. The knitted cap on his head was a dirty gray; actually, all of his clothes were dirty, from the chambray shirt to the loose-fitting jeans that rested low on his hips. His naked feet were marred by nonhealing sores.

"You see what I mean, Lucy. Obviously I must have looked harmless enough to you, or else you would not have approached me. Trust me a bit more and let me buy you a café au lait."

Lucy looked back over her shoulder at Sade, and he smiled wide enough to show that he was *not* missing teeth.

The coffeehouse had several customers all spaced out for individual privacy. Each table had a different type of candle and holder. One was a simple votive, another was a beeswax candle set on a white plate. The table nearest the door had a candle in the shape of a frog's body; the head had already burned down. The table at which Lucy and Sade sat had an elaborate candelabrum with multicolored dripping candles. The ceiling of the café was tin and the floor wood planks. There hadn't been much choice in food. Lucy had settled on a whipped cream éclair and hot honey-sweetened milk, while Sade had ordered a café au lait to be sociable.

Sade pulled a chair out for Lucy; however, she opted to sit across from where he stood. Sade merely shrugged and sat.

Lucy opened her mouth and pulled on her teeth until a set of fangs popped out. Carefully she wrapped them, first in cotton, then in a napkin.

"They look great, but I can't eat while wearing them."

"Personally I don't have that problem," Sade stated. He ran his tongue across his short but pointy incisors.

72

"Also, they're made of dental acrylic and can crack and discolor easily."

"They sound useless," Sade commented.

"I could have gotten them made of dental porcelain, but it would have cost more." She slipped the napkin into her carpet bag. "When I get home I'll shine them up a bit with a nail buffer. My parents hate them and think I wasted money on them."

"Perhaps," Sade mumbled to himself. "So you live with your parents."

Lucy nodded.

"That makes things much simpler."

"How?"

"I will not give you money to travel home alone. However, I will help you call your parents, and your father can come pick you up."

"That's an awful idea. If they knew I was out this late, they'd kill me. I was hoping to sneak into the house."

Sade smiled. "I guess, then, my other idea of going to the police for help would not appeal to you. But your parents will be furious when they wake up and not find you at home." By now, Sade knew, her parents were probably worried about her. Parents do not sleep while their babes stray. It was too soon for a missing-person report. Still, he had to move quickly.

Lucy licked some chocolate icing off the middle finger of her right hand. Sade's mouth watered.

"What kind of car do you have?"

"A Jaguar. The locks are independent, not under solely the driver's control. It's fast, it's sleek, and it's a marvelous shade of clotted blood."

"What's the color of the leather inside, scab brown?" She made a face and finished her éclair. "What year is the car?"

"Brand new, merely three months old."

"Could I try driving it?"

"You can drive us both back to New Jersey if you like."

"Why would you do all this for me?"

"I have a young niece at home." Sade's eyes sparkled. "At least she had better be at home and not wandering around as you are. I would be very angry to find out she had been disobedient. I would take away all her privileges." Sade was willing to bet that even though Lucy was of college age she was still forced to live by her parents' rules.

"I meant to be home earlier, only I was having so much fun at Dracula's Lair I lost track of time."

"Dracula's Lair?"

"A Goth place. It's a place where people who are into the darker side of life go." Lucy said this with sophistication.

"Certainly not a place for me," Sade said. "However, I would like to hear more about it."

All the way back to the car Lucy educated Sade about the Goth life. "It may be silly to you, but one never knows when one may meet a dark spirit, like a werewolf or a vampire."

"Do you still want to drive?" Sade had the car keys in his hand.

"Honestly, I'm way too tired."

Not tired enough to keep still on their ride to New Jersey.

"I plan on going to France my junior year. Do you ever go back?"

"It has been many years. Ah, *mais* I feel that soon I will."

"You have family there?"

"No, the ones I am close to are here."

Lucy cocked her head to the side in order to lean

against the car door. Sade glanced over and noticed two ruby dots on her neck. She had been playing at vampire, but he did not play games.

"You've gone way too far!"

"*Pardonnez-moi?*"

"You've passed the exit for Jersey City a while back."

"*Je m'excuse*. Perhaps a little farther up we will find a place to stop and check a map."

Sade pulled into an empty parking lot and drove around to the back of the office building.

"Please, look in the glove compartment; I should have a map there." He stopped the car, and Lucy fumbled to open the glove compartment.

"It's either locked or stuck."

"What is this?" Sade asked, reaching out to touch the pseudo–puncture wounds. "You like *donner ton sang?*" His fingers skimmed her neck in search of her carotid.

"Oh, those things. It's kind of a sexy idea to be bitten on the neck and become someone's sex slave."

"An idea that can well become true if you so wish."

He drew an arm about her, and she did not shy away. He stared into her round painted eyes and invited her into his world. She moved closer to him, and gently his grip tightened. Her fingers touched his smile. He slid his lips down her fingers and kissed the palm of her hand. The smell of sugar and chocolate penetrated his senses. The odor of human fear hid under the sweets. But it was there, and he had to move before she could regain her senses.

Quickly he moved to her neck; she screamed and hunched a shoulder. Taking his right arm from around her shoulders, he used his right hand to grab a hank of her hair and pulled her head back.

Suddenly she was out the door, running toward the front of the building, her head covered with bobby pins and clips.

"Sacrebleu!" Sade looked at the droopy wig he held in his hand. He threw it to the floor like a dead rat. His hands were stained and slippery. She had obviously used a cheap dye to attain the deep ebony color.

Should he chase her? he wondered. He would definitely be swifter than she. He looked down at the wig lying in a puddle-like mass. Somehow his appetite for this girl's blood had been vanquished by a head of hair.

"A fake Goth," he muttered, starting up the car and driving out of the parking lot onto the freeway. A car had already stopped for the girl, and she was too busy hesitating to go near that car to notice Sade drive by.

Chapter Thirteen

Sade couldn't bear the feel of the black dye on his hands, not to mention the fact that the dye was streaking his steering wheel. He pulled the car into the parking lot of an all-night diner. Once inside the diner he headed straight for the men's room.

"Hey, our rest rooms are just for customers," a male voice yelled out.

Sade didn't bother to turn to look at the man.

"Fine! Pour me a cup of coffee." He pushed open the door to the men's room and was sorry he had. A stench of vomit hit him immediately, and the person responsible was not finished yet, as Sade could tell from the retching inside the single stall.

After turning on the tap water, Sade spilled some liquid soap into his palm. Before putting down the bottle he spilled a bit more. A little water and *voilà*, soapy foam covered both his hands. *Perhaps I took too much*, he thought as he worried about getting the slippery, smelly soap off his hands. He knew, however, that he often did things in the extreme.

He heard the stall door open.

"Imbibe a bit too much, *monsieur*?"

"No, food poisoning."

"Ah! You must be married."

"Why do you say that?"

"Already you are thinking up excuses."

"It's true. I couldn't have had more than a couple of glasses of wine. And perhaps one or two martinis before dinner."

"Port? Cognac?"

"Just one snifter at the end of the meal."

"Sounds like food poisoning." Sade made room for the man at the sink. He glanced at the man's profile and then looked into the mirror to see the man's face in full. Even beneath the dripping water that the man was splashing on his face, Sade could see the incredible similarity.

"The British *espèce de crétin*, Stuart."

"Excuse me." The man crossed in front of Sade to retrieve some paper towels from the machine.

"Stuart?"

The man tossed the soaked paper towels into the trash. "Are you speaking to me?"

"I am Louis. Louis Sade. And your name?"

"David Petry." The man put out his hand to shake Sade's.

"Incredible," Sade said, ignoring the proffered hand. "You look so much like someone I met once."

"Just once? He must have made a strong impression on you."

"He changed my niece's life."

"Oh! I didn't do it, whatever it is."

"If I thought you had, I'd . . ." Sade thought for

several seconds. "You look *très* pale. You don't look like you should be driving."

"I'll hang around for a while before I drive home."

"Anyone waiting for you?"

"That wife thing again. Naw, single. Used to have a hound, but he ran away. Must have found a better home someplace else. At least that's what I hope happened."

"You like animals? My niece has a rabbit that she refuses to feed from."

"She won't cook it and eat it?"

"So to speak." Sade was thinking about what a better meal David would make. There was an edge to Sade's hunger, but this mortal could potentially bring Liliana back into the fold of vampirism. "Perhaps she would change her mind if you came home with me. Besides, you do not look well, and I am not sure a brief rest will make you whole."

"Wait a second. Are you asking me to go home with you so that I can talk your niece into cooking a rabbit?"

"No, into feeding."

"She anorexic?"

"In a way, yes."

"I think she needs a psychiatrist more than an accountant. Good luck, though." David reached for the doorknob.

"Wait! I would feel, how do you say, guilty if I didn't do something to assist you."

"I'll be fine. Don't worry about me. Sounds more like your daughter—"

"Niece."

"Niece is the one who could use your help."

"That's what I'm trying to do. Help both of you."

"Don't need any." David opened the door and exited.

Sade looked into the mirror. "Where is your charm, your *charisme*, your *savoir-faire*?"

Sade stormed out of the men's room.

"Hey, here's your coffee." The man behind the counter waved with a dish towel. He had practically no hair on his head, and his features seemed to resemble a clown's. His eyebrows were too bushy, his nose too red, bulbous and pitted; his mouth turned downward in a sulk.

"Coffee? I don't drink coffee, *monsieur*."

"Oh no you don't. That jerk before you ducked out without ordering, not you too. Pay for the coffee you ordered."

"I would gladly pay for something to drink, but I fear that you and I would differ over the price to be paid."

"I got this menu here." The counterman tossed a stained plastic-coated paper on the counter. "Even got a Gallo jug under the counter."

"Gallo? No Château Lafite?"

"Whatever you said we don't have. At least it doesn't sound familiar."

Sade walked to the counter and picked up the menu.

"No, I don't see what I enjoy to drink on the menu."

"I'm sure I can come up with something."

"Yes. Yes you can." Sade leaped over the counter and grabbed the man around the throat. When the man reached behind him to find a weapon, Sade grabbed his wrist and broke the arm over his knee. There was a high-pitched scream before Sade jammed his thumb into the man's voice box.

Sade cleaned up in the ladies' room. The soft pink tiles and the smell of menstrual blood was far preferable to the stink of the men's room. Neatly Sade cleaned the counterman's blood from his lips. He rinsed his mouth several times to eliminate any bloodstain that might be on his teeth.

The meal may not have had the delicacy Sade preferred, but it certainly had been sating.

Sade remembered the name. *David Petry*. He used his limited-edition hand-painted Namiki fountain pen to write the name on the cuff of his shirt. He meant to replace the shirt anyway; besides, this way he wouldn't lose the name.

He walked back to the dining area, over to the counter, where he left money for the coffee, then went to the door, flipped the Open sign to Closed, and left.

"You must be fully cognizant of the death you are going to undergo: this perverse blood has got to be made to seep out of you . . ."

Justine,
by the
Marquis de Sade

Chapter Fourteen

Garrett had visible bruises from the last visit, bruises that kept him away from his wife. He worked late. He offered excuses why he could not bed his wife, and she became suspicious. He had wanted to explain all this to La Maîtresse, but he feared losing her completely to another client, to another submissive.

La Maîtresse spoke infrequently to him now. Instead she demanded that he reveal secrets of his matrimonial bed. If he halted in his stories, La Maîtresse did not notice right away. Her mind wandered to someone else, he knew.

She still sought his blood. Often she seemed starved for his blood. The infliction of pain had lessened, as if she feared truly hurting him.

"Maîtresse," he called.

Her blond head rose from the crook of his neck. Blood spotted her chin. Her lips quivered and her nostrils flared. But her eyes were vacant, lost to Garrett. Slowly her hands reached up to touch her own lips.

"Garrett," she said as her eyes focused on his features.

Who is it that she sees when she is with me?

She stood. Small, he thought, with hands as strong as a workman's and a mouth more foul than any he had heard. Yet she was small. The black corset cinched her waist into an abnormally small circumference. The stiletto-heeled boots increased her height by at least six inches. Still he towered above her. Her hips and bust swelled in sensuous curves.

From the wall she took a long peacock feather and, waving it in front of him, she began to speak. "You must stay away for a while." The feather touched his cheek, his forehead, the eyelids, the nose, the mouth. "I want you strong. I want both of us to heal." The feather swept his neck and stung the wound.

He shook his head.

While beating his chest with the feather, she demanded that he not talk back. The feather roamed down his abdomen and over his belly. His wrists were manacled together behind his back, but his legs were free. He drew his thighs apart, and she circled his cock with the light touch of the feather and dragged the feather down the inside of each thigh.

La Maîtresse leaned forward to whisper in his ear.

"Come back to me bloated with life, with fresh blood. Ready to feed the desires of Maîtresse la Présidente. Your perverse blood shall feed me afresh."

Chapter Fifteen

Marie drove onto Keith's property. It had been several days since she had seen Wil, and she meant to change that. In her arms she carried a straw basket filled with scones and preserves. Her special peace offering. She shifted the load in order to rap on the door.

"What do you want?" A yellow tinge on Keith's right cheekbone reminded her of their last meeting. He did not open the door wide.

"I brought some food."

"We're not hungry. They have a soup kitchen in the next town over. Give it to them."

"Even managed to collect enough blueberries to make a favorite spread of mine." She lifted the white linen cloth covering the basket and attempted to move closer to Keith. He merely closed the door another quarter inch.

"Dad hasn't had much of an appetite since we last visited you."

Marie turned and saw Wil leaning against the front fender of her car. He stood shirtless, with a tuft of hair rising above the waist of his low-cut jeans. Grass clippings speckled his bare feet.

"It's been several days, and I wanted to invite you back."

"For what?" Keith's voice rasped behind her.

"I'm afraid there was a misunderstanding." She turned back to the father.

"This 'old fart' got the message," Keith said gruffly.

"I was overplayful."

Loud laughter spilled from Wil's lips.

"See! Your son understands it was a joke."

"My son gets off on people sticking needles in him. Not to mention the tattoos covering his hairy legs. Christ, he comes out of the shower looking like a walking mural."

"Dad's jealous. He'd like some color on his legs other than the bulging purple knots of his veins."

Marie placed the basket on the tattered pillow of the porch rocking chair. She took a deep breath and turned to face Keith.

"I apologize if I frightened you. And really, I didn't mean to hurt you. I see the bruise is practically gone." She reached out a hand, and Keith pulled back. She joined her hands and steepled her fingers to her lips. "Dinner. This Saturday evening at, say, eight o'clock. I'll invite my granddaughter. She always manages to keep me in line." She smiled. "I do owe it to you both. Lord only knows what your son thinks of me."

"Whatever he thinks would be right," Keith said.

"I think you're a lovely, stylish woman. My father and I accept your gracious offer."

Keith groaned.

As long as Wil showed up, she didn't care what the old man did. Already she had projected her strong desire for Wil onto a client. A client who was too willing to accommodate her lust and blood hunger.

Marie descended the steps.

"I look forward to seeing you both." She started for the door of her car. "And oh! Do dress casually. Shorts are fine." She winked at Wil and then entered her car.

"I'll wear my oldest boxers. Just see how much casual she can stand."

"Dad, calm down."

"Maybe you don't mind that she wants to jump your bones, but . . . well, you'd sleep with anything."

"You're jealous."

"Huh?"

Wil pulled out a kitchen chair, swept it between his legs, and sat.

"I think you've got a crush on your neighbor."

"Shit, I don't need that kind of woman hanging around me." Keith moved to the stove. "Dammit, the soup's boiling away. It'll take another half hour for it to cool. It's her fault."

"Because you happened to be heating up soup when she knocked on the door? Or because you were too attracted to her to remember the soup?"

"Wilbur, I've got a single bed, just big enough for me. I don't have any room for a woman."

"That wasn't true when I was a kid."

Keith looked at his son.

"I may have had a lady stay over once in a while."

"Whole weekends you'd be romping around in your bedroom. That's when I learned to do for myself. You and your whores would swat me out of the way when you came out for air."

"They were ladies. I never had to pay for it. Paying for sex is a sin."

"If you had gone to church on Sunday, you would have learned that sex without the blessing of marriage is a sin."

"You certainly didn't learn anything on Sundays."

"I learned lots, Dad, without having to leave my own home."

"You didn't learn to be a fag in this house." Spit sprayed the air in front of Keith.

"I'm bisexual."

"The only kind of woman chasing you is a perverted old lady." Keith grabbed a bowl off the Welsh dresser and brought it over to the stove to pour his soup. "Besides, if your mother hadn't died, there wouldn't have been any other women in this house." He slowly poured the soup into the bowl.

"God, it would have meant sleazing around cheap motels." Wil shook his head in sympathy.

Keith slammed the pot down on the stove.

"I loved your mother. I wasn't about to get married again and go through the loss of another good woman just because her maternal instinct kicked in." He placed the bowl of soup on the table and sat on one of the vinyl-covered chrome kitchen chairs.

Will listened to his father slurp down the soup. The jiggling of his father's false teeth fascinated him. *Dad's too cheap to even pay for a decent set of teeth.*

"What?" Grasping his soup spoon just above the bowl, Keith looked at his son.

"When's the last time you got laid?"

Keith dropped the spoon back into the bowl, causing a light splatter of tomato soup.

"That's why you're so grumpy, Dad. Let me treat you."

"What the hell are you talking about?" Keith's eyebrows seemed to crouch down over his eyelids.

"You still wouldn't be paying for it. I would. You're all clogged up. Let me call my favorite Roto-Rooter girl."

"Disgusting. You made me lose my appetite." Keith stood and walked to the sink with the bowl in his hand. After dumping the soup down the drain, he pulled open the dishwasher and shoved the bowl inside the machine. "You and the Wicked Witch of Rathbone deserve each other." Keith started to leave the room.

"Don't forget to mark Saturday down on your calendar. If her granddaughter's cute, we might be able to have a foursome."

Chapter Sixteen

He had the face of a young man. Liliana guessed him to be in his mid-twenties. His features, while coarse, still had some fine detail through the mouth and in the shape of the nose. His slicked-back hair gave only the faintest hint of red, while his brows and beard stubble glistened with the color. The frame of his body indicated that he had been a dedicated athlete. A dusting of reddish-brown hair covered his chest.

Young. Too young to be lying on the stainless-steel table.

She poured kerosene into the knife wound on the lower abdomen. The maggots shriveled and died. While sponging down the body with a disinfectant, she wondered about this man's life. So short, unlike hers, which was never-ending. Would death be preferable to her existence?

Stomach fluid bubbled between his lips. Quickly

she rolled over the body to drain the purge from the corpse's mouth. Later she would have to remember to tie off the trachea and esophagus before exposing the arteries of the neck for embalming. Her fingers left tracks on his discolored back. After returning him to the supine position, she swabbed out his mouth and nose.

When she grasped the palm of his hand, she felt the rough calluses marring his flesh. Gradually she flexed the arm several times, then continued on to the other arm. After bending his legs to relieve the rigor mortis, she started to massage the thick thighs as a lover would, allowing her fingers to sink deep into his crotch, pushing aside his balls. The erection caused by the settling blood stood useless; she touched it softly with the tips of her fingers. It had been so long since she had tasted the smooth tip and ridge of a male organ. Closing her eyes, she remembered the salty chlorine flavor of seminal fluid. Her hand circled the erection and moved up and down.

The sound of a moan pulled Liliana back into the reality of the embalming room. She checked his gaping mouth, but no sound had been emitted from there. A shiver and a smile acknowledged her own senseless fear. It had probably been her fantasy that had caused her to moan with forgotten pleasure.

She extended his legs and arms over the gutter circling the table. While elevating the head, she rubbed the back of her hand across his stubble. The beautician would shave him later, but for now he had the look of a sleeping lover.

Visually she sought his left and right carotids for the arterial embalming she was about to perform. No beat existed to assist her search; experience and the leanness of his body made it easier. His odor and the coolness of his flesh were familiar to her. Her own body carried the same chill, and often she awakened in her coffin to the scent of her own reposal decay. Her body healed fast, so that by the time she stepped from the casket her flesh had sweetened to the reality of life. The same could not be said of her clients, who stretched out into eternal decay.

After closing off the trachea and esophagus, she exposed the carotids and inserted hollow metal tubes in order to inject the formaldehyde and methyl alcohol mix. Before using the solution, she cut a major vein to drain the blood.

The commingling odors of the embalming fluid and the blood always made her feel light-headed. Her mouth watered at the sight of the blood dripping into the surrounding gutter. The temptation to drain the body with her own lips passed quickly. Once she had tried, and the rancidness of dead tissue had roiled her stomach. Uncle Donatien was right. They were meant to feed from the living. Vampires were not scavengers, they were game hunters. Not vultures picking at the remnants of nature.

Her fingers massaged the young man's cold flesh, helping to spread the embalming fluid that would firm up muscles that never would be used again.

Often she felt intrusive, preventing the body from taking on its final state, saving the body shell to satisfy the whims of the living. A final prep. A final farewell. The final facade with which each man must face friends, relatives, and sometimes enemies.

Intently she watched his face and hands, waiting for evidence that the fluid was entering the visible areas. And she continued to massage, feeling the ribs and hipbone dig into her palms.

"Freedom from the bonds of humanity will come. I promise," she whispered, knowing that her own blood bond was too addictive to vanquish.

When the hands showed evidence of the embalming fluid she quickly moved to apply superglue to conjoin his fingers. The nails were ragged, and some were split. The fingers were short, the knuckles knobby with the indication of early arthritis. A white scar circled his right thumb. His palm had a congestion of lines. She kissed the palm and brushed it against her cheek.

"If only I were brave enough to join you."

Gently she placed the hand over his chest.

Chapter Seventeen

From his bedroom window Louis watched Cecelia helping her mother in the garden. He had not bothered to tell Matilda that it didn't matter whether the vegetables were organic or loaded with insecticides. But he did notice a difference in flavor. So maybe organic was better, even if the ugly vegetables had to be inspected for infestations. Louis still enjoyed an occasional meal of vegetables, meat, and fruit, although his lifelong hemorrhoid problem dictated temperance.

Cecelia wore denim cutoffs cut off as high as she could go without revealing a completely bare bottom. For hours the girl would kneel on the fertile earth, leaning over frequently to plant, trim, fertilize, or weed with her glorious ass saluting his window. He thought he noticed a slight pinkish sunburn creeping up each cheek. Not as pink as he could make them if that *emmerdeuse* mother would disappear.

"Ah!" he sighed as the girl jerked the spade back and forth into the ground.

He could stand here all day *regardant fixement la jeune fille*. However, he had a project to complete, and it must be done soon or his own dear *jolie fille* would continue to waste away.

Louis blew a kiss to Cecelia and crossed the room to his *bonheur-du-jour* and sat down to write out his shortened list. He had looked up the name of David Petry in every reference he could obtain. He believed he did know something very important about Monsieur Petry. The young man had said that his niece needed a psychiatrist more than an accountant. Therefore, Louis had narrowed the list of David Petry's down to three listings. One lived in Fort Lee, New Jersey, a possibility since they had met on the Jersey side of the Hudson. Another lived in Astoria, Queens, and the least promising lived on the God-forsaken tip of upper Manhattan. Since the first two had not answered their home phones, it was the third with whom he had the evening appointment. As it turned out, the individual answering the telephone was an accountant.

At seven-thirty Louis climbed a staircase to the neighborhood called Park Terrace, which sat upon a hill overlooking the drudgery of working-class life. He had driven around the middle-class enclave for fifteen minutes before giving up and finding a parking space at the bottom of the hill. Dinnertime on a weekday was the worst time to park in a New York City residential neighborhood. He had noticed an obvious difference in the age and brand of the cars he had viewed. On top of the hill cars seemed to be less rusted, newer; more cars retained their hubcaps. At the bottom of the hill he had parked between an orange Pinto and a dented Chevette. He doubted that his feminine-voiced alarm calling for help would attract anyone, but he made sure it was turned on. Besides, the frail voice crying out his name, asking him to "please stop the rogue," turned *him* on.

At the top of the steps an elderly woman tugged a miniature mutt out of his way. The dog gnashed his teeth and yanked hard on his collar.

"Bad dog," the woman kept repeating without much enthusiasm.

One of the dog's back legs seemed paralyzed, and Louis wished he could put the animal out of its misery. Despite the warmth of the evening, the woman wore a knit hat and black raincoat. He hoped flashing was not one of her sports. Her brittle sticklike figure waved him on. Annoyance added additional lines to her already well-creased face.

"Move on, for heaven's sake. I can't be walking Ginger all night. She can't shit while strangers are watching. Move on. Hurry!"

Louis halted. The dog's gray muzzle shivered around its yellow teeth and the gravelly growl inspired little fear.

"Perhaps your dog needs a purgative."

"She needs privacy while she takes a good shit. That's what she needs."

He noticed that the woman's eyes were a cloudy gray-blue. Her nose was long, thin, and pointed, while the lips caved into her mouth. He had seen many of this kind of woman huddled around the guillotines of the French Revolution. Matter of fact, this particular woman had an uncanny resemblance to a Madame Charlotte Chénier, who sold fruits and vegetables to the voyeuristic crowds.

He didn't like either woman, but his errand took precedence over a petty grudge. As Sade moved on to his destination, the dog began yapping. Sade's ears rang with the timbre.

The heavy doors leading to Petry's lobby did not silence the sound but did at least muffle it. Sade checked the names listed on the intercom. David Petry's apartment was on the fourth floor, and he answered Sade's ring immediately with a long buzz. Sade opened the inner door and headed to the elevator.

Out of service, a four-by-six yellow index card informed him. On the way up the stairs, Sade hoped that this would not be the David Petry he was looking for, since he felt a bit famished from all the exercise.

Petry's door was painted the same dark green as all the other apartment doors, except his had a coat of arms pasted directly under the peephole. A coat of arms Sade recognized. But it would be too coincidental, too simple, too pretentious to be Stuart.

Suddenly the door opened. It was the right David Petry. *Cet espèce de crétin*, Stuart.

"Hello, Mr. Sade?"

"*Oui.*"

David extended his hand. "I'm David Petry." The handshake was limp, not surprising to Sade.

"Is it getting chilly out there?"

"Pardon?"

"Your hand feels cold. But come in."

"The coat of arms?"

David laughed. "A souvenir of my trip to England. I don't know why, but I liked it, even though I know it's kind of kitschy."

"Sometimes the past haunts us," Sade said.

97

The apartment seemed to be full of souvenirs and yard sale items. The Persian rug was well-used and fake. The sofa was draped in a deep purple Afghan that barely hid the tattered material beneath it. Two uncomfortable director's chairs faced the couch. Sade sat on the center pillow of the sofa, away from the stained and dirty armrests.

"Excuse the place. I spent four years in the armed services and then went back to school, so I'm a little strapped for cash. Not that my business isn't picking up, but I do have some hefty loans to pay off."

"Armed services? *Monsieur*, let us hope you do not repeat all your follies."

"I never thought of serving in the army to be a folly."

"It depends on what side you are on."

"I suppose you're right. Have we met before?"

"*Mais non*, I would remember. I'm very good at faces."

David shrugged. "Over the phone you mentioned that you needed assistance with some financial planning."

"*Oui*. My last accountant left the books in disarray. And I'm looking for someone who can make sense of the multitude of numbers."

David rattled off his rates.

"Your cost does not frighten me, *monsieur*. Of course, I may ask you to start with one set of books first. The ones dealing with my U.S. possessions. The European investments could be taken care of later."

"Do you have any immediate questions?"

"No. I will try to have most of my books available to you on Saturday evening."

"Excuse me?"

"This Saturday when you come for dinner."

"It's really unnecessary . . ."

"If I am to feel comfortable with you, *monsieur*, I would like to get to know you on a social level."

"If you want references, I can give the names of a number of my clients."

"No, *monsieur*. I need to get to know you on my own, not through the eyes of someone else." From the looks of the apartment, Louis didn't think that Petry could afford to turn away any job.

Grudgingly David agreed to a seven o'clock dinner engagement for the coming Saturday.

After leaving the apartment, Louis felt an enormous thirst. Luckily, David Petry did not appeal to Sade's sensuous side, or else he would have found it impossible to leave without sampling the accountant's blood. But now that he descended the steps, he realized all the exertions and stress of the day were weighing him down into a sluggish fog. His mind still had its edge; however, physically he began to move more slowly, yet not so slowly that he couldn't capture a stray human.

"No, no, no. That's enough, Ginger. We must go back inside now."

Easy prey, Sade thought, but how unpalatable. The woman and her dog came into view just as Ginger decided to crouch down for a piss. Sade was uncertain whether he disliked the woman or the dog more.

"Bad, Ginger. Naughty." The woman gave no indication that she knew anyone was coming down the stairs.

Perhaps, thought Sade, she herself wanted to be invisible at this point in time, and she hoped the person would pass by without acknowledging her.

"Ginger has gotten over her shyness, I see."

The dog immediately started yapping.

"Merely an accident. She's ten years old, and sometimes she misjudges where she is."

"Ginger does not know whether she is outdoors or indoors?"

"You startled her, and that's why she wet herself."

"She not only wet herself, *madame*, she seems to have flooded the hall."

"Are you leaving, sir?"

Sade hesitated.

"I could stay. Would you like me to stay, *madame*?"

"I would like you to leave. Who buzzed you in, anyway?"

Sade drew closer to the woman and smelled the odor of age. He encountered the smell every day when he rested inside his coffin. He hated the smell. This would be a violent killing, one that would surely cause him *d'avoir l'estomac barbouillé*. Already he thought he felt a burp coming on.

Just when Sade had come to a decision to find a tastier morsel, Ginger snagged onto the cuff of his trousers and began to rage.

"See what you did now? You have Ginger all upset."

Slowly Sade stretched out a hand while keeping the woman within his constant glare. He settled his thumb deeply into her voice box and spread the rest of his hand around her neck.

"Mrs. MacManus, if you can't keep Ginger quiet . . ."

The voice came from behind Sade. He judged that whoever it was could not see the hold he had on the old woman.

"Can I be of any help?" The voice tinkled in his ears. Young, he thought, probably a good deal younger than his current pitiful sack of a meal. But if he let Mrs. MacManus go in order to take the fresher meal, what would happen? What chaos could this old woman reek in the soggy hallway? He noticed that he stood fully in Ginger's puddle. Quickly he twisted the woman's head, and she fell dead into his arms.

Free of the leash, Ginger tried climbing his leg, gnawing holes in his trousers.

"*Madame* is ill, and I'm afraid the dog misunderstands my intent."

A woman in her mid-twenties rushed to his side. When she saw the limp body of her neighbor, she immediately offered to call 911.

"I think it would be better if I could lay her down somewhere first."

"Of course." She began to move away from him.

"The *chienne*."

"What?"

"Gin-ger," he pronounced the name slowly to keep from screaming.

"Of course." She scooped up the dog and beckoned him to follow her.

"Maybe I could take her from you. Can she walk at all?"

"*Mademoiselle*, she is unconscious. True, she is *très* thin, but still a *dead*weight."

"Are you related to her?"

"Merely a Good Samaritan who needs to lay his burden down."

She opened the door to her apartment, and Sade brushed past her before she could ask any more questions.

The living room glowed with the flickering of the television. A settee with a white lace coverlet stood opposite the flickering picture. Gently he placed the body down on the lace.

"Will she be all right?"

The dog emitted a low growl and snuggled into the young woman's bosom. The woman seemed to be wearing nothing under her cotton robe. The material defined every inch of her body, revealing a full-bosomed, narrow-hipped redhead. He could tell her hair color was true, because even in this dim light he could make out the cluster of red pubic hair under the translucent robe.

Sade looked down at Mrs. MacManus.

"No."

The young woman moved in for a closer look at her neighbor.

"What do you mean?"

"Perhaps you should lock Ginger in the kitchen with a bite to eat."

"The hell with Ginger!" She dropped the dog to the floor, and to Sade's relief the animal ran out the apartment doorway, which still stood open.

"Oh my God, what did I do? Mrs. MacManus will be furious when she wakes up and can't find Ginger." She started for the door. Sade followed closely behind. He reached beyond the young woman and swung the front door shut.

Some mail sat on a table near the door. Sade noted that the mail was addressed to Evie Springer.

"Evie, I don't think our first concern should be the *chienne*. I mean Ginger." He hated it when an English word escaped him.

"You're right. What am I thinking. I'll call 911."

As she walked to the phone, Sade noted the thrust of her ass, not broad but certainly shelflike. He moved forward, and his arms circled Evie's waist.

"There is no more we can do for poor Mrs. MacManus."

"You mean she's dead?"

Sade kissed the back of Evie's head.

"I don't want a dead body in my apartment."

"Where do you think we should put her? She must have the keys to her apartment in a pocket." He let go of Evie in order to rifle through the dead woman's raincoat.

"I can't have the police finding a dead person in my apartment. There'd be too many questions. They might even search the apartment."

Sade wondered what Evie had to hide, but it didn't matter as long as she wanted to be rid of the body.

He found the keys pinned with a safety pin to the inside lining of Mrs. MacManus's raincoat.

"Voici!"

Evie gave him a blank look.

"Take the keys."

"Why?"

"Mademoiselle, I cannot open *la porte, ce que je veux dire c'est,* the door and carry the old . . . Mrs. MacManus."

"You want me to help you?"

"I could leave her *ici* . . . here."

Evie grabbed the keys. Sade lifted his burden and followed Evie to the door.

"Perhaps I should take a peek into the hall first. Don't see anyone through the peephole." Slowly she opened the door.

"Hi, David."

Mais non. Sade wanted to pounce on them all and end this in a serious blood orgy. *Liliana, never doubt that I love you.*

"Hey Evie, have you seen Mrs. MacManus? She doesn't answer her door, and Ginger seems to be stranded in the hall."

"Mrs. MacManus? Gosh! I can't imagine where she would be."

"You wouldn't happen to have an extra key to her apartment, because I'm thinking it might be a good idea to check on her?"

Evie quickly brought her right hand behind her back. Sade could see the golden-colored keys sparkle in her palm.

"She'd never give me a key. Are you kiddin'? You know how she is. She trusts no one. I doubt she has any friends to hold a key for her. Besides, I think it would be too soon to barge into her apartment. I did see her earlier in the day. Maybe Ginger snuck out while Mrs. MacManus was locking the door or maybe Mrs. MacManus is asleep. Who knows how Ginger managed to get into the hall? She can be quit mischievous. Ginger, I mean."

Tais-toi!

"I guess you're right. I'll take Ginger up to my apartment and check in again with Mrs. MacManus later in the evening. By the way, Evie, could I stop by later tonight?"

"Not a good idea."

"Already booked with another client?"

Client? wondered Sade.

"Sort of. Good night." Evie closed the door, leaned her back against it, and signaled Sade that he should be quiet.

Sade didn't plan on revealing himself to David while holding a dead body and cavorting with a soon-to-be-dead young woman.

Several minutes passed with both of them barely breathing.

"Let's try again," Evie finally said.

This time the hall was empty. Sade waited inside the apartment while Evie unlocked Mrs. Mac-

Manus's door. As soon as he heard the squeak of the door hinges, he rushed Mrs. MacManus back to her apartment and deposited the body on the first object he saw, an old pine dresser. He stepped back and thought about how inappropriate she looked. The floor would be better, but did it matter? *If they do an autopsy, which they probably will, they'll see she has a broken neck. Hmmm.*

"What will the police think when she's found?" asked Evie. "I mean, I can't afford to have the police knocking on my door asking questions."

"What are you doing?" Evie watched Sade search through several closets, finally pulling forth an aluminum stepladder.

Sade had decided to ease Evie's qualms and to make it look like Mrs. MacManus fell from the ladder. He undid the raincoat, removed it from the body, and hung it up in the closet. He set the ladder up so that it appeared that the old woman had been searching a kitchen cabinet. Easily he hoisted the body up the ladder and dropped her from the top step. He paused to look at Evie.

"What the hell . . ." Evie's mouth and eyes were round.

He walked past her to the outside hall while suggesting she lock up. Evie followed and did as she was told.

"The keys. What do I do with the keys?"

Sade grabbed the keys from her hand and dumped them down the garbage shoot.

"She won't be needing them again. And I expect after a week or two someone will suggest breaking down the door. *L'odeur de la mort* never fails to attract the scavengers."

Evie shivered and padded her way back to her apartment, with Sade following closely behind. At the door she stopped and looked at Sade.

"I hope to never see you again."

"I have assisted you in being rid of a body."

"There wouldn't have been a body except . . . What did you do to her?"

"*Moi!* Nothing! I merely came to the aid of someone who appeared ill." Sade brushed back a red curl from Evie's right cheek. "*Mademoiselle* Evie." He brushed his thumb across her deep red lips. "It is obvious you are truly a beautiful, sensuous woman. *Une femme de petite vertu.*" She watched his lips form the sound of French poetry without comprehension. "I could promise to never speak of your contribution tonight if . . ."

"The pound of flesh."

"Literally."

Evie guided Sade into the apartment and immediately into her bedroom, a room draped in black and red with a standing bondage post. A wall rack and padded bondage table were to his right. Upon the opposite wall hung an assortment of whips, canes in a variety of materials, leather hoods, and on the aluminum table various piercing devices.

"*Mademoiselle*, the acoustics?"

"Three layers of soundproofing."

"*C'est le paradis!*"

"... I am in a state of the most violent agitation: I shall not describe the night I passed: my tormented imagination together with the physical hurt done by the monster's initial cruelties made it one of the most dreadful I had ever gone through."

Justine,
by the
Marquis de Sade

Chapter Eighteen

The Vault. Paddles. The Hellfire Club. Garrett had made his way down to the meatpacking district, a part of Manhattan bustling during the day with humans cutting and packing meat and at night with rats licking up the scraps and blood left over from the day.

Garrett took a turn onto a dark side street. A dim streetlamp revealed the presence of a few rats scurrying across the bloodstained surface of the sidewalk. The rodents didn't appear to fear him; they were busy seeking dormant flesh. Uncomfortable with the sight, Garrett stepped down from the curb into the street to avoid confrontation. Once past the rats he stepped back onto the sidewalk. He wanted to find Rapture, the fourth club on his list. Business associates had talked about their slumming at sex clubs. Just to watch, of course, they always added. Garrett decided to browse alone in case someone caught his interest. He also left his chauffeured car at home, fearing it would attract attention. If an acquaintance saw him at one of the clubs, he could turn on his machismo attitude and join his friend in having a drink while sharing a laugh over the scene they viewed. He had scanned all the s/m magazines and noticed that several of the clubs were grouped together in Chelsea and the Meatpacking District. Rapture seemed to be the hardest to find.

No one walked the streets. It amazed him how desolate the streets near the clubs were, since the clubs themselves were crowded. He wondered whether an underground tunnel existed, or whether the players never left the scenes.

An oasis of a restaurant appeared in the midst of the sweltering silence of the summer night. A cab pulled up in front of the restaurant, and a man and a woman stepped out. Perhaps they would know. But he hadn't moved quickly enough, because the couple rushed into the restaurant.

He moved closer to the restaurant and peeked in the window. On the inside the restaurant looked like a pretentious diner. Formica-topped tables with chrome-frame metal chairs crowded in on each other, and at every table customers ate their meals elbow to elbow. The young, professional couples appeared to be dressed down in their designer jeans and environmental T-shirts. Several people waited near the door for a table.

Garrett mulled over whether he wanted to go in and ask about Rapture. He didn't. He couldn't say whether his hesitancy was because he didn't want to appear out of the loop in the midst of a crowd that obviously thought they made up the loop, or whether he would be embarrassed if someone did recognize the name of the club.

The people at the table directly in front of the window started waving at him and beckoning him to come in. He knew they didn't want him to join them, since he couldn't have squeezed himself in anywhere at the table. He guessed they felt as if he were gawking at them. When he looked down at the food on the table, he saw what he expected. Meat loaf, fried chicken, and Salisbury steak. Old-fashioned diner food being served up as a culinary experience.

A deep bark distracted him away from the restaurant. A tall, bald-headed man in leather walked his Great Dane. The dog and the man wore matching spiked collars. *If anyone would know . . .*

"Excuse me." Garrett approached the stranger. The man's pale blue eyes inspected Garrett's clothing. That day Garrett had worn his undertaker special, a plain black single-breasted suit with a white shirt and a black and white paisley print silk tie. "I wonder would you know where the Rapture Club is."

The man stopped, and the Great Dane sniffed Garrett's crotch.

"Are you a member?"

"I didn't think a person had to be."

"Only for the locked portion of the club."

"So I can get into at least a part of the club."

"Anyone can. Regrettably." Garrett expected the man to sniff, but he didn't. "I should say any male with forty-five dollars can get in. Females, of course, get in free. But you look like you'd like that idea."

Not wanting to antagonize his source of information, Garrett simply asked again for the location of the club.

"You're standing in front of it."

Garrett turned around and peered at the restaurant's window.

"You mean . . ."

"It's right above Ernie's."

"Ernie's. I take it that's the restaurant."

"Yes."

"And the entrance?"

The man pointed to a fire door nestled in between the restaurant and a packing house.

"Hard to find. There's no name on the place."

"People usually don't need to see the name to find it."

"This is my first time." *Brilliant statement, Garrett.* He felt the weight of the dog's paw settle on the tip of one of his new Ferragamo shoes. If he pulled his foot away, the leather would definitely be scratched; however, if he waited, his big toe might fall asleep. Brusquely he pulled his shoe from under the dog.

"I'd better get Rin Tin Tin home. He's getting a bit antsy."

Garrett laughed. "Rin Tin Tin?"

"That's right." The man didn't crack a smile, but he continued. "Perhaps I'll see you later." He winked and walked off with the dog.

Garrett went over and knocked on the fire door. It swung open an inch and then all the way.

"Good evening." The voice sounded like a bad impression of Marlon Brando. The body looked like Mr. America on a double dose of steroids, and instead of glistening with oil his body neoned in bright-colored tattoos. "Member or a guest?"

"Guest."

Immediately the man spun around and lifted a xeroxed sheet from the table behind him.

"That will be forty-five dollars, please."

111

Garrett counted out the money.

"Thank you. We have one request, actually a list of requests." The man snickered. "We'd like you to read our rules before climbing the stairs."

Garrett quickly scanned the short list containing the typical sex club "do's" and "don't's": No public intercourse. No forcing someone to play who did not want to. Always use barriers when touching genitals. No speaking to participants of a scene. Do not engage in loud talking or laughter when near a scene. Do not touch members of a scene unless specifically invited. . . . The only unusual suggestion indicated that a customer could enlist a club employee's assistance in finding a willing partner. This club may have an advantage over the others, Garrett thought.

The edges of the cement-block stairs had rubber grip runners. As Garrett climbed each step, he glanced at the beige peeling walls. At the top of the staircase, burgundy velvet drapes blocked the doorway. A thumping rhythm pulsed the material. Cautiously he pushed the drapes aside.

Illumination dim, music loud, and a sweet odor hiding sour sweat, all hit his senses in a flash.

As his eyes became accustomed to the lights, he suddenly caught sight of several torture devices. The St. Andrew's Cross to his right stood ready for a victim. A photograph of St. Andrew hung on the wall between the two top cross beams. A plaque next to the cross stated, "According to Leonardo da Vinci, the human body displays beautifully with the poser's legs spread at a seventy-two-degree angle. Enjoy!"

"Like to try it out?"

Garrett turned to see the man who had been walking the Great Dane. His leather jacket was unzipped, revealing a bloodred tattoo of a skull and crossbones on his chest. Garrett marveled over how the image looked as if it were carved from a bleeding open wound. The brushed edges of the design gave the appearance of bleeding flesh.

"No!"

The man moved closer to Garrett. He sniffed the air.

"You have the smell of a sub." He pulled Garrett's chin upward. "The pleading eyes of a submissive. And the shallow breathing to mark you as victim."

The man started to undo Garrett's tie, but Garrett pushed the hand away. Quickly he stepped around the man and walked deeper into the dry ice haze filling the room in front of him. He turned once to see whether the man followed. The man stood stock-still, his pale blue eyes fixed on Garrett. *He's got my number, but he's not my flavor*.

Garrett moved on. Tucked away to his right he saw a schoolroom, complete with blackboard, erasers, school bell, dunce cap, and various-size rulers in varying thicknesses. The handheld school bell reminded him too much of the bell the principal in his parochial elementary school had held. The sight of the nun had frightened six-year-old Garrett, with her towering height and black-and-white habit that allowed only the center of her face to peek through the wimple. That's where he first learned not to touch himself, at least not in public, especially not in church. He recalled the sting on his cheek caused by the pastor's sharp cuff. An old one-piece school desk stood near a heavyset dominatrix. The kind of school desk he had had to lie across to receive his punishment. As he reminisced, the dominatrix made her sub lie across the desk. She chose the thickest ruler.

Garrett turned away and moved into the opposite room. Here a group of people stood around a medical examining table. Because of the crowd he couldn't see the patient; instead he only heard a low moan or two. He moved back into the hall and continued on.

A dungeon came up next with fake stone walls, several inhabited cages, an occupied spinning catherine wheel, a bondage chair, and two guillotines, one for each head. Stretched out upon a rack lay a naked female. Her master selected a whip from the wall and drew the whip's snakelike tendril across her flesh. Clamps hugged her nipples, a black gag stretched across her mouth, and her white flawless skin awaited the flushing burn of the whip.

Garrett stood and watched as the woman silently accepted the sting of the whip. Other males and females gathered around. No one spoke. No one attempted to halt the display. But, he thought, to their credit no one cheered. He backed away from what he believed should have been a very private moment. Tripping over traditional steel restraints, he moved on to the next room.

Here the three mirrored walls reflected back the spanking horse, the whipping post, and the spanking block in an infinite series of receding reflections. The fourth wall displayed the whips, floggers, crops, and paddles. The ceiling lights glowed harshly down on very human-looking bodies. Beauty diminished by wattage. A man in his late forties or early fifties stood naked in the center of the room masturbating. Garrett noticed that the man did wear white tube socks and high-top sneakers. His pack of Camels caused a bulge in his left sock.

Garrett stared at his own image in the mirror

across from him. Suddenly the bald-headed man came into view behind him. The man now had a black handkerchief tied around his neck.

"You moved through the club quickly. Didn't find anything of interest? I can get you into the locked room. There's something different waiting for you in the locked room." The man spoke in a low voice. His lips hardly moved, but his words came through clearly.

"I've seen enough."

The man smiled. A gold front tooth glinted off the mirror's reflection. "How about some active participation?"

"Not here," Garrett said. Not publicly. He needed La Maîtresse's strength, her control, her breath softly floating across his skin as she moved to his neck.

"Blood sports."

"What?" asked Garrett.

The man reached into a pocket of his jeans and pulled out a straight-edge razor similar to the one Maîtresse la Présidente used.

"You drink?"

In answer the man opened his mouth, stuck out his long fat tongue, and licked his lips.

She wanted him to build up his blood. Replenish all that she had taken. His blood flowed only for her. But she no longer found the taste satisfying. Not his flavor, but the bald man desired what she had rejected.

"Back to your place?" Garrett asked.

Chapter Nineteen

"Matilda, a bit more tarragon," Sade said as he tasted the cooking mushrooms. "Tarragon adds an exquisite citron liquorice flavor."

"I didn't want to add too much, sir."

"Too little is just as bad." Sade wrinkled his nose in disapproval. "The soup? How is it doing?"

"Fine. The roast is in the oven and Cecelia is making the salad."

Cecelia smiled at Sade as she drew a cucumber delicately from her straw basket. She washed the cucumber under running water, rubbing her hands up and down the dark green skin to remove all surface soil.

Sade sighed.

"What is all this?" asked Liliana, entering the room. "I've never seen the kitchen so busy or so lively with delicious smells."

"Matilda and Cecelia are preparing dinner."

116

"Really, Uncle, sometimes I think you get too carried away with this food business."

"My taste buds have not died," he said indignantly.

Liliana laughed. "It seems so sad that you don't have anyone with whom to share the meal."

"Ah! I have a guest coming. One that needs the nourishment of a meal."

Sade knew Liliana would understand this to mean a nonvampire.

"Where did you meet him?"

"He's someone who offered to do my taxes."

"And will he get the chance?"

He leaned in close to Liliana and whispered, "I hope not."

"Then I'm glad I will not be here."

"Pourquoi ne te joindrais tu pas a nous?" asked Sade.

"I can't join you for dinner because I've already promised Grandmother that I'd eat with her and her guests tonight."

"Mais non!"

"I'm sorry, Uncle, but I didn't know that you were planning a special meal, and knowing how these meals usually end, I'm glad I will not be here."

"Mais non!" Sade glanced over at Matilda and her daughter. Neither appeared to be listening, but Sade knew servants had big ears. "Come into the dining room and see how well Matilda set the table."

They moved into the dining room together.

"The spoons are out of place!" Quickly he redid the silverware settings.

"It does look beautiful, especially the lilies in the centerpiece."

"I promise this night will not end in my taking

anyone's life. Several days ago I took my fill." He recalled the sensual pleasure he had taken while beating and sodomizing the willing Evie. Her blood had tasted of herbs and spices. *A vegetarian, most probably.* He had feasted until he sucked her dry.

"Then who is this person who thinks he's doing your taxes? And why did you invite him?" Liliana folded her arms and waited for an answer.

"*Ma chérie,* you look lovely in that silk dress. Crossing your arms will only cause creases to form."

"He's meant for me. Isn't he?"

"A dalliance. A brief touch with the male gender in a social situation."

"I have enough touches from you, Uncle." Liliana raised her voice. "I refuse to pander to your every whim."

"Quiet," he whispered. "The servants will think—"

"Uncle! Stop calling them servants. Matilda is a housekeeper, and Cecelia just comes here to help out her mother, not to wait on you."

"By extension, Cecelia waits on me."

"I'm going upstairs, getting my bag, and then leaving for Grandmother's."

"When will you return?"

"Don't bother keeping him here, because I may stay over at Grandmother's."

"You never like to stay there. Her work disgusts you."

"But she makes no demands on me."

"Your . . ." Sade remembered the mother and daughter in the kitchen. He moved closer to Liliana. "Your coffin is here with your home soil."

"I'll rest when I return in the morning."

"Ah! Then you will be back."

"Good Lord! You intend to keep him here until I get back, no matter when that may be."

"*Oui.*"

"Mr. Sade, I've added more tarragon to the mushrooms. Would you like to try one?" Matilda stood in the doorway.

"Don't follow through on your plan, Uncle. One of these days you will lose me completely if you continue this pressure."

Sade watched his niece walk away. Finally he looked over his shoulder and found that Matilda waited for an answer.

"Children." He sighed and watched a rare look of sympathy appear in Matilda's eyes.

Chapter Twenty

Grandmother baked delicious breads and pastries. Her preserves could even make a vampire's mouth water. But Uncle Donatien was right about the rest of her cooking. *Quelle tragedie!*

However, it didn't seem to bother her male dinner companions, who wolfed down large portions of everything. Liliana simply pushed the mashed potatoes and asparagus around the overcooked garlic lamb. Meanwhile, Grandmother never touched the meal. Blood lust had shined in Grandmother's eyes all evening, making Liliana feel out of place, especially since the young Bridgewater seemed more interested in her than in Grandmother.

"Are you currently in school, Liliana?" Wil asked.

"She's an embalmer," her grandmother answered.

"You're way too young to be working at that kind of job."

"She's older than she looks." The fingers of Grandmother's right hand started performing a tattoo on the dining table.

Liliana didn't want to leave and go back to her uncle and the poor, unsuspecting fool he had invited to be her dinner. However, her relations with her grandmother were being severely strained.

The older Bridgewater knocked over a water glass while reaching for the sliced meat.

"Liliana, dear, could you run and fetch something to dry up the table?" her grandmother asked.

Immediately Liliana left the room, but she felt Wil's stare follow her. Not what her grandmother had wanted, she was sure.

In the kitchen Liliana wasted a few minutes collecting a bunch of paper towels. If she left right after dinner, her grandmother would be relieved and Uncle Donatien would be elated. Liliana did not permit herself friends, for she feared the hunger might take control one day. She could drive around, but the bright headlights hurt her sensitive eyes. She, like her uncle and grandmother, had to use sunglasses night and day while driving. Mingling at the singles bars would be just asking for trouble for some poor guy.

"Do you need help?"

Wil had joined her in the kitchen.

"My grandmother . . ."

"I thought I'd give the old folks some time alone."

Just what Grandmother wouldn't want.

"You have very pretty eyes, Liliana. And your skin is so translucent." Wil reached out to touch one of her cheeks, and she backed away. "The paleness of your complexion makes you look delightfully delicate. Any man would like to reach out to hold you

121

and protect you. Would you mind if I gave you a hug?"

"Yes, I would."

Liliana attempted to walk by Wil, but he grabbed her left elbow.

"Don't misunderstand me, Liliana. I feel a strong attraction to you, but would never act upon it unless *encouraged* to do so."

"Have I encouraged, Wil?"

"You've been very polite."

"I hope politeness in your world isn't taken to mean 'easy mark.' "

He smiled. "It's taken as a maybe." He allowed her to walk past.

"Thank God you're back with those paper towels. We've been swimming here while waiting for you."

Liliana noticed that her grandmother glanced at her briefly, then settled her gaze on Wil. "What were the two of you doing so long in the kitchen? It's sort of like one of those jokes. You know. 'How many people does it take to retrieve a paper towel?' "

Liliana spread the paper towels over the water stain. The white linen tablecloth had already soaked up the water.

"Would you like more water, Mr. Bridgewater?" Liliana asked.

"Another beer would be better."

"I'll get it for him," called Wil on his way back to the kitchen.

"Grandmother, I think I'm coming down with something. It may just be a bad cold, but . . ."

"I understand if you must go, dear. Perhaps Keith could take you home."

"I'll take her home," said Wil as he put a beer in front of his father.

"It's your father's car, Wil. I should think he'd want to drive," said Grandmother.

"Lately I've been driving the car more than Dad."

"Actually, I drove myself here, and I'm sure I can drive myself back home," Liliana said.

"Not if you're ill," Wil protested.

"Wil, if my granddaughter says she can drive herself, then she can."

"Maybe I ought to follow you a ways. My stomach doesn't feel too good, so I should be leaving also." Keith groaned.

"If Dad's going, then I guess I am."

"Why?" Grandmother's voice sounded too high-pitched.

"Because I drove Dad here, and if he needs to get home . . ."

"Son, I'm not going to stand around and argue. Before it got settled I probably would have barfed all over this woman's table."

"Your father is so eloquent. However, I would like to speak to you alone, Wil. I can always drive you home later." Grandmother's eyes glittered with hunger.

"I don't feel up to driving," Keith said solemnly.

Liliana noticed the father's color was just a shade lighter than bile green.

"Grandmother, why don't I take Keith home, and Wil can use his own car when he wants to leave."

"Good idea." Keith burped.

In Liliana's Saab, Keith didn't look any better than when he had been seated at the dinner table.

"Your granny is a strange lady."

Liliana remained quiet.

"She's a powerful lady, too. You know, she

knocked me down one night because I got in between her and my son."

"I'm sure it was an accident."

"No. But the thing that gets me isn't the fact that she hit me. No. It's the power to her punch. It's not a ladylike punch."

Liliana couldn't keep herself from smiling.

"I'm serious. There's something about her. It's something supernatural."

"Supernatural?"

"Yeah. Not only does she pack a powerful wallop for a woman, she's also mighty strong for a man. And I don't think it's just getting laid that's she's after. Excuse me for talking like this about your granny, but I thought you could give me some insight into where she's coming from."

"The family doesn't know what to expect of her next."

"And the family consists of . . ."

"Just my uncle, myself, and Grandmother."

"Never met your uncle."

"It's better that way."

"He and your granny are related by blood?"

"Yes and no."

"That's ambiguous."

"Are we almost to your house, Mr. Bridgewater?"

"How come you have no interest in my son? He was certainly trying hard to get into your—impress you."

"All we need are the spotlights, and this would definitely be an interrogation."

"I'm an old man that doesn't have many interests and no friends to speak of. Certainly not your granny." Keith shook his head. "She is a really weird lady. What was her husband like?"

"She hasn't been married for years, Mr. Bridgewater, and I barely remember him."

"You were that young when he died?"

"No. He was that busy."

"So she had to make it on her own most of the time."

"Mr. Bridgewater, were you a psych major in school?"

"Never went to college. Went to work right after high school. Matter of fact, I started my job the day after I graduated. Didn't meet Wil's mother until years later. Played the field for a long time." Keith laughed in remembrance.

"There seems to be a fork in the road. Which way do I go?"

"Go left."

Keith remained silent for a long time, and Liliana left him alone with his memories.

"Make a right here."

"But, Mr. Bridgewater, this is a cemetery."

Liliana turned onto a gravel road. A plain iron gate stood before the car. The doors of the gate seemed to be haphazardly closed.

"I'll open the gate." With effort Keith got out of the car and walked up to the rusted latch on the gate. The latch squeaked as it gave up its security. Keith opened the gates and came back to the car.

"Why are we stopping here, Mr. Bridgewater?"

"I want you to meet Emmeline."

"Your dead wife?"

"She lives here."

And he thinks my grandmother's odd.

She drove slowly into the cemetery. Weeds had started to fill in gaps in the loosely packed gravel. The surrounding trees cut off the view of the public road.

"Just up ahead and to your right."

Liliana followed the instruction. She arrived at a sort of cul-de-sac of tombstones and stopped.

Keith got out of the car, and Liliana wondered whether she should follow or allow him time alone with his wife. Just when she decided to stay in the Saab, Keith beckoned to her. High heels were not the best shoes to wear on gravel, she decided as she limped along.

Keith took off his white shirt and started dusting a tombstone.

"Haven't been here in a while. I like to shine it up when I visit. Usually I even bring a bottle of spray detergent."

His potbelly hung over the belt of his trousers. Several moles spattered his back. One particularly large mole looked injured, as if it had been scratched or were possibly seething with a disease Keith didn't know about.

"We were together for fifteen years. Did everything together. You know, through that fifteen years we never spent a night apart. I couldn't sleep unless her little round bottom was smack up against my big bottom."

Keith looked around.

"You have anyone buried here?"

"No family. Only a few acquaintances of my uncle."

He nodded.

"She had to have a baby. Wouldn't have felt that she was a woman unless she gave birth. Me, I didn't care. I had nothing special to leave my kin. We spent several weekends fucking our brains out trying to get her to conceive. Finally, on a rainy afternoon, she got the word from her doctor. She was

126

tickled pink, and I was happy for her. The child wasn't important to me. She was."

"Did you ever love your son?"

"I love my son as a son. I didn't choose to have him come into this world to murder his mother. But I guess the boy didn't chose to commit his sin."

"I don't believe it was a sin. It was unfortunate and hurt him as much as you."

"He never knew her. How can you miss someone you don't know?"

"He knows he doesn't have a mother."

"She started taking up knitting and crocheting. Was really bad at them. She'd lose stitches. Forget an armhole. Emmeline was a petite woman, must have been no more than four-eleven in bare feet. Slender hips, not meant for birthing."

When he turned to look at Liliana, she saw his eyes shine under the light of the quarter moon. He used the shirt in his hand to mop his face.

"Why does your granny want my son so bad?"

"My grandmother is friendly."

"No. Not even his body would satisfy her. The woman wants his soul. She wants to reach in and tear it out."

Liliana's shoulders shuddered. *She wants your son's blood, Mr. Bridgewater. She wants to own him. Live off him.*

"I was a bare minimum father. I took him to the doctor when he was sick. I saw him off to school each morning. Checked his homework at night. When there was a father-son function, I was there. Called the police on him when I found marijuana hidden under his mattress. I knew the sheriff would put a scare into him. Knew he wouldn't put my son away for more than a night."

"You sent your son to jail?"

"Spent only one night in juvenile detention. Picked him up the next day, and he was as brazen as ever. I tried to follow the rules and regulations of fatherhood, but I never allowed my heart to interfere. Never exposed myself to anyone else after Emmeline died."

He took a step closer to Liliana.

"But I don't want any harm to come to him. I can't say I love him as a person. I do love him, though, because he's my . . ." He glanced back at the tombstone. "Our flesh and blood. He's a part of Emmeline I can't put behind me and forget. Memories fade in and out. But when I see Wil and touch Wil and breathe his scent I'm in Emmeline's presence again." He looked at Liliana. "Please don't let your grandma hurt my son."

"Send your son away."

"He won't go. He thinks he's looking out for me. Wants to prove he loves me. But he can't, you know, because I didn't teach him how."

Something moved. She looked around to see what it was.

"Scared? Don't have to be. It was probably some animal scurrying across the cemetery. We probably invaded his property. Or at least he thinks we did.

"When I was a boy I wouldn't go near cemeteries. Dad used to tell fiendish tales about flesh-eating ghouls and bloodsucking vampires. Where he came from, if they thought someone was a vampire they would dig up the grave, cut the head off, and put it at the feet of the body. Facing downward, just in case the vampire was able to reach down and stick the head back on his shoulders. That way the vampire couldn't see where he was going. Guess they didn't think vampires were smart enough to twist the head around.

"But ever since Emmeline died, I'm no longer afraid of at least this cemetery. After she died I spent a lot of time reading." He laughed. "Still do. One book talked about the Aztecs and their belief in *cihuateteo*."

"Female vampires that died in childbirth," Liliana mechanically said.

"Yeah." His voice displayed his surprise. "Anyway, I used to come here and wait for her to rise. Hell, I would have let her bite me if I could have spent eternity with her."

Keith fell down on his knees before the tombstone. He muffled his sobs with his shirt. Liliana went to him and placed her hand on the back of his wrinkled neck. Her hand slid down across the keratoses and moles, resting finally on the large festering mole.

Chapter Twenty-one

Marie fingered the doily on the arm of the settee. Wil had offered to retrieve a bottle of champagne from the refrigerator.

Her eyes hurt. She stood and walked to the other end of the room to dim the lights. Keith had insisted on turning the lights on maximum. *Thank God he's gone.* She felt guilt and relief that her granddaughter had left.

Liliana had certainly looked fragile tonight. The diet she was keeping obviously sapped her strength. Her fingers were long and thin, and Marie couldn't help but notice that the skin withered under the girl's fingernails. Marie wondered what Liliana's body looked like under the layers she wore. When Sade had been forced to go on a bloodless diet and sleep without his coffin in the Bastille, he had become bloated. Her stupid daughter, Reneé-Pelagie, had believed it to be the rich food. Marie had known better. Once she had learned of Sade's secret blood lust, she had never let the man walk free in Paris until he shared the eternal gift with her. *Bloated on rich food!* More likely his gaseous pomposity enlarged his corpse. Vampires didn't absorb food the way the living did. They had no need. Blood sated a vampire's hunger. Blood and sex, she thought as Wil called from the kitchen.

"We'll have to open a fresh bottle of Veuve Cliquot 'La Grande Dame.' "

"Go right ahead, my dear."

It couldn't hurt to have him a little—no, completely drunk, she thought. As for herself, she missed the elegant highs she had when living. Her serious highs now only occurred when drinking blood. And she wasn't sure the dead blood that her granddaughter consumed was absorbed. *How unnatural!* Perhaps for once she would join forces with Sade and attempt to make Liliana behave as a true vampire. But Liliana couldn't have Wil. That would be the only line Marie would draw in helping her.

Marie had worn a revealing black dress, hoping to emphasize her blood-hungry white skin. Alas, Liliana in a heather gray turtleneck dress still seemed to outdo her. Somehow Liliana had managed to shine like silver against the bland heather hue. *How silly to envy one's own granddaughter,* she chided herself.

"Where did you go?" asked Will, staring at the empty settee.

"I'm here," she said quietly, and rapidly moved herself directly behind her prey.

She smiled what she hoped was a pretty smile, but she had become a vampire too late to retain the freshness and youth that marked Liliana.

131

Marie walked around him and settled herself once again on the settee, placing her hand on the cushion next to her as an invitation. He handed her a fresh glass of champagne before taking the seat immediately next to her.

"I must say that I'm impressed with the quantity and quality of champagne you can afford."

"Why?"

"Your husband must have left you quite well-off."

"Husband? What makes you think I depend on a dead husband for financial support?"

In fact, initially the money had come from her husband. However, she was proud that her crafty investments had transformed the modest legacy into a fortune. The fees her clients paid her were pin money, taken merely to assuage her clients' guilt.

For the first time she noticed that Wil's eyes had a touch of gold in them, a shine that appeared only when he thought something amusing. She meant to prove that she was more than just amusing.

"What did you want to talk to me about?" asked Wil.

"Truth."

"How solemn."

"So many people waste their time in games. I never waste a minute."

"Recently you seemed to have been biding your time." That horrible shiny glow lit his eyes once again. But those eyes could turn darker, she knew, and she would bring out the ebony in them.

"There's a difference between biding one's time and being . . . polite. And I think we know enough about each other to drop the charade."

"You mean from now on you're going to be impolite." The amusement in his eyes had begun to sting her.

Marie rose and began to disrobe—not with any special speed. No, casually she discarded her dress and stood before Will in a heavily laced black corset. She lifted the cushion on which she had been seated and pulled out a flogger, one of her fanciest with gold leaf on the handle and studded with emeralds. She allowed the deerskin thongs to fall across her right thigh.

Wil leaned back on the settee and stretched his legs, resting his feet on the coffee table. Whimsy didn't leave his pupils as he sipped the champagne.

"What's your preference, flogging or whipping?" she asked.

"The floggers I use are made of harness leather, not deerskin."

"I have a selection."

Suddenly Wil leaned forward and made a grab for the flogger. Her hand instantly tightened on the handle, and she could feel the tension spread up her arm into her neck, tensing her lips.

Wil simply turned his hand palm upward and waited until she released the handle of the flogger into his palm.

Placing his feet back on the floor, Wil moved forward in his seat and began to brush the thongs against Marie's shapely leg.

"Your body's in good shape."

"For an old bag."

"Better even than many young purses."

They both laughed. Wil put his glass on the table and stood. He kept his long body straight as he removed his jacket.

"And the shirt," she suggested.

He smiled. That damn shine of amusement never

seemed to leave his eyes. He switched the flogger to his left hand and rubbed the back of his right hand across his lips. After taking several steps backward, he practiced using the flogger in the air.

"From the way your chest had looked the other day I wouldn't have expected you to be able to use the flogger so expertly."

"I switch."

The amusing shine in his eyes glowed.

"I don't."

"Shame. You can't be good at one without being good at the other also."

"Bullshit." She smelled him now. Not just the odor of his blood but the testosterone violence building in his body's cells. Maybe that had been what she had sensed all along. Not the weakness and submissiveness of this young man, but the potential cruelty and power he could wield. He definitely needed to be tamed.

His movements were fluid, confident, and professional.

"Another way you earn a living?"

"And now I know how you can afford all that expensive champagne."

"I don't do it for the money."

"And you don't do it for free."

"No, a good psychiatrist always makes sure the bill is paid."

His eyes lit up like fire as he went into a fit of laughter. He attempted to speak, but garbled his words. Finally: "It's my turn to say bullshit."

"I do it for the blood." Her voice sounded stern and level, filled with no humor.

"For the sight of blood?"

"For the feel of the thick juice rolling across my tongue, settling into my pores. Keeping me alive."

"A wanna-be vampire. I don't give of my blood until I've drawn my partner's."

Wil tossed the flogger onto the settee, picked up his jacket, and walked to the front door.

"Will you be seeing me out as a lady should?"

The sarcasm sparked the fire of her need. She lifted the flogger and came at Wil.

Quickly he dodged her swing. She heard his laughter through the door he had slammed behind him.

"One has no conception of what anguish is suffered by the wretch who from hour to hour awaits his ordeal, from whom hope has fled, and who knows not whether this breath he draws may not be his last."

Justine,
by the
Marquis de Sade

Chapter Twenty-two

Garrett stood over the toilet retching. He heard his son's loud music as a thumping through the wall that separated him from his son's bedroom. After puking on and off for several hours, Garrett now had the dry heaves and painful cramps. His teenage daughter screamed at her brother so loudly that her words sounded garbled.

He used a wet towel to wipe his face.

A gentle rap introduced his wife's voice.

"Honey, are you all right? I can call the doctor's service, or perhaps I should drive you to the emergency room."

"No! God, no! Just leave me alone."

"Whatever it is, I hope it's not catching." She lowered her voice. "Remember the children are here."

The old family Saint Bernard barked wildly. Garrett's son and daughter had most likely come to blows again. The battles never amounted to much, but Garrett didn't like the idea of his son hitting his sister. He didn't like the idea of any violence within his household.

He rubbed another layer of Preparation H into his crack. He had the shits all morning, and now the burning and pain made it difficult for him to walk. Quickly he had disposed of his silk boxer shorts lest his wife see the blood staining them. Black and blue marks covered his ass. He checked his cock for any blisters or sores. Too early, he supposed, but hell, he couldn't believe the bastard didn't bother to use protection. He guessed his real worry would be the cum that the guy had squirted up into his asshole. His stomach roiled with the memory of having the fag's dick shoved into his mouth. He remembered the hooklike shape that seemed to force its way down his throat and the metal ball piercing the tip that had slid against his tonsils.

Talking about assholes. Why the hell did he allow the fag to tie him up? Because he was stupid? Because he was suicidal? Perhaps because he wanted to bring a little gift back to Maîtresse? Whatever the reason, he rued the previous night's activities.

Painfully Garrett bent over to pull up the black silk pajama bottom from around his ankles.

The bastard didn't even get into any blood sports. That probably was a blessing. His nipples were sore from the clamps that had looked like miniature wine presses. Cautiously Garrett picked up the pajama top. He hated slipping it over his tender nipples, but there were some suspicious bruises marking his back, and his wife would surely notice them. Stiffly he stretched his arms into the sleeves, but before buttoning up he pulled the Band-Aids from the medicine chest. He placed an inch-wide strip on each nipple, then closed the pajama top. Not perfect, but better, he thought.

Another gentle rap.

"Honey, the lawyer's on the phone."

Damn it! He was in the midst of closing an important business deal, and he couldn't clear his mind of the pain to think straight.

"I'll call back."

There were a few seconds of silence.

"Okay." And she was gone, for good, he hoped.

"Dad!"

"Aw shit!"

"Dad, Robbie hit me again."

He wanted to tell his daughter to shoot her brother, but he knew that would be unwise because she took things too literally.

"Yeah, yeah. Get your mother."

"But, Dad . . ."

He heard his son let out a loud raspberry.

"Mom!"

Garrett let down the top of the commode and tried to sit. There was no comfortable position that he could assume.

Why the hell did he do it? Nice and safe, that's how it had always been with Maîtresse. *She's a professional. The turd last night was a pervert.* And the jack-off had even invited him back for another session. Told Garrett his name was Letcher. Rin Tin Tin and Letcher. Garrett shook his head and almost began to laugh, but caught himself when the pain kicked in.

Chapter Twenty-three

"A Cohiba?" asked Sade.

"Wow! They're hard to come by. Whom do you know?"

"I get them myself. I bring them back via Canada. I can't resist the leathery spiceness and dark chocolaty rich flavors."

David hesitated a moment before choosing a cigar.

"But it is a tough draw, and I've heard you have to be careful of fakes while you're up there."

Sade almost dropped the lid of the box on David's outreached hand.

"I bring them in via Canada, but buy them in person at a state shop in Cuba. Of course I could purchase them at the Davidoff shop in Toronto, but I enjoy the trip to Cuba because I visit some of my old friends."

"Then this should be the real thing."

"I assure you that I don't replace the originals with fakes just to fool my guests."

Sade lit the cigar for David.

"I don't normally smoke, Mr. Sade; however, when someone offers me a Cohiba, I think of it as a special occasion."

Sade sat in a burgundy leather wing chair.

"And it is, David. At least I hope it will be."

"Mr. Sade, I've enjoyed the meal and the company, but shouldn't we get down to discussing business?"

"A cognac? The Cohiba is always enhanced by a good cognac."

"I'm sure it is, but I'd like to get down to discussing business."

"It'll take me *un moment* to pour each of us a snifter."

Eat rapidement, ma petite Liliana. Sade had begun to tire of his guest and wished to move on to his own nutritious dinner awaiting him on the streets.

"Is this a working fireplace?"

"Mais oui," answered Sade. He poured out a hefty snifter for each of them; after all, it could be a long night. "We rarely light *un feu* since *les flammes* unhinge me." He walked back to the sofa where David sat and handed him a snifter. "A spark any bigger than what's on the tip of this Cohiba . . ." Sade held up his cigar in his right hand. "Seems totally useless and dangerous to me. I've lost many of my brethren to spiteful bonfires."

Sade returned to his chair.

"In fires?"

Sade nodded but refused to elaborate.

"David, you haven't tried the cognac yet."

"Actually I think I may have had enough to drink.

141

When you give me the work papers, I want to be able to make some sense of them, and hopefully I'll make sense to you. You do have the papers, don't you?"

"The papers . . ." Sade halted. He heard the sound of a car pulling up in front of the house. "Did I mention that I have a niece?"

"You have a dependent?"

"*I have a niece*. She's quite charming. I think you'll enjoy meeting her." The front door opened and closed. "And here she is," Sade said, rising from his chair. "Liliana!"

A wilted young woman entered the doorway. Her hair looked uncombed, half moons hung under her eyes, and her makeup appeared to be smeared.

Sade wondered whether he should send her upstairs and try again another night.

"Uncle?"

Sade sighed and dared to persevere.

"Liliana, I would like you to meet my guest, *Monsieur* David Petry." Sade stood aside so that she had a clear view of the sofa.

"Good evening," David said while attempting to stand from the plush sofa's feathers pillows. When he finally stood, he noticed he didn't have a free hand to offer and immediately put down the snifter so that he could extend his right hand and walked over to greet the young woman.

Sade turned back to his niece and saw that her skin had paled nearly to the point of blotting out the dark circles under her eyes.

Liliana watched the young man move awkwardly across the Persian rug. Did he have a limp, or had his foot gone to sleep? The hand he extended looked smooth and soft. His cheeks showed no sign of war wounds. But the blond hair, the blue eyes, the features were there.

"Stuart?"

Liliana did not accept his hand. He let his right hand droop to his side.

"Don't I know you?" he asked.

"Ah! You feel a certain déjà vu when looking at my niece."

"No. It's you, sir."

"*Moi!*"

"Yes. At a diner in New Jersey."

"Hardly the kind of place I would partake in any culinary pleasure."

"In the men's room. This is quite embarrassing. You don't remember me? Perhaps I should leave it that way."

"*Oui*. Come join us, Liliana."

She felt the tug of her uncle's fingers on the sleeve of her dress.

David stepped aside to make room for her.

"You're the young lady who's queasy about eating rabbits."

Rabbits. Diner. How had her uncle found this impostor?

Liliana allowed herself to be pulled into the room, but directed herself to the wing chair. Sade tried to alter her path, but stopped when she dug her high heel onto his left instep. There was no cry of pain, only a slight tearing of the Marquis's eyes.

Sitting down in the wing chair, Liliana said, "I'd love to know more about your first meeting with my uncle, Mr. Petry."

"His name is David. And you did hear him say that he was rather embarrassed about some meeting we supposedly had."

"Tell me about it, Mr. Petry."

Sade began to pace the room. David, unsure whether he should stand or sit, decided to lean against the mantel of the fireplace.

"Call me David, please, Ms. Sade."

"My name is not Sade. It's Liliana Plissay, but do call me Liliana."

"Or even Lil," muttered Sade midway across the room.

"I'm sure my uncle wouldn't mind if you sat while he worked off his *anxiety*."

"Oh, do, please," said Sade. "Your cognac is waiting for you."

David took a seat on the sofa and looked around.

"An ashtray, Uncle."

"Excusez-moi." Sade retrieved an ashtray from inside a cabinet. "Matilda, our ser—housekeeper likes to put everything away."

"You met my uncle in a diner?"

"Yes." David cleared his throat several times. "I had never been in that diner before, and surely I never plan on returning."

"I presume you don't even remember the name of the place," said Sade.

"I don't even remember the town I was in." He blushed when he looked at Liliana.

"Well, so much for that *petite histoire*."

"Were you dining there, David?"

Sade loudly harrumphed.

"Not exactly, Liliana. I became ill while driving and stopped to use their men's room. Your uncle came in to clean up, I believe, and we basically met at the sink."

"Simple, boring *histoire, ma petite chérie*."

"Now you remember it, Uncle?"

"Vaguely."

"And my uncle invited you home with him to do his accounting books?"

David took a few moments to think about this.

"I guess I gave your uncle my name. Honestly, I don't remember telling him that I was an accountant. At the time he wanted my assistance in getting you to eat some rabbit.

"It's odd that you should have called me, Mr. Sade. Did we speak of doing some work?"

"Only on the telephone." Sade stopped pacing to stand behind the wing chair.

David downed almost the whole snifter of cognac.

"I admit I'm confused as to how you managed to locate me. I mean, there are tons of accountants out there."

"But none like you," Liliana softly said.

The young man fidgeted with the cigar he had placed in the ashtray. A blush again flushed his face.

"I take that as a compliment, but I haven't proven myself yet."

"I'm sure you'll get the opportunity. Don't you think, Liliana?"

"Uncle, I hate you."

Chapter Twenty-four

Stupide jeune fille!

Sade recalled the debacle from the previous evening. He had been certain that Liliana could easily seduce David. Not only that, she was obviously mesmerized by the resemblance to Stuart. Why did she have to ruin a perfect situation with her *stupide* declaration of hate?

Sacrebleu, what a waste of some fine, warm, young, and live blood. He would see to it that she had another opportunity, but perhaps in a more intimate setting.

How long would he be able to put David off? he wondered. All the young man seemed to talk about was business. Sade had gone to great lengths to appease his business manager, Gaspard François Xavier Gaufridy, who had certainly been irate when he had learned that Sade had made him a vampire. He had promised Gaufridy that he would compensate his family for the loss of their sole financial support. Unfortunately, while the family was alive, the Marquis had run into serious financial problems. But whom was to blame for that?

Gaufridy still kept the books, very stingily, Sade recalled. Sade could not ask Gaufridy to turn over the books to this boy, even for a short period of time. Gaufridy would balk, threaten again to cut off contact with Sade. This threat had been present ever since their boyhood days.

Sade mulled over the situation in the wing chair while Matilda cleaned house around him.

"Matilda."

"Yes, sir."

"What would you consider a romantic evening for a young person?"

"How young, sir?"

"*La jeune fille* is seventeen. A very mature seventeen."

"Seventeen, sir!"

Sade noted that she had instantly stopped her work.

"And the gentleman, Matilda, is in his late twenties, early thirties."

"What kind of girl is this?"

"*Une jeune fille!* What more do you need to know?"

"She sounds way too young for the gentleman."

"More likely the other way around."

"You feel this girl is very experienced?"

"Far more than most people know."

"But you know?"

"In practically every way."

"Except?"

"We have not been intimate. As yet." Sade smiled to himself.

"I think you—or whoever this gentleman is—should stay away from her."

"How prudish, Matilda."

"I'm certain the girl has family that would not look kindly on the relationship."

"Kindly?"

"They'd probably do him in for the crime."

"What crime?"

"She's underage."

"Nonsense, Matilda. Besides, I'm family, and I'm trying to set this romance into motion."

"You're related?"

"Liliana, my niece."

"Thank God!"

"You needn't make it sound like she's an old maid, Matilda."

"She's not an old maid, but I did think she was older than seventeen, not by the way she looks, of course. However, she holds a job and has for some time."

"Why do *femmes* choose to make everything so complicated? Perhaps she's older. I never remember birthdays." Sade rose from the chair and paced the room. "What would be a romantic evening for you, Matilda?"

"I'm sure my idea of a romantic evening is very different from your niece's."

"Hmmmm. So is mine." Sade sighed.

"Does your niece have any interest in the gentleman?"

"She used to."

"Then they've been separated for a while?"

"Very much so."

"What initially attracted her to him?"

"The uniform, the scar . . . hmm. His shyness.

148

But with her he opened up. I must work on him, then."

"You can't remake a person, sir."

"I'm not changing him. I simply want him to be as he used to be."

"Sometimes time can't be turned back, depending on the gentleman's experiences."

"He has similar experiences. He was in the armed services. He still blushes."

"How charming!"

"*Les femmes* do appreciate that. Although he may not be as shy as he once was." Sade recalled the contact David had made with Evie. "But then, that may be a plus. Before he never knew where to put his hands, never mind his—"

Matilda cleared her throat.

"*Excusez-moi*. I am interrupting your work schedule. Please finish up."

Matilda ran for the exit to the kitchen, but stopped when Sade called her name.

"How is Cecelia doing?"

"Fine." She turned back to exit.

"By the way, she mentioned a dance recital that she's going to perform. Has the date been set yet?"

"It's been canceled, sir." Speedily she withdrew from the room.

Chapter Twenty-five

Seeing the gates of the cemetery in daylight chilled Liliana's soul. When she had been with Keith, it had been dusk, and she couldn't make out many of the fine details—or at least they hadn't attracted her attention.

The bars on the gates were closely fitted, and the top of each bar ended in a sharp point. No one would be able to gain entrance *or leave* the cemetery. Did spirits waft through the narrow spaces between each bar? Certainly vampires couldn't. Unlike the stories fed to the mass market, vampires were not able to turn into a puff of smoke.

Liliana left her car on the triangular dusty space to the right of the gates. Today she had dressed comfortably in sneakers and jeans. An old sweatshirt with the logo of an outdated rock 'n' roll band topped the outfit.

When she touched the door of the gate, she

thought she felt an electric shock and immediately pulled her hand away. But there was obviously no circuitry hooked up to the gate. Only her imagination, she thought. She picked up a medium-size branch and used it to pull back the gate. The gate barely swung open, but it was enough to allow her to squeeze through.

The gravel road she traveled immediately forked into three different paths. Straight ahead she would find Emmeline. Before paying a visit to Keith's wife, Liliana took the path leading to the right. Evidently this led to the old part of the cemetery, for it was less maintained, with tombstones either leaning or fallen over. There did not appear to be any mausoleums, only a few crosses interspersed among the tombstones. Most of the writing on the stones was illegible. Once in a while she could make out an unfamiliar name. Most of the surnames were very English-sounding: Stafford, Vaughn. An occasional Irish or Scot name broke the monotony. The tombstone dates preceded the American Revolutionary War. Nettles stretched out onto the road, causing her to trip occasionally. She wondered whether any vampires lived here. She had heard of a mysteriously impaired line of vampires that spent nights looking for food and days hiding underground or in mausoleums. These vampires led a primitive existence. Although she herself had never encountered any of these, she believed the stories about them to be true. There was even talk that some of the impaired vampires had once been fully functional, but that something in their brains had broken down and that they had become something closer to ghouls than true vampires.

The trees here were old and tall. Only an occasional ray of sun poked through the thick branches, comfortable for Liliana and perfect for the impaired vampires. Yes, she decided, if any vampires existed in this cemetery, this would be their dwelling place.

She looked for dirt that had been recently moved or a path disrupting the weeds that grew among the tombstones. Nothing—until she caught sight of a yellowed piece of lace resting next to a fallen cross. The material did not fly in the breeze; instead it seemed caught in a clump of earth. She walked to the lace and picked it up. She smelled the cloth. Blood, stale, perhaps a week old. She touched the material with her tongue and tasted human baby's blood. Not healthy blood. The child must have been quite ill. The faded blood appeared as pink slashes across the material. After feeling the cloth between her fingers, she could tell the cloth had not belonged to the baby. Instead the lace had been aged well over a century.

Again she searched for moved earth. Did these vampires really dig back into their coffins each daybreak? Or did they hide during the day behind bushes and in hollowed-out trees?

Many weeds but few bushes covered this part of the cemetery. Most of the trees were old and gnarled. A squat dead tree stood to her left. On closer examination Liliana noted some remaining greenery on its branches. She walked around the tree and saw a hollowed-out pit. The hole in the tree was big enough for a child or very small adult. She couldn't see inside. Blindly she slipped her hand into the opening. She could feel the uneven surface of a walnut, and she broke several webs. Certainly the pit hadn't been occupied in a long time. But then her hand caught onto something rubbery.

When she pulled out the object she recognized that it was a baby's pacifier.

Now she noticed something she had missed earlier. There were no ants running up and down the bark of the tree. No insects at all. And birds seemed to avoid this area of the cemetery completely, although she couldn't remember whether she had seen any birds near Emmeline's tombstone.

She continued along the path until she reached the ivy-covered fence. No squirrels. No insects. No birds.

An old French hymn came into her mind and she began to hum. She couldn't remember the words, but the tune kept ringing inside her head. It had been a century since she had heard this music. Why would the hymn come to her now? She sensed that at least one ancient vampire slept nearby, one of the primitive ones that survived by the sufferance of a disbelieving public. Could this thing that she tracked be considered human anymore?

She retraced her steps, humming and attempting to memorize as many family names as she could. When she had returned to the fork, she took the center path. The path that led to Emmeline.

Here a mixture of tombstones and mausoleums shared the earth. Flowers had been left at most of the plots, and some plots even had small gardens, carefully planned and colorful as if to deny the emptiness of the cemetery. The doors on the mausoleums were closed. None stood ajar.

She saw Emmeline's tombstone before her. The charcoal-gray granite shined in the sunlight. The simple and legible legend on the stone stated her birth and death dates and that she had been the wife of Keith Bridgewater and the mother of Wilbur.

Liliana investigated Emmeline's neighbors and found that Emmeline was the youngest female buried in this part of the cemetery. One male child slept to her right. The rest had died in their seventies or eighties and one had barely reached one hundred. Wives and husbands buried together for the eternal rest.

"What are you doing here?"

Liliana turned quickly. How had anyone sneaked up on her? Her hearing was acute, and her sense of smell was definitely sharp. Obviously she had allowed herself to be drawn into a deep reverie on death.

"I'm sorry, Wil. I didn't know family would visit today."

"Hadn't planned on it, but the old man's been giving me a hard time all morning. Thought I'd come here and draw on some of my mother's famous patience."

"Famous?"

"Whenever I was bad, my father would wish that mom were around to deal with me. She had the patience, he said."

"Were you that wayward as a child?"

"Willful, as he called it."

Wil walked past Liliana and stood at his mother's tombstone in silence. Liliana was ready to move away when he spoke to her.

"Dad takes good care of the grave."

"He loves your mother."

"And because of that he hates me."

"Your father and I talked about you and your mother yesterday evening. My impression is that he's confused."

"Why are you here?" he asked. "Out of curiosity?"

"I wanted to see how . . ." How the dead really *lived*. "Your father talked about her a lot. He even got me to drive him here to the cemetery before taking him home."

"He had to spit-shine the stone."

"I think he missed her and was trying to figure out how to connect with you."

Wil faced Liliana.

"When I was a boy I used to spy on my dad. See that tree over there?"

An oak nestled its roots outside the cemetery; many of its branches hung over several stones near the fence.

"Yes."

"I climbed that tree as a child. Used to watch Dad cleaning the stone, planting flowers, even kneeling in prayer. I had to be careful, though. See that big branch that glides out over the fence?"

"Yes."

"Sam, a boyhood friend, used to climb up there with me sometimes, until once he nearly fell right down on top of the spiked fence. I grabbed him in time, but he never climbed that tree again. Almost found himself truly staked out over the cemetery." Wil laughed.

"Bet Sam didn't think that joke was funny."

"How did you guess? Do you know him?"

Liliana turned away and began her walk back to the cemetery gate.

"Wait up," Wil yelled.

She stopped for a second, then continued. When Wil did catch up, he was slightly breathless.

"You doing anything special tonight?"

"Yes, I am."

"Okay. How about tomorrow night or anytime within the next six months would you go out with me?"

"No."

"Because of your grandmother?"

"No. I don't want to."

"But let us consider matters from another viewpoint. Is this a personal chastening I'm getting? and as if I were a naughty little boy, the idea is to spank me into good behavior? Wasted efforts, Madame. If the wretchedness and ignominy to which I have been reduced by the Marseilles judges' absurd proceedings, who punished the most commonplace of indiscretions as though it were a crime, have failed to make me mend my ways, your iron bars and your iron doors and your locks will not be more successful."

Letter (1777)
To Madame la Présidente de Montreuil, by the Marquis de Sade

Chapter Twenty-six

It had been just over a week since Garrett had met Letcher and his dog and Garrett's body had just started feeling better. Not well enough to have sex with his wife or to return to his regular workout program, but comfortable enough not to mind the potholes his chauffeur couldn't avoid.

Garrett set aside the legal pad on which he had been doodling and leaned against the backseat of his Lincoln. Useless. His brain was useless today. He couldn't concentrate. He couldn't forget. He glanced out the window. The road they were on did not lead home.

"Philip, where are you going?"

"It's Tuesday, sir. I always take you upstate at this time."

They were coming up on La Maîtresse's home. He could see the house and the bright colors of her garden. He had no appointment with La Maîtresse.

157

She had told him she would call when she could take him back.

Philip turned and pulled up in front of La Maîtresse's garage. The chauffeur immediately got out of the car and opened the back door to allow Garrett to exit.

An older man stood on the porch of the house and stared at the car. He had white hair and his stance appeared haughty. Could he be the favored slave?

Garrett stepped out of the car and walked up to the porch.

"Is Marie expecting you?"

"Marie." Garrett had never known her real name. Hadn't wanted to. Fantasy began when he crossed the threshold of her home. The home of Maîtresse la Présidente. He paid in cash and never asked anything about her own life.

"Is . . . she here?"

"No. But I am. Perhaps I can help you." The man's smile was a cross between a leer and humor.

This man knew why Garrett came here.

"Do you live with her?"

"No, *monsieur*, but I'm quite familiar with the place."

"Are you her husband?"

The man with the French accent guffawed.

"Son-in-law, *monsieur*."

"Sorry."

"Ah! Sad it is, because she drove my own Renée-Pélagie away from me. May she rest in peace. But you are not here, *monsieur*, to inquire about my relationships. Instead, I think, you seek pleasure. *N'est-ce pas?*"

"Will she return soon?"

"Not soon enough for you, I'm sure, *monsieur*.

Perhaps you could help me with this Eton bench. I want to bring it down to the *donjon*. Perhaps I may even set it up now, *monsieur*. It has not tasted flesh against its platform in some time."

Why did his fucking cock ache? wondered Garrett. Hadn't he learned his lesson? The bruises had been slow to fade. His butt still had a yellowish cast from the last beating. On the other hand, this would allow him access to La Maîtresse's house and a world with which he was familiar.

"I assure you, *monsieur,* that Marie allows me full use of the *donjon*. At least when she is not here. By the way, I introduced her to many of *les instruments de travail*. And with my expert guidance she has become a well-educated dom."

Garrett's breath caught. Sweat beaded on his forehead. His body tingled. A breeze carried the sweet smell of honeysuckle to his nostrils, almost turning his stomach.

"I can't wait for your decision, *monsieur*."

The man on the porch walked over to the Eton bench and lifted it easily. As he started for the front door Garrett quickly reached out for the knob.

"Thank you, *monsieur*. I will certainly need your assistance when I reach the *donjon*. If you remember, there's a terrible kink in the stairs."

Garrett remembered. He remembered the placement of the whips, floggers, canes, manacles. He remembered his lowly position. On his hands and knees. Head down, ass raised in the air. He thought of all this as he moved through the house, knowing where the dungeon door was without thinking.

The dungeon always remained cooler than the upstairs. When he opened the door a cool breeze sped by him.

"Thank you again, *monsieur*. Would you mind

leading the way down the staircase? You can then warn me of any obstacles that may be in the way."

The wooden steps were unfinished. Rough splinters protruded from the pine. Garrett grabbed the metal hand railing. The steps were steep, and he did not want to add to his bruises. At least he didn't consciously think he did.

"It is *très gentil* of you to assist me. Often I have been down *ici*, but with such a large load I thought it best to have someone along."

"Then why didn't you wait for . . ."

"Marie?"

"Marie."

"I wanted to set up before she got home. *Une surprise.*"

Garrett reached the kink in the staircase and turned to face the older man.

"We may have run into a problem. Would you like me to help squeeze that thing around the turn?"

"Eton bench, *monsieur*. Patterned after the one designed at the school. It is used for the birching or caning of *les élèves*."

"My French is poor, but you did say for caning students?"

"*Oui, monsieur*. Some extra restraint straps have been added for my special purposes."

The older man cleared the turn easily. His strength and agility amazed Garrett. The rest of the trip down the stairs went swiftly. At the base of the staircase the older man did not bother to rest; instead he carried his burden over to the opposite end of the dungeon—an end that sat in complete darkness. Garrett recalled that La Maîtresse always kept the stairway light on, but the dungeon lights she adjusted to the situation.

"Are you okay?" Garrett called.

The man came out of the dark with a smile and not a hint of being out of breath.

"*Ça va très bien.*" A lean man, he stood perhaps five feet two or three inches, but exuded confidence and knowledge. His features were attractive, and his blue eyes seemed to send out an inferno of warmth.

"Who are you?" Garrett asked.

"Louis Sade."

Letcher, Rin Tin Tin, and now Sade.

"What's your real name?"

"Donatien Alphonse Françoise de Sade."

The man's eyes sparkled. Garrett would have laughed except . . . *No*, Garrett thought, *this is ridiculous. This old man is simply taking on a persona, a rather twisted historical role that conveniently portrays his fantasy.* This Garrett could understand.

"I guess I should admit to being Leopold von Sacher-Masoch."

"Ah! But his encounters were only with women. Can you say the same?"

Garrett felt a heat flush through the skin of his face. He wished he could answer "yes." Staring into the other man's eyes, he knew the man couldn't be lied to.

Louis walked over to the controls of the track lighting and slowly raised the level of light, but still kept the light dim enough to cast shadows across his own face.

"I would appreciate additional assistance from you, *monsieur*. The Eton bench, it must be set up and *tested*."

161

Chapter Twenty-seven

Marie watched Wil fill the car with groceries, a mundane chore of which she willingly followed every nuance. The tattered chambray shirt rode closely on his muscles. The rolled-up sleeves revealed the definition of his blood vessels. His hands were large but slender, with a recently made paper cut marking his right thumb. The smell of the blood reached her quickly. Luscious and warm. The low-slung jeans draped his hips the way in which she wanted to, curving into his loins to capture his heat. The taste of salty blood and semen, only a wished-for phantom on her tongue, drove her to approach him.

"Your father lets you out alone?"

Wil turned toward Marie, arching an eyebrow and at last smiling.

"Didn't know I'd run into you, or I would have taken my cane with me."

"To drive me away."

He moved close to her, his body reeking of testosterone and heat. Her cold body reacted instantly, as if a flame had been set to her clothes. The stinging nerves sharpened her senses.

"You must use canes once in a while," he whispered.

"On you it would be a pleasure."

"No role reversal yet, my dear." He turned his back on her.

"You're not dismissed."

"Shit, woman, you've really got the patter down." He looked over his right shoulder at her. "Now you need a lesson in humility."

Wil returned to loading the car.

"I have no reason to humble myself, Wil."

"If you want me, you do." He threw the last of the bags into the car, slammed the trunk closed, and smiled at her. "Think about it. Dream on it. Or do you already? Are you trying to come to terms with your lust? Do so soon, because I'm thinking about heading back to the city."

"When?" She didn't mean to seem eager, but she also didn't plan on letting him slip away.

"Haven't decided. But I don't have any reason to hang around. Dad doesn't want me here, you've bulldozed your granddaughter into staying away from me, and verbal sparring is simply foreplay. I want the real thing."

"Give me a ride home?" she asked.

Wil looked around.

"How did you get here?"

"Doesn't matter."

He laughed and gleefully spoke.

"I've got eggs and milk in the car, can't afford to dawdle today. Besides, you're not contrite yet."

163

"Contrite!" she screamed.

"Beg for it, baby. You know how. The same way you make your clients grovel."

"I already know you 'grovel' from the marks that I first saw on your chest."

"Yeah, but I've got something you want real bad." He slowly drew his hand up his thigh.

He's right, she thought.

He drew his wounded thumb across her lips and her tongue automatically flicked out to taste it. He pushed his thumb between her lips and allowed her to suck. She knew he would be startled by the coolness of her mouth and attempt to pull away, but she caught his hand and held it until his own warmth heated her mouth.

The sucking motion caused the cut to reopen and the sweet metallic taste of blood raked across her bloated taste buds, seeping slowly down her throat. The eternal chill inside her body softened but did not disappear.

"I've got something that tastes even better," he said.

Better, she thought. *The only thing better would be to be saturated in his body's blood.*

Wil slowly withdrew his thumb and looked down at it. Blood dribbled up out of the cut.

"Kinky."

Marie lowered her mouth onto the cut and let her tongue sweep away the bubble of blood. The odor of his rich burgundy blood drove her forward into his arms. Her breathing came in gasps, and the thrill hazed out her sight.

"Maybe if you're a good girl," he whispered.

Her hand reached into his crotch, evidently awakening Wil's awareness, since he immediately pulled away from her.

"Slow down, baby. Remember we're in a parking lot in a respectable small town. Not everyone will understand our lack of inhibitions."

"Come over to my place tonight," she said, feeling blood dry tightly across her top lip.

"When I do decide to come, so to speak, you'd better be willing, because you only get one more chance." He got into the driver's seat of his father's car.

"Tonight?" she asked.

"Naw. Dad and I watch sports games tonight."

His brown eyes sizzled with the glow of satisfaction. He shoved the car into gear and didn't bother to say goodbye.

Marie stood watching the car leave the parking lot. Her hunger needed to be sated. She looked around. Too public, she thought.

She walked to her car and vowed that she would return home and not feed. Not allow Will to win.

Chapter Twenty-eight

Upon arriving home, Marie caught sight of Garrett's car parked in her driveway. The chauffeur had his hat pulled low over his eyes, and his head rested comfortably against the leather headrest.

I told him to stay away. I warned him.

She shut off the motor and got out of her car. As she passed the Lincoln, she checked the backseat. Empty.

Damn him!

A powerful wave of hunger drew her to the house. Once inside, she sensed a strong scent of blood tinged by the sourness of sweat. The odor came from farther back in the house. The sour sweet smell led her to the dungeon door. But she kept the door locked, as it was now. How could Garrett gain entrance? Only Sade—

Marie struck out wildly with her right forearm

and the wooden door splintered. On the second blow the door caved in completely.

"Sade!" she shrieked.

The odor of blood and sweat exhilarated her. She lunged down the stairs.

"Sade, how dare you!"

A relaxed Sade stood shirtless before her. His left hand grasped the handle of the bullwhip. Just beyond him, stretched tautly across the Eton bench, was Garrett. Naked. The skin on his buttocks split with raw gashes. Sweat formed a sheen over his entire body.

"*Ma* Marie, don't get so upset. You weren't here, and I thought I could fill in for you. *Votre client* was in need of service. As a favor . . ."

"You beat him with the bullwhip."

Sade looked down at the glistening braided leather of the whip. "Should I have started with something *plus doux*?" Sade walked to the wall of the dungeon and selected another whip. "A signal whip, perhaps?"

"Don't ever touch my slaves." She put out her right hand palm upward. "The key."

Sade stooped a bit to look up the staircase.

"*Mais* you don't have a door to lock."

"Never. Never will you be permitted to use the dungeon again. Is that understood?" Her body trembled from anger and hunger, a hunger that kept growing stronger the longer she remained with the bleeding Garrett.

"Marie, we have been too long together to argue over a mere . . ." Sade looked over at Garrett. "Meal."

"Too long we've tolerated each other."

"Ah! But you got what you wanted, Marie. You are immortal. A bloodsucking immortal who stands gasping from the smell of her next meal."

"Out!" she screamed.

Sade walked over to Garrett and ran his right index finger across a wound. His finger came back drenched in a bright red. He used his tongue to lap at his finger several times until the red had disappeared. He frowned.

"You deserve something richer, *ma* Marie. This man has been bled too often. A favorite, perhaps." Sade smiled. "One that needs to be given a rest, or his life should be ended this day." With full force Sade used the whip to break open another wound.

Marie shrieked as she ran at Sade. Her fingers tightened around his throat. Sade flung the whip aside and grabbed her hands, pulling them slowly from his neck, and with each movement Marie could hear the bones in her hands crack and break.

"You will never be as strong as I, *garce*. I would be pleased to rip your body apart for all the trials you have put me and my Reneé through. But there is one who would miss you." Her hands seemed to shrivel in his grasp. "Liliana. She would blame me even if she was not sure that I had rid my life of you. Liliana begs me to protect dear *grand-mère*. You tyrannical *vieille bique*."

Sade forced Marie onto her knees. The cement floor was cold and hard, but that didn't matter, for the excruciating pain in her hands had taken her to a level of pain that brought numbness, and she felt that he could not take her beyond that pain. Suddenly Sade released her hands and backhanded her across her right cheek. The sound of smashing bone sounded loudly inside her head. The pain echoed throughout her skull as she fell sideways onto the floor.

"This is not the late eighteenth century. There are

no authorities to back your pronouncements. Now you exist at my whim, not the other way around. Do not speak rudely to me. Do not forbid me anything. Do not attempt to set limits on my behavior. *Plus jamais ça!*"

Sade lifted the signal whip from the floor and lashed Garrett three more times before flinging it across the room. Sade stared down at Marie and tsked.

"You look *malade, ma pute.*" The last word he spat at Marie. She closed her eyes as the wetness of his saliva hit her face. "*Voici* your medicine," Sade said, indicating Garrett. "*Voici* your medicine."

Sade fetched the white silk poet's shirt that he had neatly folded and placed on the unused rack. He walked past Garrett and Marie as if they didn't exist in his world. Marie knew that he perceived them as too lowly to exist on his plane.

With a straight back and an easygoing gait he climbed the steps.

"Bastard!" Marie's throat burned, but he never turned back.

"Not my manner of thinking but the manner of thinking of others has been the source of my unhappiness. The reasoning man who scorns the prejudices of simpletons necessarily becomes the enemy of simpletons; he must expect as much, and laugh at the inevitable."

The Marquis de Sade,
in a letter to his wife

Chapter Twenty-nine

The confused Garrett had heard the fight. He had heard the breaking of bones, but had not viewed the scene. He knew, though, that La Maîtresse whimpered now, and he could not go to her.

His armpits ached from the taut way in which he had been tied to the Eton bench. His legs he could barely feel. His stomach ached from the pressure of the bench. His buttocks stung. And he needed water to help bring back the saliva to his mouth.

Until Maîtresse had interrupted them, he had been flying on a wave of elation, spinning in a heaven of euphoria. This man, Sade or whoever he was, knew how to mete out pain. He satisfied his slave before thinking of himself, unlike Letcher. Briefly from a corner of his eye he had seen the man licking a bloodied finger. To whom had the blood belonged? Garrett hoped it had been his own, for he had wanted a very personal bond to be formed with the man.

He heard no movement, only the soft whimpers of a woman crying. Of La Maîtresse crying. Crying over spilled blood. Garrett heard the humor in the phrase but could not smile. He tried to form words. *I wanted this. I enjoyed this.* The words came out only as incomprehensible guttural sounds. The words defied his Maîtresse and brought shame to his soul.

Marie's fingers throbbed as she tried to move them. She used the back of one hand to feel the broken cheekbone. Sunken in. The touch sparked a flame of outrageous pain. Her fingers hung limp and useless. She could not even untie Garrett. Did she want to untie Garrett?

The smell of his blood sent the top of her body reeling in a circular motion. Sade had tasted of this one's blood in front of her. Had Sade taken blood from Garrett earlier? Had she interrupted Sade before he could?

Marie got to her knees and slowly crawled to where Garrett waited on the bench. When she drew closer, she saw among Garrett's new wounds the yellow tinge of week-old bruises. She had not caused them.

Voici your medicine. Sade's words held truth. There is her medicine. Her cure for the bones broken and the bruises caused by Sade's wrath. Garrett's blood would hasten the healing of her body. Garrett's blood would make her stronger.

"*Voici,*" she whispered, stretching out her neck to bring her lips closer to Garrett's flesh. Closer but not within reach.

The cure or the bane? she wondered.

Long ago she had forced Sade to give her this . . .
not life, but a strange compromise with death. She
had starved him of blood in prisons and would have
let him die at the hands of the French peasants.
How magnificent it would have been to watch his
head bounce into the basket of the guillotine. She,
of course, would have had to be in disguise amid
the mob; still, he would have been dead. She would
have stolen his head and gouged his eyes out,
racked at his brains, and then set the mess afire.
But he had offered her the same immortality he had
if she would free him. Yes, she saved him from the
mob, but no, she could not bring herself to turn the
monster free to go back to her daughter and grand-
children. She forced the animal into an insane asylum, where he learned of his true strength and
eventually feigned his death.

Thank God her daughter, Reneé, had died in a
convent before he could reach her.

Garrett's gurgling noises distracted her, and she
moved to where his flushed face could be seen.
Could he even see her? There is nothing you can
offer him, Marie, she thought to herself. He smelled
of blood, sweat, semen, and feces. Odors that mingled, and yet the scent of blood seemed singled out
by her senses. She knew the taste of this blood. It
had always been clean, healthy blood, blood she
could dream of during her long respites. However,
now it seemed tinged by a budding germ, not a simple cold. No, something heavier, muskier. Something possibly terminal. Something Sade had given
him? No, vampires did not carry germs. Diseases
could not survive in a vampire's dead body. Bereft
of nutrition, the disease died shortly after entering
the vampire's body. Sade could not pass on any-

thing living to Garrett. And the disease flourished in Garrett's blood.

Poor Garrett didn't know, couldn't know as yet, but unless something else happened to him, he would find out.

Voici *is your medicine*. A medicine marked with an expiration date. *Use before the man with the scythe claims him*.

Marie ached. Marie's eyes slowly closed. Yes, she needed sleep. Her coffin awaited upstairs on the second floor. It had been relined with a soft peach satin, although the home soil still supported her body. Sleep would bring back the freshness of her skin and bones. She dreaded the preamble to sleep. She always did, but especially now. Her body each day would semi-decay into the soil to be rejuvenated. Her wounds would make the decay more intense. The decay would spread to a greater portion of her body, and as it did, the smell would frighten her. The decay always made her sleep uneasy, and the decay seemed to worsen with the centuries. Always on awakening she would be whole. The staleness would still be there inside the box, but that she could escape for at least a while.

Garrett gurgled some more. What did he want, she wondered. To be freed? To be beaten? To be fed upon?

She bent her head back and looked up into his eyes. Glassy pupils stared back at her. The whites of his eyes held a network of intersecting red blood vessels.

"Can a future be told by studying one's blood vessels, Garrett? I think I see your future." Delicately she brought her hands up so that he could see them. "My hands cannot rescue you."

"Chauffeur" he said hoarsely.

"My integrity cannot save you either. You were my most obedient slave. The most willing and giving. My favorite until . . ."

No! He did not want to hear these words. *My favorite until* . . . La Maîtresse never finished the sentence. It wasn't necessary, because he had known all along. She had sent him away to make room for another.

His blood no longer nourished her fantasies. Instead she had thrown him aside like a used condom filled with spoiled desire.

He looked at her damaged face and knew he would never see her again. He wished for a strong Maîtresse who could command and be obeyed.

Sade had diminished her. Perhaps the ghost of the real Marquis de Sade had taken over the man's body.

"Sade," he whispered and watched Maîtresse's eyes harden.

"Sade," he whispered again, because he wanted to see that hate shine in La Maîtresse's eyes one more time.

"Sade is a strong-willed child, a demanding bully who will never grow up."

She used the back of her right hand to wipe away the sweat dripping into Garrett's eyes. It was not clear what color his eyes were, and she felt ashamed that she couldn't recall. Weakly she lay back on the floor to stare up at Garrett. *Careful, Marie, fall asleep here and the body will not recuperate.* Instead she would wake weaker, without her soil to replenish with her native minerals.

"You have family, don't you, Garrett? A wife, children. You never told me how many children. You have people to return to at home. It would be foolish to use you as my medicine, Garrett. I would have to flee. Inconvenient, given that my casket needs to be specially packed, with me stored safely inside it."

Maîtresse speaks of death as if it were upon her. Could she be hurt far more than he thought?

Garrett's body throbbed with pain. He saw La Maîtresse, and then she disappeared into the dark, for how long he did not know. But then she appeared again. The same mutilated face, the same brown eyes that had nourished his obsession. Her voice seemed softer, kinder. Too kind. *Where is her strength?* Her upper lip started to swell. He thought he saw the lip pulse.

Fear paced his pain. Hate weakened his spirit. Still, he caught glimpses of her, briefer now. The coldness of her body chilled his sweating flesh. He smelled waste, his own brought on by the torture.

Only La Maîtresse and he existed, bound together in a spiraling darkness that would take them both.

"I'm sorry, Garrett." She had just realized that she would never be able to make it back to her coffin before passing out. "I'm so sorry, Garrett. I sent you away to save you. Now I must have you."

She lifted her head to kiss him on the mouth. Pain passed between them. She glided her body from under his and stood.

The wounds on his buttocks had clotted. As she bent down to look more closely at his wounds, her fangs automatically pushed out from between her lips. Touching the wounds, her teeth bit into the young scabs on his flesh and he bled anew. Her tongue lolled across the blood. She heard her own little lapping sounds. Evidently Garrett had heard also, for he squeaked out a "Thank you."

No, thank you, she thought and would have said, only she couldn't draw her tongue back from the blood.

The tension in her body began to ease.

No, thank you, Garrett, for the gift of your life.

Chapter Thirty

Liliana fed her pets. The rabbit her uncle had given her had become more docile. A raccoon with singed fur licked her hand as she put down his dish. She had saved him from one of her uncle's temper tantrums. Minerva, the eighteen-year-old cat, yawned and plopped her fat body down for a delicate meal of sardines.

These were animals she didn't have the heart to feed from. The others; the mélange of rats, mice, hamsters, and ferrets, she kept apart in an enclosed shack that had little light but was kept clean. The animals were so small that she had to drain several at one sitting, or perhaps, as she would put it, standing. Often she would stand in the shadows of the woods at twilight and swiftly wring the neck of her chosen meal, suck the animal dry, and discard the corpse quickly among the trees. What she didn't eat scavengers would pick at.

"Miss?"

"Yes, Matilda."

"There's a young man here asking to see you. His name is David Petry."

"Oh!"

"I'm ready to leave for the day. Is there anything you'd like me to do first?"

"Is my uncle home?"

"I haven't seen him all day. Would you like me to wait around until your business with Mr. Petry is finished?"

"No. Go on home, Matilda."

Liliana noticed the relief in Matilda's expression. She hadn't wanted to stay another minute. Matter of fact, she had already slipped off her apron and stood in the doorway holding her pocketbook and vinyl tote.

As the two women said goodbye, Liliana caught a glimpse of David Petry waiting in the salon. His build seemed almost identical to Stuart's, and he paced with the same nervous energy that the young soldier had possessed.

"You wanted to see me, Mr. Petry?" Liliana drew her shoulders back and walked with a forced indifference.

"Mr. Sade said that you would have some papers for me." He walked to where she stood and then retreated three steps.

"My uncle didn't give me anything for you. Are you sure you were not supposed to see him directly?" Of course not; this was another try at getting her to drink fresh human blood. If she hadn't taken Stuart's blood, whatever made Sade think she would rob this young man of his life?

"I feel awkward, but I'm sure it's what he told me."

"My uncle is not at home right now, so it's impossible to ask him; however, I'll remind him of this tonight." She certainly would.

David started for the door.

"Mr. Petry!"

He turned quickly.

"David, please."

"Then you may call me Liliana. My uncle is trying to hook us up." *Why the hell had she said that?*

"You mean like in dating?"

"It goes beyond that."

"I'm honored that he would consider me as a potential boyfriend."

"You wouldn't be if you understood his motive."

"Nothing so petty as to have me encourage you to eat rabbit, I hope?"

"Nothing *so* petty."

"I'm not sure what I'm supposed to do now. Ask you out? Smile? Say I understand and then gracefully leave? What do you think I should do?"

"Whatever your emotions lead you to do."

"Is that an invitation to ask you out or an objective view of the situation?"

"Both."

David smiled broadly. His shoulders relaxed, and he heaved a great sigh.

"In that case, why don't we humor your uncle and go to dinner this Friday evening?"

Liliana turned her back on David. Curiosity kept making her want to see where the similarities between Stuart and David ended. Most probably she could sit through one date without jumping David's carotid.

"My job is close to the city, so why don't I meet you in the city at the Four Seasons Grill?"

David cleared his throat.

"Sure."

"Has my uncle given you a retainer as yet?"

"A small one."

"Don't settle for small, David. Ask for more. There's peril to your assignment."

"Is he in trouble with the IRS?"

"My uncle will pick up the dinner bill."

"No. I mean, I couldn't allow that. I would really like to take you out to dinner, but perhaps you'll allow me to select a restaurant." He gave a crooked smile. "One that I can afford."

Liliana's cold body tickled with the hint of warmth that sounded in his voice. She nodded agreement.

The front door slammed shut, and a loud voice was singing a joyful aria from *La Belle Hélène*.

"*Evohè, que ces Déesses . . .*"

Sade's white complexion glowed. His long white hair flowed freely over his shoulders. The open poet's shirt revealed enough of his chest hair to emphasize his virility.

"*Monsieur* Petry, I forgot you would be *ici*."

"I'm certainly glad you're here. Your daugh—"

"Niece," Liliana corrected.

"Sorry. Your niece said that you had forgotten to give her the papers we had discussed over the telephone."

"*Un désastre, monsieur.*"

"Excuse me, sir?"

"A disaster."

"What happened?"

"Way too complex to explain right now, but maybe later. If you promise to stay for dinner."

"I can't this evening, sir. Is there a good time I can call you? I'm probably going to be out of the house most of the evening, but I can put aside some time to call you."

"What will you be doing, *monsieur*?"

"Uncle! It's none of our business."

"Your niece is right, sir. I've made several special trips out here at your convenience; however, this can't continue. Perhaps you could fax the papers to me or—"

"*Monsieur*, I have given you cash as a retainer."

"Not enough cash, I would guess, Uncle. At least not for what you expect him to do."

Sade glanced at his niece; his blue eyes had darkened into a stormlike gray.

"Did you want more money, *monsieur*?"

"How could I? I haven't done anything for you as yet."

"Except to travel around at my uncle's whim."

Sade brightened.

"Certainly, *monsieur*, you must charge me for the time it took getting here and leaving."

"I had planned on it."

Liliana couldn't decide whether her uncle had given a smile or a sneer as he turned away to walk over to the bar.

"You seemed to have enjoyed my cognac the last time you were here, *monsieur*. Would you like one now?"

"No, I have to be driving back to the city. If you find the papers, sir, give me a call and we'll figure out some way to get together.

"I look forward to this Friday evening, Liliana, and would certainly be glad to pick you up somewhere, unless you're driving in."

"Don't like to drive. The glare of the headlights bothers me."

"Then why don't you call me with the location of

your employer, and I'll pick you up and take you home."

"Thank you, David. I'll speak to you later in the week. I'll get your number from my uncle."

She walked him to the door and waved goodbye while he drove his car back onto the road.

"*Ma petite chérie*, why make it so complicated?"

"What?"

"Waiting until Friday. I'm sure with your help we could have gotten him to stay for dinner. Ah! *Je suis très heureux pour toi*."

"Happy for me, Uncle?"

"Yes, that you are returning to the fold."

"I'm merely meeting him for dinner."

"*Oui*, but he will bring you back here."

"And you will mind your own business."

"I will help with the cleanup."

"It won't be necessary, Uncle. I have far better self-control than you."

With his right index finger he rubbed her left cheek and crossed downward to run the same finger across her lips.

"When I made you immortal I gave you my blood. The hunger is always there, Liliana. *Toujours*."

Chapter Thirty-one

Tap, tap, tap.

The chauffeur didn't budge.

Marie rapped harder on the window of the car.

The chauffeur moved a bit but did not waken.

Marie banged on the window.

Suddenly wide awake, the chauffeur seemed embarrassed. He pushed the button to make the window on his side open.

"Normally I don't sleep so soundly. I doze a little. What time is it?" He checked his watch and shook his head. "Is Mr. Winter angry?"

"He's beyond caring, I'm afraid."

"Did he call a taxi?"

"No, he doesn't need a taxi. It's so awful." Marie tried to cry, but it seemed impossible now after all she had been through. She, too, was beyond caring. "Mr. Winter is . . . dead. Come in and see for yourself."

The chauffeur lifted the cellular telephone and was about to close the window when Marie stuck her head inside the car.

"Whom are you calling?"

"Mrs. Winter."

"Do you think his wife really wants to hear this over the telephone? Especially since he . . . I'm sure you know."

"And I bet she does too," he answered.

"Still, it's a very delicate situation. I wish you would come in and take a look for yourself."

"I believe you."

"Then come in." She reached for the door handle.

"Please, I believe you, and I definitely don't want to see anything." He brushed her hand out of the way.

Marie admitted to herself she had not thought this situation out completely. The chauffeur should have been willing to dash into her house to at least check whether his boss was dead or simply in need of medical assistance. *So much for loyalty*.

Using violence on this man seemed so dirty, so *sadistic*. Violence should be consensual, and she had always managed to keep it that way in the past, but if she had to strong-arm this chauffeur, well . . .

"I assure you, madam, this is not completely unexpected."

"What do you mean?"

"His wife warned me that he had a congenital heart problem and told me to call her if something should ever happen. Her or Dr. Lowrey."

"Garrett's doctor?"

"No. I believe he's related to Mrs. Winter in some way. She especially did not want the police to be called if he should . . . experience a problem while visiting *you*."

"She knew about me?"

"Indirectly. You see, I think Mrs. Winter had hired people to report on her husband's activities."

"How do you know that?"

"She hired me. Mr. Winter always seemed too busy to worry about details. Therefore, all staff was hired by Mrs. Winter."

"I guess it wouldn't look good for Garrett to be found enjoying certain pleasures."

"No, ma'am." The chauffeur started to punch out the number and Marie allowed him.

She pulled her head back out of the car and patted her cheeks. Garrett's blood had proven to be the perfect medicine. The fact that she had been using his blood for some time probably helped in the healing process. This was not completely foreign blood that she had used. Her body had already adjusted to the chemical differences of Garrett's body.

Garrett waited, washed, dressed, and propped up in the salon.

She returned to the house after the chauffeur told her that Dr. Lowrey would be coming out, but no police.

Garrett looked so pasty white that Marie tried applying some makeup to his face and neck. He had closed his own eyes toward the end, enabling her to escape an accusatory stare.

"I'm sorry, Garrett. You know I tried to avoid this. Part of it is your fault for coming back before I asked you to. The majority of the blame, however, falls on my son-in-law, the ignoble Marquis de Sade. I promise I'll find some way to destroy him."

The wounds on Garrett's buttocks hadn't looked so bad after they were washed and dressed. At least they didn't look as if they would have caused his death. On the other hand, if the medical examiner found no blood, then there would be a problem.

A knock interrupted her thinking. Walking to the door, she stopped briefly to look at herself in the mirror. She actually looked refreshed, but she didn't want to look too good. She grabbed at a couple of strands of hair to give herself the halo of disarray. She sighed deeply, turned down her mouth, and opened the door.

"I'm Dr. Lowrey," the tall gentleman said immediately. "I believe Mr. Winter is in some distress."

"Not anymore. Come in."

She led him to the corpse. The doctor made some fluttering movements around the body but was really interested only in Garrett's pulse.

"He is dead," he pronounced wisely.

"I thought so."

The doctor's handsome face hid behind a facade of solemnity. His hands were large and quit hairy, with tufts covering each of his knuckles. He reached into an inside pocket and pulled out a pair of rimless glasses and put them on at the bridge of his nose. Presbyopia, she thought. Poor dear is getting on in years, although she judged that he couldn't be more than forty-five.

"Mr. Winter has many business connections and social obligations, madam. You realize also that it would be best for his family if he was discovered dead in bed. At home, that is."

The doctor's hands were sweating.

"Indeed I do, Dr. Lowrey. What do you suggest?"

The doctor cleared his throat.

"I'm sure we can trust the chauffeur, if we could get you to agree to our transporting his body elsewhere."

"Dare we do that?"

"Only three of us, four if you include Mrs. Winter, know about this."

187

"And I doubt Mrs. Winter wants to be included."

"This is a terrible shock for her."

"I would have thought she might have expected it, given the condition of his heart."

"His heart?"

"The chauffeur told me that Garrett had a congenital heart defect."

A light suddenly dawned on the doctor's face.

"Yes, that's right."

"One would think immediate cremation might be best in this situation. Then Mrs. Winter wouldn't have to go through all the distress of planning a long wake."

"I agree, madam. If you allow me to call the chauffeur, we'll remove his body right now."

Marie nodded. Her curiosity got the best of her.

"Dr. Lowrey, you're not related to Mrs. Winter, are you?"

"No. We've been friends for several years."

And lovers, Marie silently added, watching the doctor cross the threshold of the front door.

Several minutes later the awkward, uncomfortable chauffeur entered the house behind the doctor. The chauffeur looked around the place, no doubt stunned that naked people weren't hanging from chandeliers. He must have expected to see at least one naked body tied to a rack. But then, that's probably how he expected to find Garrett.

Marie looked at the corpse. *It's never really a secret, Garrett.*

"If there's any financial recompense that's due, I'm willing to settle it now." Dr. Lowrey reached into a jacket pocket and pulled out a thick roll of bills. None of them were in small denominations.

"No, Doctor." Besides, she expected someone else to pay.

Chapter Thirty-two

Sade wistfully watched Cecelia collect a bouquet of flowers.

"You would make a wonderful Justine," he muttered, not expecting to be heard.

But the girl had sharp ears, like most servants.

"Shakespeare's Romeo and Justine," she said excitedly.

"Romeo and Juliet, *ma chère*."

Her cheeks flushed, and she almost dropped the bouquet.

"How embarrassing! I read *Romeo and Juliet* in school; I'm really familiar with that. I don't know why I made such a mistake." She thought for a moment. "Maybe it's because I've never heard of Justine."

"*Ma chère*, I believe that I, too, misspoke. I know of no Justine either. I must have been thinking of one of Brontë's characters."

189

"Jane Eyre?"

"That is it, *ma chère*."

"I'd rather be Juliet. Willing to die for the one she loves. Willing to give completely of herself." Coyly she looked over her shoulder at Sade.

Sade envisioned her soft high rump over the Eton bench.

"We should read some of the French classics together, *ma petite enfant*."

"I would love to," said Cecelia, turning to face Sade. "Only, Mother would be angry if she found us reading instead of my doing the chores. Unless . . ."

"*Oui?*"

"I have dance class three nights a week. Usually my girlfriend drives us there and back. If you would happen to show up at school before class began, perhaps I could skip at least one class."

"And what would you tell your friend?"

"Make something up. You're an uncle. Hell, I wouldn't have to make up a story. My friend would never rat on me."

"What does your friend know of me?"

"Nothing right now."

"Good." Sade stood and stretched. He had built up quite a muscle in his left arm after favoring Garrett with his attention. "This day is *magnifique* and you are *une belle femme*." Sade had an itch but didn't know how to scratch it. Young girls had always been trouble. Such sweet, tender trouble, he thought, looking at Cecelia. The poor child looked disappointed. *You couldn't be any more disappointed than I.* Sade never could resist temptation. "Your mother has a very busy schedule during the day. I mean between her work *ici* and taking care of her family."

Cecelia, not a simple girl, smiled.

"Yes, often I find myself at home alone."

"It gives you great freedom, *ma chère*."

"Except that I don't have my own car yet. I depend on friends to take me places."

"To what sort of places do you like to go?"

If she said the malls, Sade decided he would give her up.

"Beaches. There's a beautiful lake not far from here. Whippet Lake. Have you been there?"

"*Mais non.*"

"Then you must go. I'd be willing to direct you."

"I am so poor at following directions."

"I mean I'd go with you. To make sure you got there."

"What if it should rain?" Sade hated sitting out in the sun for long periods of time. The sun sucked too much of his energy.

"No problem. There's an old cabin right on the lake. Been deserted for several years. We could always duck in there."

"The cabin must be a favorite, *comment dit-on ça....* hangout for you and your friends."

"Most of my friends hang around the mall. I've used the cabin by myself sometimes when I want to be alone, or my girlfriend and I have secret picnics there. We have a little hibachi set up."

"Roughing it, *ma chère*."

Cecelia laughed, and when she did her breasts jiggled under the white cotton T-shirt. Her teeth were very white and straight, thanks most probably to a good orthodontist.

"So what do you think, Mr. Sade? Want to go sometime?"

"We could roast some of those *Americain* weenies."

"I prefer those fat hot Italian sausages."

"There are some good-size French sausages, *ma chère*."

"But are they as hot as the Italian ones?"

"They can burn the tip of your . . ." Sade reached out his left hand and held his index finger in front of Cecelia's lips. She responded by sticking out her tongue. *"Langue,"* he finished his sentence. The tip of his finger barely touched her tongue for a brief moment, and then he pulled his hand back.

"How about tomorrow?"

"You are eager to learn the French ways. That is *très bien*. I like teaching eager students. Do you know where Belinda Road crosses the railroad tracks?"

"Sure."

"You think you could meet me there, *ma chère*?"

"I'll bicycle. Three o'clock?"

"Oui. Three o'clock."

"Will you bring something of your own?"

"Pardon?"

"Something you've written."

Her eyes shined with eagerness, and Sade thought of many writings he'd like to bring, but decided to be cautious.

"I'll have to look through my work and see if there is something that would interest a *jeune fille* like you."

"I'm sure I can learn something from anything you've written."

I am sure many people have, he thought.

"May I put this bouquet in your bedroom, Mr. Sade? Oh, I know your bedroom is off-limits. What I mean is I could put these flowers in a vase and leave it at the foot of your door."

Ah! Such a pupil, thought Sade.

"But, *mon enfant*, then you would have to pick a new bouquet for the dining table."

"I don't mind. Really!"

"Then *merci, mademoiselle*."

"Will these do? I could pick another bunch, if you'd like."

"You have been holding this bouquet for so long that they must have picked up some of your own fragrance, and tonight that would be *une très bonne mémoire*."

But hopefully not as lovely as la mémoire *of tomorrow*.

Chapter Thirty-three

Liliana had climbed Wil's childhood tree. The limbs were sturdy and healthy, and the view of the sunset eased her rampaging soul. A squirrel sat on a distant limb, obviously trying to decide whether he wanted to share his tree with a stranger. A branch of leaves gently brushed her cheek with each breeze, and the scent of nature lulled her into a semidoze.

She had been eight years old when last she climbed a tree, and for that she had been reprimanded by her nanny. Unladylike, she had been told. "I don't want my trees destroyed by a wayward child," bellowed her father. Her mother merely stifled a chuckle, while her brothers displayed some weird sense of bravado at having snitched on her.

Her nanny and her family were long gone. Unable to say goodbye to them, she still imagined them alive and waiting. Waiting by her grave for the minister to end his sermon. Her family believed in her death, and why not? To all appearances, for several days she was dead, until her uncle brought her coffin to his villa in Italy. There he fed her fresh blood from a toddler, a scrawny child of a poor family who thought they were selling the little boy into servitude to a wealthy family. Instead they had ensured his early death.

Many times she liked to think her family would all come together again. But her brothers had died in wars. Her mother died most probably from grief, having lost all her children. Father had simply withered away into a crippled old man without family and without his mind.

Leaves in the next tree shivered loudly when the squirrel also decided to abandon her. He scurried deep into the leaves, leaving behind his old home in favor of the safety of an undisputed tree. Liliana smiled and silently wished the little guy well and hoped he'd have a more peaceful life than she had known.

The gray shadows of night were bringing their bland coloring to the earth. The bright green of the grass dimmed. The colorful wreaths and bouquets of flowers dulled. The tombstones and mausoleums took on the eerie complexion of a haunted night.

Movement. Close near the fence. It was late for someone to be in the cemetery. Most mortals avoided the reminder of death at this hour.

Movement again. It seemed to be edging from the old part of the cemetery to the new. A scurry like a wary animal, except its size and shape seemed more like a human's.

There it was again. Rags dripped from a moving object. A human-size object. Another smaller shape joined the first. Lingering shapes hesitated to join their scouts.

Liliana shimmied down to the ground and ran for the cemetery's gate. Ajar, the gates invited her curiosity inside. Not wanting to make a sound, she squeezed between them. The gravel beneath her shoes crunched. She halted. No other sound and no other movement. But she was sure she had seen shapes moving about, and she was determined to find them.

Slowly she walked up the trail to the old section of the cemetery. Flashes of movement kept their distance from her. They were too quick to be caught. She began searching behind tombstones and trees, hoping to surprise a shade. She found nothing until . . .

A yellowed scrap of muslin clung to the bark of an oak tree. Her hand shook as she reached out for it. She wanted to know about the mutants, but she didn't want to believe it was true. When she touched the material her fingers stung, but she refused to pull away. Gradually the sting faded and the material fell into the palm of her hand. Bits of flesh clung to one side of the muslin, and the other side appeared bloodstained.

Liliana brought the muslin to her nose. The odor of decay, of blood, of earth and age pervaded the threads. Upon tasting the material, she realized it did not come from anything living. Instead, soil freshly covered the entire patch, almost drowning out the flavors of flesh and blood.

Hunger spiked in her body. Blood hunger. Not thinking, she sucked the cloth until the metallic taste of blood ran across her tongue. Human blood. Blood of the dead.

She spat out the muslin and turned in the direction she thought the shapes had traveled in. They were crossing over into the new part of the cemetery, into the active section.

Guessing their course, Liliana cut through several swaths to again reach the main path. No one walked the path. Several yards away, beyond an ornate mausoleum, she thought she saw movement again. She travelled in that direction until a foul odor caused her to stop.

Fear throbbed inside her, a fear of seeing the mutants, of beholding the wretches that had been mere speculation and gossip among the immortals. Fear of seeing her own desires played out on this deathly stage. Her embalming work allowed her to brush near the dead without having to accept the culture to which she had been doomed.

Mentally setting aside the smells, she continued on to the far mausoleum. Beyond the mausoleum the land was generously landscaped with weeping willows. Most were healthy, but one tilted too much to one side. As she approached, she noted that some of the tree's roots were above ground. The tree seemingly readied to make a mad dash out of the cemetery. What had it seen? she wondered. Too much pain and hurt. Too many tears. Or unnatural scenes of grotesquerie.

Not far away she could hear the sound of animals digging. Following the sound, she came to a hilly mound. At the top of the mound she dropped to her knees. Before her were human forms digging, hands performing the work of claws. They worked quickly. And they worked as a pack on the freshly dug grave.

When they reached the coffin, each repeatedly slammed weighty stones against the lid until one of the pack howled. All the others stopped. The leader leaned over, and Liliana heard the sound of wood being ripped apart. Long dangling ribbons of drool hung from the spectators' mouths.

Finally a body rose out of the grave, but not on its own. No, the leader passed the corpse to his brethren. The corpse seemed fresh, not more than a day old. Never embalmed, thought Liliana. *Immediately interred*. Still full of the blood that these creatures sought. A plump body of a woman, a middle-aged woman wrapped in a white shroud. The pack ripped the protective shroud from the corpse and went to work trying to extract as much of the body's blood as they could.

Liliana rose to her feet and slowly glided down to the scene of the feast. The leader spotted her and howled. Each in turn howled and made vicious hand movements in her direction, but never moved away from their meal. Gradually they returned to their sucking and munching, and only occasionally would a pair of wary and mindless eyes look at her. They all had the eyes of frightened animals. All were ugly, fangs grown disproportionately long, lips partially chewed. The faces were discolored and blotched with singes from the sun. Hair was matted with the decaying flesh of their prey, nails uneven and bent, fingers like stalks of wilted wheat. Most wore shredded rags, some hovered over the corpse naked.

"Can you understand me?" Liliana called out, praying no one would answer. She moved closer, but the frenzy had become such that they no longer took any notice of her. "My name is Liliana," she said, surprising herself with the calmness of her voice.

She had to stop. Her stomach roiled. Their breath

seemed hideously foul and oppressive in the summer's night heat.

The fangs worked as a hindrance, piercing veins way past the necessary prick. The tongues lapped at the rivers of blood spreading across the corpse. One held a torn-off breast, sucking the flesh between its mangled lips, forcing its tongue deep inside the hollow it had dug.

Some squeezed portions of the body over their mouths, catching drops deep inside their throats. Gobs of flesh were swallowed with the liquid.

Cannibals, she thought. But what was she? Actually, as an embalmer she stole from the grave robbers. What did they do when formaldehyde instead of rich blood squirted into their mouths?

Mesmerized, Liliana waited. She watched. The sex of each diner could be determined only by the shape of the body. The faces no longer differentiated one from the other. Gentleness and strength had been leached from their features. Even facial definition blurred in the mass of sucking and chewing.

But she watched. To learn about her kind. They were all vampires. The family of vampires. They dramatically depicted the ancient peasant stories of what vampires were. Not romantic, sophisticated lovers, as her uncle portrayed himself. How had the line been drawn? And who were the freaks? The pack before her? Or the evolved lineage of her uncle? Or did it all eventually come down to the scene in front of her?

She envisioned her uncle howling and commanding even in dementia.

Like dogs burying bones, the pack gathered the waste and brushed it back into the grave. Rapidly they returned the soil to the site and stomped the muddied soil tightly into the grave.

A single member of the pack made a movement toward her. She faced the thing full-on and drove it back a step. It could smell the blood inside her veins. They all could. The pack waited for the member who dared to step back into Liliana's reach. It scowled and hissed and moved in jittery motions. Its hunger had not been sated. When Liliana put her hand out to it, immediately it tried to gnash its fangs into it. But her speed exceeded the mutant's.

The leader, tiring of the pathetic display, led the others back to the old section of the cemetery. Feeling alone and unsure of itself, the last mutant followed behind the pack.

Chapter Thirty-four

In the morning Marie canceled her clients' appointments. There were few clients now. She guessed it was because of her behavior, edgy and preoccupied. Only Garrett had seemed to be turned on by her indifference. But her work demeanor would change after today. She would see to it before noon.

She had chosen blatantly suggestive attire: a black lace bustier and a black half-slip that she used as a skirt. She had eliminated a layer of clothing. The spike-heeled shoes had straps that wrapped around her ankles several times, and the hose shadowed her still-shapely legs in opaque black.

He thinks that I can't portray the sub, does he. She buckled a simple leather collar around her neck, its only decoration a chrome ring meant for attaching a leash. On her eyes she had used kohl. Her red lips bled redder than blood onto the blotting tissue. Her cheeks were dusted a pinkish-red that only really seemed to work on teens.

Marie couldn't decide whether she looked like a siren or like *Whatever Happened to Baby Jane*. But she had tried everything else. All that she could hope was that the harsh sun would spend the morning behind the growing clouds.

She wore no jewelry. Marie slipped on her Nikon aviator sunglasses and topped herself off with a broad-brimmed Panama hat. She threw a large leather satchel over her left shoulder, lifted her house keys from the hall table, and left her home.

On the drive to Keith's she tried to decide how to approach the two men. Keith didn't trust her, and Wil played his game.

Wondering whether the two men were late sleepers, Marie pulled into their driveway. No signs of life, but, as she knew, that didn't prove life wasn't there.

As she climbed the steps to the porch, she listened intently. Soft noises came from the house. At least one person was at home.

The rap on the door received no reply. She moved to the right and peeked into a window. Only shadows were visible, and they weren't moving. A tap on the pane of glass drew the angry-looking Keith to the window. He made motions indicating that she should go away. She wouldn't.

The door opened and Wil stepped out onto the porch.

"What are you done up for?" he asked.

"I wanted to prove that I could handle both sides." She drew a leather leash from her satchel and attached the end to the collar around her neck. When she handed the leash to Wil, he took it and gave it a powerful yank. Quickly Marie moved toward him.

"You mean serious business, don't you, lady?"

"I know what I want."

"Me? But you don't know what you're getting."
Marie ran her tongue across her lips.

"I'm in it for the surprise." Marie considered how unusual that statement sounded.

"Somehow I think you expect to surprise me." He yanked her closer. "It won't be easy. Meeting my requirements, that is."

How right you are, she thought.

"What the hell is that?" Keith appeared at the door.

"This is a leash, Dad."

"Give her back her leash and tell her to go home, Wilbur."

"Aw, can't I keep her?"

"She's not properly house-trained."

"But that'll be my job. I promise to feed and chastise her if she breaks any rules. Please, Dad?"

"She's dressed like a . . ."

"Sub. A subordinate."

"None of that stuff will go on in my home."

"Can I play over at her house, then?"

"No, Wilbur. Now get her the hell off the property."

"I guess that means I can't come out and play today."

Wil rolled the leash into a ball and shoved it down the front of her bustier. He clapped his hands.

"Go home now, girl. Go home."

A test, she knew, but a hard one to pass. Marie managed to nod her head and descend the steps.

"And don't you be hanging around here, girl. I know where to find you if I yearn to play games."

Her gut clenched and a sour taste filled her mouth, but she walked to the car and got in.

"If you're a good girl, I might bring over a bone for you to suck on."

She had canceled all her clients for the day. She needed something to relieve the tension. She looked up at the porch and saw Keith pulling his son back into the house.

You old bastard!

"I'm scared. You have to help me. He never listens to me, but maybe you could talk your granny into leaving my son alone."

Liliana had let Keith into her home fifteen minutes before and still hadn't had a chance to speak.

"Wil is warped, I'd admit that. But your grandma, no offense, is psycho."

"This is enough, Mr. Bridgewater. All you've done is denigrate my grandmother since you got here. Your son is a grown man and my grandmother is a mature woman. They make these kinds of decisions for themselves."

"No, he can't. He always had very little self-control. That's why I was always trying to save him from disasters."

"Maybe your tendency to control his life is what drives him into bad situations. Leave him alone. Up until now you haven't been able to save him. Give it up. He's not a small boy anymore."

"You don't understand. Your granny weaved a spell around him. They're playing a game of tag, and your granny is sure to win."

"Mr. Bridgewater, my grandmother is not a witch. She doesn't wear silly pointed hats, she doesn't have a big hook nose, she doesn't boil up any specialties in a pot. You tried her food, you should know that. She doesn't even own a pet to use as a familiar."

"You should have seen her in the hat she had on today. It wasn't pointy; she looked more like a floozy."

"I can't believe I'm sitting here listening to a distant neighbor recite a litany of names to call my grandmother."

She did because she knew Mr. Bridgewater was right. Her grandmother would win, and perhaps at an awful price.

"I don't know what will happen to Wilbur," pleaded Keith.

Liliana remembered the scene in the cemetery the night before. Not all vampires were made whole. They lost not only their souls' blessed graces, but sometimes their minds.

"You're not even listening to me."

"None of my family should be here, Mr. Bridgewater."

"Shit, I don't care about you and your uncle. At least you two mind your own business and don't bother anyone. Your grandma, on the other hand, starts up trouble wherever she is."

"Mr. Bridgewater, you took me to the cemetery the other day to see Emmeline. Remember?"

"Sure, and I told you she's the reason I have to protect our son."

"Yes, but you also said that if she rose from the grave and asked you to join her as a vampire, you would agree. Would you really agree?"

Keith sat silently for a few moments.

"You'd really have to think about it, wouldn't you?"

"I'd do anything to have Emmeline back and anything to save our boy."

"Are there no boundaries?"

"When it comes to family, there shouldn't be."

"Grandmother's my family."

"She looked tawdry and dirty this morning. An old matron dressed like a slutty teenage prostitute. Maybe you should think about getting help for your grandma before someone is forced to stop her."

"Are you threatening my grandmother?"

"She threatens my son."

Keith stood. At the same moment Sade walked into the room.

"A guest. *Ma chère*, you never told me we had company in our parlor."

"Keith Bridgewater, sir." He even extended his hand.

Great, thought Liliana, *he's going to try to enlist Uncle's help.*

Sade took Keith's hand briefly. Liliana was sure Mr. Bridgewater was not the kind with whom her uncle cared to associate. Too peasantlike, he would say. However, if he saw a use for the peasant, he could pretend great friendship.

"I'm here about your . . . mother?" Keith looked at Liliana.

"Mother-in-law," corrected Liliana.

"Is Marie causing problems, *monsieur*?"

"Yes, she's after my son. She's trying to seduce him."

"How old is your *fils*?"

"Huh?"

"Son," Liliana translated.

"Twenty-seven. Way too young for a mature woman like her."

"You are so right, *monsieur*. She has centuries on him."

Warily Keith looked at Sade. "I'm serious, sir."

"I too. But what can I do?"

"If you have any influence over her, maybe you could speak to her."

"I assure you, *monsieur*, that my influence is limited. But I will certainly think about it, for she has become a bit too assertive."

"She's always been assertive, Uncle."

"To family, *ma chère*. Now she is out bothering *un étranger*."

Keith immediately looked at Liliana.

"A stranger," she explained.

"Yes, exactly. Why, she came over to my house and began chatting as if we were old friends. She forced her way into my and my son's lives."

"Mr. Bridgewater, I don't think that's completely accurate."

"Hush, *ma chère*. Let us not antagonize a good neighbor and turn this thing into a petty brawl.

"We know that Marie can be difficult, *monsieur*, and will try to temper her behavior toward your family."

"Thank you, sir. You're the salt of the earth." Keith gently punched Sade's left arm.

Chapter Thirty-five

Marie had gone home and changed clothes. Quickly she had washed her face, not bothering to reapply any makeup. Now, in town, she felt lost. She needed an outlet for her peevish anger, but she also had to practice caution.

She marched the streets looking for a victim. Too close to home, she knew, but her driving had become too chaotic to travel any further.

Women lunched in the old-fashioned ice-cream parlor. Businessmen grabbed hamburgers at the local bar. But everyone seemed to be in groups today. She needed someone alone. Someone preferably who was a stranger.

Children balked at their mothers' reprimands. Pets waited patiently for their masters in the hot sun.

Her gut tightened. *Wait patiently*. If that old man

hadn't been around, I wouldn't have to stalk in broad daylight.

Soon she realized she had stopped seeing the people passing by. Instead she squinted into her own thoughts, blindly making her way from one end of town to the other.

Suddenly a German shepherd in a two- or three-year-old Jeep took to barking. She turned to curse the dog and stopped in her tracks when she saw who was causing the animal to bark. Wil stood just beyond the Jeep, trying to get the dog to hush up.

Could she be lucky? She had paid her dues recently. It was owed to her. Ducking her head, Marie walked away from Wil. She had a visit to make.

Just as Marie arrived at the Bridgewater home, Keith pulled up in the car. He got out, leaving the motor on and slamming the door.

"Get the hell off my property, hag."

"But I thought we were the best of friends, dear," Marie called from the inside of her car.

Keith went up to the driver's side of her car and smashed his fist into the back window.

Marie opened the door, ramming the metal into the old man's stomach. Keith doubled over and stepped back.

"Keith, how rude you've become."

Keith caught his breath in a gasp.

"Damn, woman, I just want you gone."

"I've tried to be a good neighbor. Stopped by to see how you were. Invited you and your son to dinner. Even shamed myself in the supermarket by buying that dreadful beer instead of spending my money on a decent bottle of wine. Introduced you to my granddaughter. Shared special moments with you. Such as when I had your son at my feet and pulled back his head by the hair."

"And told him to come back 'without the old fart.' "

"You do remember. I never thought you stupid, Keith, just absurd in your belief that you had to be the Father Protector of your son. Especially since you've done such a poor job so far."

"Why the hell are you here? To tantalize me?"

"No."

"Well, my son isn't here, and I don't want any blow job from you."

Marie struck out, dragging her long fingernails across Keith's cheek.

"Shit!" As he spoke he sprayed saliva into the air.

Three of her nails were clotted with his flesh, and she turned her palm up so that he could see, then she licked and chewed the skin free of the nails.

Keith's feet stumbled backward, encumbered by old, heavy work boots.

"Listen, I've never hurt any woman, but you come at me again, and I'm going to defend myself."

She watched the blood slide down his cheek. He raised his hand to his face to feel what she was looking at. The wounds must have burned, because she saw him wince when his fingers came into contact with his cheek. She took a step toward him.

"I'm a lot bigger than you. What, you about an even five feet? I've got a good head over you. I could seriously hurt you, and I don't want to do that. Just go back to your car and get off my property."

She shook her head and extended her right hand. Keith tried to bat the hand away, but it was immovable. Suddenly her nails were ripping across his throat. Again her fingernails were clotted with his flesh.

"Want a taste?" she asked.

"What the hell are you?"

"Taste your flesh, old man." She moved in closer. Keith's body hit the side of his car.

"You're a real nut job."

"Taste," she whispered.

He tried to run by her, but she lunged and grabbed the back of his head, squeezing the lower part of his skull until she brought him to his knees.

"Have a headache, Keith? Pop any arteries?"

Keith's face was red. His breaths came in pants, but he tried to speak. The only sound he could make was a mewling noise. She slammed his face against the side of his car and bit into the back of his skull, cracking bone to reach the brain. Her tongue darted into the folds, lapping out a small portion of the brain. His body shivered in her arms.

"I'll not kill you, Keith. Alive, you can watch me take your son. Your greatest fear." Marie rolled the old man onto his back and peered into his eyes. "I can never tell how disabled a person is. Somehow, though, I still see intelligence in those watery eyes. Speak, Keith, speak." Marie flicked an index finger across his lips. "Speak. Try." She lowered her ear to his lips. Nothing but a gurgling sound. "Can you protest anymore? Can you interfere again?" She raised her head and looked into his wide eyes. "Scared?" She allowed his head to slide from her hands and hit the ground.

Marie drank sparingly of his blood and shared only enough of her own to keep Keith in the limbo between death and vampirism.

Using a portion of his T-shirt, Marie wiped the blood from her lips.

"Now you will not die. Of course, you will not have much of a life, either. You will be a vegetable and be cared for as I care for my pretty delicate flowers."

Chapter Thirty-six

The lake reflected the blueness of the sky. Earlier
Cecelia had feared that it would rain, but once she
and Louis pulled up to the lake on his Harley, the
sun seemed to rush from behind a cloud to wel-
come them. Leaping off the cycle, she hurried down
to the small sandy beach. There were rumors that
the water had been polluted by the last major
storm. Waste sludge supposedly had been carried
in streams that led to the lake. Cecelia didn't care.
Immediately she kicked off her sneakers and ran
into the water. The water was chilly, but not cold,
and if the sun stayed out, she figured the water
would warm up quickly. She walked into the water
up to her thighs, still a good distance from the ends
of her cutoff denim shorts. Resisting the temptation
to remove her halter top, Cecelia stooped over to
pick up a handful of water, which she released
above her head. Knowing that the white material

of the halter would become transparent when wet, she scooped up a second handful, tossing it against her breasts.

When she turned to get Sade's reaction, she found that he had already headed for the shack.

"Louis!" she dared to yell. "Louis, come into the water."

He never turned around. Instead he twisted the knob on the door and let the door swing open on its own. She watched him poke his head inside, but he seemed reluctant to move his entire body into the ramshackle hut.

"It's safe," she yelled. "Besides, we're not going to need it. See, the sun is out." She raised her hands to the sun in adoration.

Sade slipped off his black leather jacket and let it fall to the ground. She always marveled at what tight buttocks he had in his jeans. Tight certainly for an old man. His black silk shirt was a contrast in texture and fit to the jeans. The sleeves of the shirt were blousy. The cut of the shirt was full but still tapered.

His white hair, cut just short of his shoulders, blew in the swiftness of a summer breeze. A few shaggy strands fell onto his forehead as he looked down at the two steps leading into the shack.

"Louis!" she called again, but he climbed the steps and disappeared inside.

Reluctantly Cecelia made her way back to the beach, picking up her sneakers on her way to the shack.

"Louis, you should try out the water." She jogged up the two steps and ran into the shack.

Sade sat with bent knees on the wood floor, his back against the fake wood paneling of the wall.

"Sit down, *ma chère*. First close the door behind you."

"But we should at least let some sun in, or it'll be real dreary in here."

"Shut the door, Cecelia."

Compelled by the sound of his voice, she followed his instructions. As soon as the door closed, Sade pulled off his aviator sunglasses.

Even in the dimness of the shack, or perhaps because of it, Cecelia could see how white his flesh appeared under the blackness of the shirt. He seemed to glow, and his eyes shined a warm invitation. What the hell, she'd be able to reinforce her tan tomorrow.

She flung her sneakers across the tiny room, but when she sat down in front of Sade she felt the sharp pierce of a splinter enter her right buttock.

"Owww," she moaned. Lifting her buttock off the floor, she tried to locate the splinter.

"A problem, *ma chère*?"

"I have a splinter in my fanny."

"*Viens ici*, let me help." He moved forward, tucking his knees under him.

She felt his hands gently touch her flesh. His fingers were long, the nails well-manicured. But his touch was cold. Frigid, she thought, as he kneaded her flesh in search of the splinter.

"It's farther up," she said, rising to her knees so that he would have a better view.

His left hand moved to her left buttock, and he massaged the soft baby fat of her ass.

"It's on the right side of my fanny," she said, not pulling away from his touch. "Ow! Right there. You've found it."

"Much too soon, *ma chère*."

Her rear shivered when he plucked the splinter

out. She slipped her hands under his and began rubbing her own ass.

He pulled himself up onto his knees and pressed his body against hers. She could feel the hardness of his cock. With a gulp Cecelia cleared her throat.

"Have you seen the rest of the place?" she asked.

"I've seen only a portion of what I want to see," he answered.

Immediately she pulled away and stood.

"Over here we keep our cigs," she said, walking to the far wall. She pulled up a beige tarp and revealed several packs of cigarettes. "Sometimes we have weed when one of us can afford it. We're broke now." She looked back at Sade and found that he hadn't moved. His hands appeared to be turned palms outward exactly where her buttocks had been.

"Louis?"

"Oui." He stood and faced her with an obvious bulge disrupting the smoothness of his denim jeans.

Her eyes lingered a bit too long on his groin.

"Would you take pity on me, *ma petite chérie?*"

"Huh?" Confronted with the opportunity that she had been fantasizing about, her confidence wilted.

What if she was too inexperienced? What if he didn't like her body? Oh my God, when was her period due?

"The hibachi is over there," she said, pointing to a sooty object in a dark corner of the room. "My friend and I can stay here all day. We'd probably sleep here, except our parents would blow a gasket."

"With whom do you spend the day?"

"My girlfriend, of course. Once I invited Joey down here. He's my . . . a guy who kind of likes me."

"And what did you and Joey do here?"

Cecelia was confused. She wasn't used to the burning flush stinging her cheeks.

"Do?"

"Yes. That day that you spent here with Joey. What did you two do?"

Sade stood perfectly still. A meanness seemed to creep into his blue-eyed stare. He opened several buttons of his shirt, and she could see the curly gray hairs that lay flat on his chest. She wanted to fluff up the hair, feel their downy softness.

He opened the rest of the buttons and removed his shirt.

"Ah, it is hot in here."

"That's why we should be in the water," she replied mechanically.

Sade used his right thumb to undo the snap on his jeans. He continued to stare at her.

Cecelia swallowed several times. Being with Joey was never this excruciatingly embarrassing. Things just seemed to happen when she was with him. Here the world had gone into slow motion, and she felt that she had to make a real decision. Making love with Louis Sade would not be an unbridled passion that she couldn't contain. She had to make the choice.

Suddenly she smelled the odor of her own sex. The moistness of her genitals fed the burning heat of her vagina. Her nipples ached, and the coolness of the water had dissipated while her breasts burned to be touched.

Another gulp of saliva slid down her throat as she undid the tie on her halter top.

Joey liked her breasts, but Joey had been with only one other girl. What did he know?

On the other hand, she was sure Sade had tasted

the most exquisite of actresses and models. Women both young and old.

Cecelia took a deep breath and dropped the ends of the halter top. She saw a smile widen his thin lips. He liked what he saw. She, too, undid the snap on her denims, but she had to use two fingers, since her thumb couldn't steady itself on the snap.

"Shall we play Simon Says?" Sade asked. *"Oui?"* Again the decision had to be made consciously.

"Yeah," she answered.

"Simon says . . ." Sade slipped the jeans down over his hips and let them drop to his ankles before stepping out of them.

This is not Joey, she thought, staring at the ampleness of Sade's erection.

"Are we still playing the game, *ma chère?*"

This isn't a game, she thought. *This is the real thing. A true man and not a boy.*

She rued the baby fat clinging to her hips and belly. But if she let the moment pass, he might not give her another opportunity.

She squeezed out of her tight denim cutoffs and pulled her thongs off with the shorts.

"Come here, *ma chère.*"

He did not use the French word *ici*. Instead he spoke in clear English. She had to give herself; he would not take unless offered.

Slowly she moved closer, feeling sweat form under her armpits, smelling the odor of her sex, even stronger now.

"Touch me." He spoke the words softly, but with a firmness she dared not ignore.

She reached out to touch his chest, and he shook his head. Her hand dropped down to his erection, and it quivered in her hand.

Sade and she lowered their bodies onto the floor.

"*Ma petite fille,* taste me."

She heard demand mixed with patience.

Her free hand felt the down on his chest. *Silky.*

He placed his hand atop her head and gently pressed down until her mouth was even with his penis. Again he whispered.

"Taste me."

Her lips parted, and she filled her mouth with the breadth of his passion.

Chapter Thirty-seven

Slow, Sade reminded himself. The young dove would flee if she realized the extent of his passion. As her head bobbed, her butt rose high. Such a morsel, he thought. An ass that could take the sting of a thousand lashes. An ass that could be made to take the fullness of his cock.

Sade lay back on the wood floor and vowed to control his needs. A step at a time, he told himself. To beat or draw blood now would rob him of the future delights that he had planned. Let the young one feel that she is in charge now. Later he would have his turn. Eager to prove herself, she would gladly meet all his demands, he knew.

Sade reached down and drew her body up against his. He noticed the pulsing in her neck. Not yet, he reminded himself. He would feast on her in degrees until she submitted to his every command.

Her need for him would grow in proportion to the confidence she had in her skill.

His hand felt the excessive wetness between her legs. The probing of two of his fingers revealed the heat inside her. Her body moved without her control. Instead her flesh fed on primal concupiscence.

He pushed her shoulders back and grabbed hold of her thighs, setting her astride his groin, his cock pressed against the smoothness of her slightly rounded tummy.

Cecelia raised her body and spread herself apart with one hand while guiding his cock with the other.

Little by little he slipped inside her. Her desire to fully take him in overcame the moment of pain that flashed on her face.

Sade restrained himself for a few seconds, allowing her body to adjust to the forced expansion. Cecelia began moving first. He allowed her to pace the movement. *She must think she wields some of the power,* he thought, *until I show her the inevitable truth. Her body is mine. Her will has been broken.*

She moved faster, the pulse in her neck more pronounced, making him remember the taste of blood. *Ah, to see rouge blood stain her neck.*

Her breaths came in pants, and he heard her mewl when he touched her clitoris.

Control. He had never given up the control. He would only lend the control to her so that she would have none of her own left.

Chapter Thirty-eight

Sade dropped Cecelia off where he had picked her up. The sex had been good, and under his tutelage he knew she would get better. His blood hunger overcame his senses as he sped ninety miles an hour down the deserted road.

He needed to feed. Some needed to light a cigarette; he needed the metallic taste of blood.

He knew shanties existed down the road, hovels in which families tried to survive, scared families that avoided authority. They settled disputes themselves. They educated their own, and births hardly ever got recorded.

He had taken a few lives there. Children were the least likely to be missed, since a child's death meant one less mouth to feed.

The dirt road leading to the shanties was nearby. Sade slowed to catch his turnoff.

A crumbling fence and a useless mailbox marked

the spot. He had been told that originally a large, mostly inbred family had lived in a rambling Victorian house on this land. The house burned down one summer evening and the family scattered, although most town people believed that the residents of shantytown were the progeny of that old family.

The scent of beans and ham cooking reached Sade. Not a meal he would enjoy, but he understood that the people here were able to grow their own beans and successfully raise pigs. Quite a limited diet, he thought.

He chuckled. And what would the shanty people think of his diet? There were vampires that only drank blood, never touched the food meant to fatten their prey.

Before seeing the shanties, Sade pulled to the side of the road. From here he would go by foot.

One child would not be sufficient to sate his sexually charged appetite. The elderly sat around in groups waiting to be plucked by death, but not by Sade. His blood needed to be refreshed, rejuvenated.

The sudden barking of a dog reminded Sade of how fond these people were of their pets. A cross between a Saint Bernard and a German shepherd approached him. One of the dog's eyes was clouded over, the other seriously drooped. However, the dog's sense of smell still allowed him to locate trespassers. The dog's gimpy back leg slowed him down considerably.

"Go home," Sade commanded.

The dog walked up to Sade and sat. His coat was matted and his teeth weren't all present, but his tail worked enthusiastically in his greeting of Sade.

"Great *chien de garde*."

The dog whimpered and lay down at Sade's feet.

"Guilt won't work with *moi*."

When Sade attempted to move on, the dog followed.

"*Chien*, I cannot have you following me."

The dog again whimpered and lay at Sade's feet.

Sade heard a sound. A crunching of leaves. Feminine pheromone came swirling in the air around him, and the precious smell of blood enfolded his senses completely. He drew back beneath an old tree and waited. The dog stood and stared at Sade like a bloodhound directing the hunter toward the kill.

A lissome girl of twenty stepped into view.

"There you are, dog. What are you doing out here?" The girl approached the dog and ruffled his dirty fur. "Come on back before you get lost. Johnny won't sleep unless he's cuddled up next to you."

The dog never moved. The girl nudged him with her knee, and the dog sat down.

"Aw, please come back. I don't want to be standing out in the woods all night. And neither do you. Remember how you got that old droopy eye chasing rabbits in the dark? Thinking you could fit inside the hollowed-out tree like the rabbit? Bruising that face of yours so badly that we weren't sure whether it would be kinder to shoot you or patch you?"

The dog steadfastly ignored her.

"What's the matter with you?"

The presence of the menstruating woman drove Sade's hunger to the brink of carelessness. His body stiffened to leap.

The dog growled.

"Is there some dumb animal in those trees?" she asked the dog.

"If I chase it away, will you come home then?" The girl shook her head and tried to peer into the blackness of the woods.

Come to me, ma petite fille.

Sade could not make out the color of her eyes, but her features looked carved. Her braided black hair reached down to her narrow waist. Her small pert breasts jutted out against the knitted cotton dress. The sash she used around her waist appeared bleached and old. Her legs and feet were bare.

"I don't see anything, dog." Again she attempted to get the dog to move. This time it stood and moved closer to the trees where Sade hid. The girl followed, passing by the dog and determinedly heading for the woods.

The sexual energy and menstrual blood turned Sade into a quivering shadow.

"Is someone there?" she asked.

Sade withdrew further into the shades surrounding him.

The girl stopped and called a name. A name that Sade did not catch. She called several other names, and Sade's mind calculated the leap he would need to make to capture her.

The girl turned toward the dog.

"What do you have me doing? Making a fool of myself?"

The dog growled in reply.

"What the hell's bothering you?" With an exasperated sigh she turned again to the woods and walked into the shadows.

The dog barked once before he fell silent, a matted twisted jumble of fur and flesh.

Sade sated his sexual hunger. This time he felt the complete release of thirst quenched and desire punctuated by orgasm.

"But no one opens his arms to the guilty person. . . . People blush to be in his presence, are embarrassed to offer him their tears, as though terrified of contagion; he is banished from every heart: pride impels us to heap abuse upon him whom we ought to succor out of a feeling of humanity."

Ernestine,
by the
Marquis de Sade

Chapter Thirty-nine

Marie wrapped the collar around her neck and tightened the buckle. Each day she would perform this ritual until he came. He would inevitably, driven either by the suspicion that she had something to do with his father's condition or simply to direct his wrath at someone. And she would be here waiting, hungry, and willing.

Before noon Wil did show, his hair greasy and disheveled. His dark eyes had no glow. Shadows darkened the puffy bags under his eyes. His stale breath soured the air around him, and his body's stench revealed all the fear, pain, and anger that he had so recently experienced.

"I knew it had to be you the instant I found him."

"Wil, it sounds more like a crazed dog than any human. From what you're telling me, it sounds like your father was mauled. Perhaps some beast. A wild cat. A wolf."

"They don't exist around here."

"The gory details you've told me certainly indicate to me that it had to be something from the wild that did this to your father."

Wil let himself drop onto the settee.

"He can never get better. He's permanently a . . . vegetable."

"Do they know how much he understands?"

"He's still unconscious, but hell, his brain was dripping out of his head onto the ground when I found him." Wil steadied his elbows on his knees and rested his face in his hands.

Marie fingered her collar.

"I didn't come home to hurt him," Wil sobbed.

"Yes, you did."

Wil looked up at Marie, tears sliding down his cheeks, eyes a lackless dark ebony.

"You always tried to hurt your father, Wil. You wanted retribution for having been abandoned as a baby. Oh, he took care of the child in mundane ways, but he deserted his son as soon as his wife died. You were never part of their family. Not for your father. His family consisted of two people, and you killed one of them."

Marie watched Wil's chest pump from the heaving roiling his insides. Suddenly Wil sprang to his feet and ran for the bathroom.

At least he still remembers his manners, she thought.

She didn't really like this aspect of Wil. The sniveling. The self-pity. She would have preferred a raging bull.

When he returned to the room, he carried one of her best hand towels, the one with the stitched poppies bordering each end. He had soaked one corner

227

of the towel with water, and he kept rubbing it across his face.

"Want a drink, Wil?"

He shook his head and sat on the settee.

Marie fingered the collar. He didn't seem to notice.

"I could give you a little arsenic in a bit of champagne."

"I can't go back."

"To your father's house?" A smile rounded the corners of her lips.

"Back to the city."

"Do you want to?"

"I can't go back."

"Don't cryptic. I don't have time to give you therapy, Wil."

"I owe a lot of money."

"The pimping business is that bad?"

"I don't do that shit anymore."

"Drugs? Gambling?"

"I borrowed money for a business I was starting."

"What kind?"

"An escort service."

"And you say you're not pimping anymore."

"It was going to be legit. There's a lot of people who need to show up at functions with a companion. Some are closet gays who need to rent a date just for the evening. Businesspeople who don't have the energy for a real relationship, but don't want the boss to know."

"How much did you borrow?"

"Two hundred thousand."

"What fool lent you that kind of money?"

"A guy who would like to step over my dead body."

"Ex-lover?"

228

He nodded.

Marie unbuckled the collar and removed it from her neck. She studied the collar, trying to decide whether it would fit Wil.

"You want your father dead."

"No! Damn it! I thought I could stay with Dad for a while until . . ."

"Until he dropped dead."

Wil flung the towel across the room.

"You need a shower, Wil. You stink. There's an open shower in the basement. Use it."

"I'm not good enough for the upstairs bathroom?"

Marie sat next to him. She measured the collar around his neck.

"You need something to relieve the tension. I can help you."

Wil undid the buttons on his denim shirt.

"I can make you forget for a time."

"I don't want to forget. I want to be made to pay for what happened to my father. And you, bitch, know how to do it."

Marie chuckled. If she had only known sooner.

"Take the collar with you and put it on after you shower. Wait for me downstairs." She dropped the collar into his lap. "Now!"

A flash sparked his eyes, and by the time it disappeared Wil had taken the collar in his hand. They both stood. Marie slipped the denim off his shoulders and down his arms. His muscles sagged a bit, the confidence and power gone from his body. She unbuckled his belt and undid the trousers. He was erect beneath his trousers; a horizontal bar with a metal ball at each end pierced his cock head.

When she finished undressing him, she held his clothing at arm's length.

"Bet you've had these on for several days. This what you were wearing when you found your father?"

"Yeah." His voice sounded defeated and tired.

"I'll burn them." She started for the doorway, then stopped. "You're dismissed."

Wil looked down at the collar he still held in his hands.

"After the shower you can put it on. I don't want the leather getting ruined."

He moved past her. As he walked, she took in the colors covering his legs. The Grim Reaper flexed on the back of his right leg, wielding his scythe over his head and just under the curve of Wil's right buttock. Tombstones covered the back of the other leg. Skeletal limbs were scattered among the tombstones.

She didn't have to show him the way to the basement. He homed in on the dungeon, or perhaps she had said something previously about where the dungeon was located. She couldn't remember, and it didn't matter.

"Remorse is no index of criminality; it merely denotes an easily subjugated spirit; let some absurd command be given you, which forbids you to leave this room, and you'll not depart without guilty feelings however certain it is your departure will cause no one any harm."

Justine,
by the
Marquis de Sade

Chapter Forty

Wil touched his father's hand. Milky white, he thought. The ragged nails had been trimmed by a nurse. The misshapen knuckles no longer gave his father pain. The age spots appeared to be more prominent against the flaccid flesh. Wil slid his own palm under his father's. Slowly Wil's fingers closed around his father's hand, but as when he was a child, there was no response. He felt the weight of the hand and tried to lift it, but it seemed to be made of a heavy material that looked like flesh, only looked like flesh.

"Dad, I'm going to be taking you home soon. The doctor said he could do no more for you. Hell, I don't know what I can even do. Nothing, I guess, but bathe and feed you. And maybe pray, if I can remember any prayers. What should I be praying for, Dad? Your recovery? Or for you to die a peaceful death?"

He waited for tears to shine his eyes, but nothing blurred the vision of his father lying against white sheets, tubes keeping the old man alive. The hospital bed seemed too narrow for his father's bulk. Too confining. Too unreal.

"Hey, when I get you home I'll slip an old T-shirt and boxers on you. Get rid of this piece of cloth that passes as a nightgown. Besides, you're too macho for a *gown*."

The nurse's call button dangled uselessly from the headboard.

"The nurses don't know how lucky they are that you can't use that button. You'd really be living it up bullying around the staff."

Wil smiled, but didn't feel any emotion. He used his thumb to rub the back of his father's hand, attempting to bring back life.

He knelt down beside his father's bed and kissed the old man's hand. The smell of antiseptics overpowered Wil's breath. His stomach roiled, and his own hands began to shake.

"Don't know if I'll be able to duplicate all this clean stuff. Home might smell more like . . . a sewer. I think I finally fixed that toilet. I've been flushing and the water hasn't spilled over. Still think you could use a new septic tank, except that you're so damned cheap you'd rather live with the stink rather than part with a cent."

An empty bed lay stripped down next to his father's bed. A boy had been bunking there, or at least he had looked like a boy. Yet Wil and the boy had been the same age. Born two months apart, they had been able to communicate and share jokes. The kid had kept talking about going home, had kept apologizing for Keith's condition, even though he had had nothing to do with the *accident*. The kid had never been farther than fifty miles outside his town until he had the stroke. They had rushed him to the nearest hospital, one hundred and five and a half miles from home. He had to learn to walk all over again. Had to work on the slight slur that had marred his speech. His intent to overcome the remnants of his stroke had camouflaged the boy's fear. However, when the boy had died, fear and surprise distorted the expression on his face. Briefly Wil had caught a glance of the chiseled dead face. A second stroke had taken away the boy's second chance.

Wil wanted to start all over. His father wouldn't let him. Marie wouldn't let him. He couldn't allow himself to forgive his own indiscretions. His own warped and depraved pleasures eased the pain. Made him forget. Made him purge himself of the guilt.

"I'm so sorry, Wil."

He turned to the door and saw Marie standing with the door open, the knob still in her hand. Gently she closed the door and slowly walked to the bed.

"Can he hear anything?"

Wil shook his head. *Why had she come?* he wondered. *Out of hate, spite, or curiosity?*

"Get up off your knees, Wil."

He found himself obeying.

She stood on the opposite side of the bed, facing Wil.

"You look like shit."

Wil sought escape by looking down at his father.

"Can you hear me?"

"Yes."

"Not you, idiot. I'm talking to your dad. Think they could close his mouth? He looks a bit demented with his lips parted like that."

"He's a vegetable."

"Keith has always been an old turnip."

Shut up! Get out! Stay away from me!

"Where are you placing him?"

"In his old bedroom, of course."

"You're taking him home?"

Wil nodded.

"Why?"

"I'm going to take care of him myself."

"Too late. May as well pass him on to a health care provider. Or is the cost a problem?"

"I want to take care of him."

"I can set up a trust fund for him. We'll find an exceptionally good nursing home and move on with our lives together."

"No!"

He faced her steady glare. She softened and turned back to look at Keith.

"I'm sure Dad would feel better in a home." Her hand reached out and stroked Keith's gray hair. "He hated you, Wil, and from what I have observed, the feeling seemed mutual."

"Not true," Wil replied mechanically.

"Stop this stupid denial." She leaned over Keith and blew a few fine hairs off his forehead. "You don't want to see your son come home with the welts from my whips, the bites from my teeth, and the slashes from my canes. Do you?"

Wil watched his father's body twitch and shake. Immediately he ran from the room, calling for a doctor.

When he returned to the room, he saw Marie bending over his father, whispering into and licking his ear. Wil reached out to grab her shoulders, but his hands were scorched by her icy skin.

"Seizure!" he heard from behind him. People

235

pushed and shoved until he found himself in the hallway, watching Marie heading for the elevator bank. Her mauve dress fluttered around her calves. Her high heels tapped out the retreat.

A nurse's hand pulled him back toward his father's room.

"Your father has had a seizure. The doctor isn't sure what brought it on, but given your father's unstable condition, it's unlikely that he'll be able to go home with you for a while. Have you thought about a nursing home? They could give your father twenty-four-hour-a-day care. It will be impossible for you to do the same."

"He's coming home."

"Not a very wise choice, but it's certainly your decision."

The nurse took the same path as Marie and ended up getting on the same elevator. They smiled at each other. Neither spoke.

"Damn you!" he shouted as the elevator doors shut.

Chapter Forty-one

"Remember when we were translating *Venus in Furs?*"

Sade nodded while removing his banded-collar navy linen shirt. He had removed the black sheets from the windows of the cabin tonight. Instead of illumination by candlelight, the moon would spray ghostly shadows on the two lovers.

"I got a book of my own." Her hand dipped into her red canvas bag and pulled out a thick newspaper. Playing magician, she slid a blue-colored, large-format paperback from within the pages. *Screw the Roses, Send Me the Thorns*, shouted the title in white letters. Cecelia giggled.

"I've been studying this book," she said ominously.

"And?" The child learned faster than he had thought she would.

"And I have a special surprise for you."

"Will it hurt?"

Cecelia nodded sagely.

Sade tossed his shirt to the floor and quickly undid his black leather jeans. He carefully shed his outer layer of animal skin, paring down to his own white flesh. Alerted, his cock stretched forward and out toward the scantily clad teen. Her skimpy white shorts and halter top barely covered her loins and the tips of her breasts.

Cecelia tucked the book under one arm and again reached into her canvas bag. This time she pulled out a new clothesline, still wrapped and sealed.

"I shall demand your full cooperation, sir."

"Or . . ."

Confused, she hesitated. Suddenly she exchanged the position of the book for the rope. Quickly her fingers brushed across the multiple Post-its indexing the book.

"Why don't I stand in front of this coat hook," Sade suggested.

"Yes, that's a good idea."

She placed the canvas bag, book, and newspaper on the floor and began to undo the cellophane binding the rope. Unfortunately she broke a fingernail and stopped to suck on the injured finger.

"Let me do that for you, *ma chère*."

The wrap disappeared in a flash.

"Now raise your wrists up to the hook," she demanded.

Sade followed her order.

Clumsily Cecelia wrapped the smooth rope around his wrists and around the hook. One burst of energy and Sade could easily break free, but he wanted to play the game to the conclusion.

"*Mais, vos* clothes, *ma chère*."

She stood tall and did an abbreviated striptease, giggling and blushing through it all.

The baby fat on her ass shimmied as she walked back to the canvas bag.

"I'm going to brand you mine," she said while dipping into her bag one more time. "I'm going to heat up the hibachi and stamp my initials across your rump." And from the bag she pulled a branding iron that displayed her initials across the tip.

Quelle merveilleuse surprise! The girl showed herself to be quite willing to seek out the tools necessary to enhance their relationship. He wondered how embarrassed she had been while purchasing these *sensuelles* goodies.

She placed the hibachi near Sade and started the fire.

"Now for the blindfold," she announced.

Again the canvas bag and yet another toy for their amusement. She fingered the black blindfold lined with a furry, cream material, attempting to tease and worry her victim.

Sade allowed her to slip the blindfold over his eyes; however, he did not tell her that he could still peek out from the bottom of the blindfold. No, he wanted to observe his *mignon* as she attempted to bring pleasure to her lover.

Cecelia rubbed her body against his. Her nipples were hard, but the skin felt smooth and soft. She spread her legs so that she could rub her mound against his thigh.

Wet! A perfect beginning, he thought.

"You'll be all mine forever," she whispered.

"Oui, vraiment!"

"Huh?"

"True! We *will* be together for eternity." He

smiled, thinking what a treasure he had found in the *petite coquine*.

Her fingers brushed a few gray strands of hair off his forehead. Her lips came nearer to his, and he could feel her breath tickle the fine hairs inside his nostrils. Finally she placed a kiss on his lips and forced them apart with her tongue, searching his mouth for the taste of wet pleasure.

Sade's cock ached, but he would wait for her lead. Her hard nipples stabbing into his chest abraded his white flesh. Her long legs meshed with his as her hand found his cock and she began to draw her fingers in an up-and-down motion. Something cold and metallic scraped the ridge of his organ. He remembered the silver and onyx ring that she always wore.

She pulled away and shouted, "Enough!"

Hardly.

"I am now going to brand you with my initials."

Sade watched her jerk the branding iron in and out of the hibachi's heat, purposefully causing the loud crash of coal against metal.

She stopped, placed the iron on the floor, and slowly tiptoed across the room. He could not see her open the door; however, a slight squeak gave away her location.

What marvel could she be hiding outside the cabin?

Her toes daintily returned to his view.

A Pepsi? And a hamburger patty? Did she plan on stopping for a snack? Sade's sense of the erotic would be badly ruffled. *La fille* would need true punishment.

"Now I'm going to mark your white flesh and bathe in your pain," she said.

Her lines would get better with practice, he assured himself.

Cecelia lifted the branding iron and made a plentiful amount of noise hitting it against the hibachi. Quietly she put the iron back on the wooden floor, lifted the hamburger patty and Pepsi. In two swift movements she flipped the burger onto the hibachi grill and slammed the frozen can of soda against his left buttock. The sizzle and smell of burning meat.

No doubt she wanted him to believe that the burn from the icy can of soda actually was the branding iron.

Dramatically he sucked in air. His body shivered, and he heard her giggle.

When she removed the blindfold she held the can of soda in front of his eyes.

"It was only a frozen can of soda, silly. You think I would consider marring such white, beautiful flesh? I read that it's the fantasy that really counts. I got the idea from the book."

She tried to untie his wrists, but only seemed to manage to tighten the knots. Sade snapped apart the rope, freeing both his hands.

If her wide blue eyes were any indication, she seemed impressed by the feat.

"You could have freed yourself anytime, but you trusted me."

"*Oui*. Just as you should trust me, *ma chère*. It is now my turn."

"Nothing is as persuasive as the eloquence of lovers; theirs is a logic of the heart that the mind's logic can never equal."

Ernestine,
by the
Marquis de Sade

Chapter Forty-two

Marie's red-stained tongue licked the surface of his penis in slow, long movements.

"Seems I may have a problem, Wil."

"What is it?" He sighed, delighting in the pleasure she gave him.

"One of my clients has died. And . . . my name has somehow been mentioned in connection with him. Very embarrassing, as you can imagine. I try very hard to be circumspect about my business, not only for my client's sake but also my own. This has forced me to think about going back to Paris sooner than I had expected."

"You're going to leave me."

"No. However, we will have to travel separately, since I'll need you to look after an important . . . piece of luggage." Marie had found that the most comfortable way for her to travel was in her coffin.

"I can't leave my father."

"Your father has already left you, Wil. He's not coming back. As a matter of fact, it's probably better that he not return to us. I mean, given the condition of his brain, he will never be able to function as he once did."

"I can't leave him."

Marie noticed the change in the timbre of his voice. He wanted to pull back from the passion in order to find his own integrity. Swiftly she took him fully into her mouth. She took his groan as an indication that she had overcome his moment of guilt.

"Before I leave . . ." She hesitated, licking the tip of his cock. "I have someone special that I want to see stopped."

"Stopped? We're not talking murder, are we?"

"Oh fie, he's already dead."

"Are you stopping the burial or cremation?"

"Cremation. I like that. Burial would be useless in his case, but a nice bonfire would work very well."

"I must admit I'm not following you."

"I want you to destroy a coffin, preferably with a body inside it."

"Me? Why me?"

"How unladylike it would be for me to do it. Besides, my granddaughter would never forgive me. I want to be able to look Liliana in the eyes and seem shocked when she tells me."

"Will she be returning to Paris also?"

Marie flicked the switch she held across his penis.

"My granddaughter's not for you. Actually she's dating some math whiz quite happily." She gazed up into Wil's face. His dark eyes had lost the glisten of sensuality. His face paled from the volume of blood she had siphoned off. "One would think I don't make you happy."

"You remind me of the life I can't escape."

"We're put here for pleasure, Wil. Not to wallow in guilt. There should be no such thing as guilt. We do what is best for ourselves."

"A man who takes a life should not feel guilt?"

"No, Wil." She stretched her body across his, fingering the ropes that bound him to the bed. "Death can be a treasure or a waste, depending on one's ability to control the grim reaper's sleep."

"You mean if I were to kill you—"

Marie laughed. "You couldn't. I'm long past the fear of death. Only my body can be destroyed. My soul is now bound to the earth."

"You mean you're not going to heaven? That's a surprise." He smirked.

"I gave up heaven for pleasure."

"Then all those saints I learned about in Sunday school missed out big."

She shrugged her naked shoulders. "Everyone has their own idea of pleasure. Mine is to exist forever."

Blood had crusted on his neck. She would have to be careful not to take too much. She needed to make him drink her own blemished blood. He would make a very masculine, sensual vampire once he recognized the strength she could give him.

"Mine is to make up for all those years I ignored my father."

"Your father is beyond any pleasure. He needs to pass on and return to dust."

"You want him dead?"

"I want you. That is all I can think about."

"And what about me and my happiness?"

"I will make you more than happy. I will share a secret power that I have."

"Is this going to be in a potion made up of mashed frog legs, bat's wings, and whatever other witchy brew you can come up with?"

Marie bit down hard on her wrist. Blood bubbled to the surface. She squeezed the break in her flesh to allow the blood to flow freely.

"Shit! What the hell are you doing?"

"Share my brew now." She brought her wrist up to his lips and he turned his head. "Only a fool would turn from my gift."

"Hey, I let you nuzzle up and suck some of my blood, but I've never had the desire to lap up anyone else's."

"Never?" She pursed her lips. "Never in a fit of passion have you drawn your tongue across a wound you have inflicted? Never in a blur of desire have you bitten down to taste the metallic juice of a lover? Never have you lapped at the remnants of a woman's bloody life-giving tissue?" She stared at his profile, seeing the turmoil twitch his flesh while he remained silent. "You have. Sometimes we can't control the sweetest temptations." Slowly she moved her wrist around to his lips. He did not turn away this time, but he did not suck on her flesh. Instead he allowed the blood to flow across his full lips, rivulets moistening the parchness of his flesh.

Gingerly Marie used her other hand to guide the drops of blood between his lips.

"Swallow, my love. Let me seep into your body."

His tongue met her bloodied fingers, licking, savoring the salty sweet taste.

Chapter Forty-three

Liliana found herself laughing more as her dates with David became more frequent. He startled her darker side into believing that life had not been wasted on her. He touched her gently, and she savored each embrace they shared. Again as she remembered him in a former life, he cautiously approached intimacy, and Liliana slowly recalled the thrill of a passionate embrace, the rhythm of united bodies, even though it had never been with him.

David had tanned since first she had met him. His skin had turned from a pale white to a warm earth shade.

"How come you named him Françoise?" David asked as he scratched the rabbit behind its ear.

"I named him after my uncle."

"I can't imagine your uncle being pleased about that."

"Causing pain pleases him."

"I don't understand." David placed the rabbit back into its cage.

"My grandmother and uncle aren't speaking. Hell, they can't even tolerate the sight of each other." Liliana latched the cage door shut. "Grandmother refuses to say what happened between them, and Uncle implies that Grandmother is overreacting. To what? He won't tell me. Caught in the middle, what the hell am I supposed to do?"

"Not allow yourself to be pulled into their feud."

"I try, but I don't like the bitterness between them. They've never been on good terms with each other; however, they used to at least talk."

"Time will help."

"No, David. My gut tells me this is too serious."

"I've never met your grandmother. Is she as much of a terror as your uncle thinks she is?"

"He's spoken of her to you?"

"Yes. Her name was mingled in with some French words that I didn't understand, and I thought it best not to ask for a translation."

Liliana shook her head. Why must she give up a beautiful Saturday afternoon to her kin's feud? She took David's soft, firm hand in hers.

"Let's forget about the skeletons in the closet."

"Are there many, and do they bite?"

"Only a few . . . but they do bite."

David laughed. "Your family is probably no worse than the average."

Liliana stroked his hand with her thumb.

"Come over here and sit down with me, Liliana."

They crossed the yard to a white gazebo. The paint job had been shabby. Globs of bubbles marred the various planks of wood. A vine attempted to cut off their passage onto the elevated natural wood stage. Dressed in hot-pink bell-shaped flowers, the vine extended itself from one side of the doorway to the other. David reached out a hand and batted the vine out of their way. As they moved across the wood floor, Liliana could measure the weakness of each board. The bell-shaped flowers surrounding them had a subtle sweet odor. A hint of honey and chlorophyll impinged upon their bodies.

"Why don't we sit on the bench for a while and talk." David swept a hand across the dust that had collected on the oddly curved bench. "I think the builders were attempting to make a love seat. Obviously they failed."

David sat and drew Liliana down upon his lap.

"Too much the gentleman to have me sit on a dirty bench?"

"Naw, it's just an excuse to get closer to you."

She wrapped her arms around his neck and rubbed her fingers through his hair. His hair seemed fine, baby fine, but there was no thinning. She touched his pale eyebrows and licked each eyelid shut. His nose twitched, causing her to giggle.

"You look just like Françoise when you do that."

"I hope you mean the rabbit, not the uncle."

She giggled, and kissed the bridge of his nose.

"A little lower," he said.

She kissed the tip of his nose and then his lips.

Immediately he parted his lips, and Liliana's tongue ventured into his mouth. Gently he sucked and circled her tongue with his.

She felt his right hand slip under the sleeveless denim blouse that she wore—a move Stuart never would have attempted. But then, David's age easily approached thirty; perhaps with maturity Stuart would have become more aggressive. He undid her bra and brought his hand around to cup one of her breasts. He weighed her breast and fondled the nipple with one finger.

Foreplay, she thought. Dare she allow both their passions to be freed? Could she make love and not draw blood? Liliana knew that passion peaked the hunger. Whether it be the passion of love or hate, they both awakened the hunger that animal blood, dead blood, could not satisfy completely. She pulled away and heard him moan and whisper her name.

"Lil," she corrected.

David opened his eyes and smiled.

His lips formed the name Lil, but the name remained unheard.

Using his free hand, David cupped the back of her head and pulled her down into another kiss. This time the kiss staggered Liliana's senses. She wanted him. She deserved another chance at love. She wouldn't allow her uncle to continue to cheat her of her flowering youth that he had stolen many years before. With one hand she opened the buttons on her blouse. As the material slid down her back, David pulled away to see her blossomed breasts. She let the bra slip onto his lap. Immediately he suckled at her breasts, passionately moving between the two.

Liliana opened the snap on her jeans and permitted his fingers to pull down the zipper.

The combined smells of his baby-fine hair and his masculine sweat drove her beyond a point at which she could deny him.

"I love you," she muttered into his soft hair, bringing several strands closer in order to smell and taste him.

He stopped, and rested his lips on her bare midriff.

"I can't promise you love, Lil."

"And I can't ask it of you. Allow me to at least share what I am feeling. What I have felt for so many years."

He chortled and kissed her skin.

"We've only known each other for a month."

"You've been in my heart for centuries," she whispered.

David looked up at her. "Funny, you don't look like such an old crone."

"I never will." Liliana scooped up his chin and rushed into a breathless kiss. "Make love to me," she cried out as he lowered her to the floor. "Make love to me like you always should have." The chaste love's name, "Stuart," almost passed her lips, but she caught herself and settled for a protracted hiss that fed the steam in David's hurried movements.

Clothes cast aside, the two lovers explored each other. The dampness of his flesh stirred the hunger within Liliana, and she lapped at the dewy salty flesh. When she reached a pulse point, she immediately withdrew her tongue in favor of biting down on her inner cheek. She thrust her hips up toward his tumescence, her hands gripping his buttocks to bring him closer. As he slid into her, a burst of blood dribbled onto her tongue. She had broken her own flesh in order to drink without stealing his life. The blood did not quench her thirst, but it controlled the hunger.

Wrapped in the scents of bell-shaped flowers, sex, and blood, she heard the panting and felt the slapping of flesh on flesh as she reached her orgasm.

Chapter Forty-four

"God, you've become so lazy. I can't get you to do a thing for me, and if you do something for me, I can't get you to do it right."

Matilda emptied the grocery bag, noting that half the items she had requested were not there.

"What did you do with the list I gave you?"

Cecelia shrugged.

"You go out with your friends and forget the rest of the world exists. What did you and Linda do, spend the afternoon mooning over boys at the mall?"

"I don't moon over boys, Mom."

"Listen, young lady, remember you're not as old as you'd like people to think. And what's this?"

"A new shirt."

"Did you need a new shirt?" Matilda asked, holding up a long-sleeved denim shirt.

"Mom, you've never liked my halter tops. Think you'd be happy that I'm covering up."

"You have started to look more like a respectable young lady, I have to give you that much credit. Where are all those flimsy tops and shorts, anyway?"

"Here and there."

"Does that mean they're all in the hamper and you're too lazy to wash them?"

"No. They're in closets and drawers. I was thinking about taking them down to the church."

"The church? What are they going to do with your clothes?"

"Give them to people who need them."

"My God, do you think the church is going to pass out your old snatches of material? They'd be more apt to burn them, I'm sure."

Thirsty. Cecelia couldn't drink enough to quench her thirst, and it seemed to be getting worse each time she visited with Sade. She wondered whether he could have passed some disease to her. She didn't know of any venereal disease that caused constant thirst, but then, she hadn't really read up on the diseases. She had been too busy memorizing the how-to books.

"I have to be honest with you, Cecelia, I'm of two minds about you not being willing to help me out at the Sade residence. I used to think that you spent too much time bothering Mr. Sade, but you were also a big help to me."

"I told you, Mom. I don't feel comfortable there anymore."

Besides, Sade had recommended she stop the visits to his house in favor of the trysts they frequently had either in the middle of the afternoon or evening.

"Did Mr. Sade ever do anything or say anything to make you feel uncomfortable?"

"Mom! I told you it was nothing he did. I just don't like being around his niece and that strange menagerie of animals she keeps. And what a sicko job she has. I'm surprised you continue to work for them. I know you could fill that space of time with another client. Why don't you?"

"Because no one pays as well as Mr. Sade, and I actually find Liliana to be quite nice."

"Ms. Plissay to you."

"You're right. One of these times I'm going to slip while I'm talking to her, although she has invited me to call her by her first name."

"Big deal. The princess has deigned to acknowledge you." A bottle of room-temperature soda water sat on the kitchen table. Quickly Cecelia grabbed the bottle, twisted off the cap, and drank a third of the bottle in one swallow.

"You couldn't put that soda water in a glass? Are we supposed to drink out of that bottle after you've had your mouth on it?" Matilda put her hands on her aproned hips and waited for an answer.

Cecelia's only reply was to drink another third of the bottle.

"Drink like that, and you'll be complaining of tummy pains. All that carbonation."

A nap would be nice now, thought Cecelia. She checked her watch and noted it was half past noon. Seemed like every day at this time she was ready for a nap. Made her feel like a kindergartner again. Her eyelids felt weighty, as if each slender lash had the heft of a ten-pound dumbbell.

"Has your brain stopped working completely?" Her mother's voice came from a distance, from another planet, for all Cecelia could tell.

255

"Are you listening to me?"

No. Why should Cecelia listen? Her mother had nothing good to say. Always complaining. Always criticizing. Always pulling Cecelia back to a dull little house on an innocuous street, surrounded by drones that followed orders to the letter.

"What is wrong with you, Cecelia?"

"Nothing. I'm going to take a nap."

"In the middle of the day? Let me feel your forehead."

Matilda reached out, and Cecelia swatted her hand away.

"I only want to see whether you're running a fever." Again she stretched out her arm and finally touched her daughter's forehead. "My, you're exceptionally cool."

"Cool. That's me, Mom."

"On a hot day like today, I would have expected at least a little sweat." Matilda removed her hand from Cecelia's forehead.

"Too hot. Too cold. I'll never be just right. Mom, you're never happy."

"Don't get smart. I worry about you."

"Mom, I'm fine. I didn't get enough sleep last night, so I want to lie down."

"Well, tonight there'll be no running around for you. You can cancel your date with Joe and get to bed at a decent hour."

Cecelia's arms and back ached. Perhaps she should cancel tonight. But no, she wouldn't. He would be waiting at the cabin. Her dry mouth needed one more sip. One more drop of his blood.

"You know what? I'm really not so tired. Why don't I go back to the store and pick up the things I forgot?"

"And who will drive you?"

"Joe. He's probably home now."

Matilda sighed.

"Oh, for heaven's sake, take a nap and see him tonight. No sense running yourself into the ground." Matilda pulled her daughter close for a hug.

While slipping her arms around her mother, Cecelia noticed a heightened awareness of her mother's body odor. A mix of sweat and stale cologne. A touch of cleanser and . . .

Suddenly she became aware of her mother's pulse, the steady throb expanding and contracting her mother's fleshy neck, the bubble and gurgle of surging blood. Cecelia nuzzled into her mother's neck, savoring the scent and vibration. She licked the pulsing flesh, and her mother pulled away.

"What are you doing acting like a little puppy? Go off, nap, and see your Joe tonight. I should be happy anyway that you've lost interest in Mr. Sade."

Chapter Forty-five

Dampness surrounded Liliana. Caught in a whirl-pool of blood, splattering the leaves, splattering the earth. Soaking her clothes and skin.

Piercing cries. Frightened squeaks.

Life fluttering away in her hands. Struggling. Twitching. Still.

What rodent had she just thrown away? Dazed, she couldn't center her vision on her surroundings. Didn't want to.

A rat. A mouse. Something bigger in her hands. Something that clawed and fought. As long as it was not human but had a pulse.

She ravaged animal after animal at the edge of the forest near the cemetery.

The cemetery.

Her stomach rumbled. It roiled. But her mouth seemed eternally parched. No amount of blood appeased the hunger. She sucked on furry flesh. Bits of hair caught in her throat. Mites and fleas tickled her nostrils. She sneezed and felt bits of flesh hit her hands.

Liliana fell to her knees and began her predator crawl, sensing life deep in the shrubbery, deep in the earth.

Her fingers scratched at the soil. Dirt crusted under her bloody fingernails.

She sniffed the air and heard the crackle of a branch.

She sprang and pounced on an animal. Her fangs sunk into the flesh, ripping out the throat. Shivers. The giving up of a life. Nosing into the wound, Liliana caught the odor of fresh kill. The stink enhanced her appetite. The taste would always be inferior. She recalled savoring the live kill of a particular man long ago. The richness of his blood, the viscous volume of blood, the peace that came with holding the man near. The rush of power. Winning the battle without a struggle. He had come passionately into her arms, stroking her body with large rough hands, entering her, as she tensed her muscles.

The animal slipped from her hands. Only a token sacrifice, only a temporary satiation of hunger.

She sat on a bundle of leaves and looked around. Tiny misshapen bodies circled her, unrecognizable animals already starting to rot, already sending out pungent invitations to the maggots and ants and worms and other scavengers.

She touched her wet cheeks, wet with blood, not with tears, primal blood that dripped from her jaws. She looked at her hands and began to clean them. Licking the waste away, she preened and fidgeted, aware of the compromising scene. The chirping birds had fled; a single crow that cawed out its song remained.

A short distance away a stream flowed. She slipped out of her tainted clothes and stood, naked. After she bathed she would burn her jeans and tank top. She always kept a change of clothes in the car. Better to be discovered naked than slick with sin.

No path led to the stream, but her senses guided her. Within a few paces of the stream a breeze carried the coolness of the water. She relaxed into the cold swirling water.

The soles of her feet seemed padded, protected against the pebbles and stones underfoot. She squatted, then scooped up handfuls of water to bathe. Her thighs, still sticky with David's semen, spread apart, allowing her to drip the cold water across her mons.

Tadpoles wriggled around her feet. Gritty pebbles sprouted between her toes. She bent over and lapped at the water, cleansing her mouth. Never would she be able to cleanse her soul. Her soul would forever be bound to the earth both spiritually and physically; she rotted and rejuvenated within the confines of this world. The love she made would always be spare, limited to urges for blood and death.

A song sounded above her head. An overreaching limb supported a swallow. The lilt of his tune seemed normal even while the blood colored the stream.

She increased the pace of her movements, wanting to be rid of her history. Wanting to make believe again.

She played at having a normal family. Often her uncle laughed at her and teased her, but always he protected her.

If you didn't allow her to feed from animals, she would have to get over her ridiculous aversion to taking blood from living humans. Her grandmother made this statement to her uncle when she thought that Liliana could not hear.

Her uncle had taken away her humanity, but there existed a soupçon of guilt in his soul. His touch frequently reminded her of that. Guilt, however, never clouded her grandmother's soul. Instead, if it were not for Uncle Donatien, Grandmother would pull everyone's strings for an eternity.

Dusk covered the forest with a pall. The trees appeared to stoop in the shadows. Branches reached out at abnormal angles, deformed by the decreasing light. The leaves would hide as one among themselves. The grass would take on the blackness of night, but the gurgle of the stream would penetrate the dark with its own hysteria, slipping over rocks, cradling tadpoles, and absolving the treachery that had defiled it. The stream ran clear again, casting away the sludge of life.

Chapter Forty-six

Sade slammed the door shut on his Jaguar and breathed in the crisp night air. He felt refreshed— no, invigorated—by his evening with Cecelia. *La pauvre fille* would certainly be hoarse tomorrow from all the screaming she did tonight. He smiled and flexed his hands. His grasp on the whip had been too tight. The knuckles of his hands hurt. He had switched hands frequently to vary the strength of the whipping. His right hand never seemed to have the stamina and power of his left.

For a taste of his blood *la fille* would submit to anything.

His silk shirt ruffled slightly in the breeze as he walked to the front door of his house. From the corner of his eye he noticed David's car. *Splendid*, he thought. *More than one of us will be content this night.*

The door had been left unlocked, and Sade made

a boisterous entrance into the front hall. A vaguely familiar voice filled the house with a grating yip. And kept right on yipping even when scooped into Liliana's arms.

"Uncle, how do you like our watchdog?"

"*La chienne,*" Sade whispered.

"Meet Ginger. Ginger, my uncle Donatien." Liliana waved one of the dog's paws at Sade.

Sade's chest puffed up to utter a loud condemnation.

"*Arrête de faire l'idiote.*"

"Sir." David stood in the doorway next to Liliana. "I didn't mean to cause any problems. Just that I knew how Liliana liked to take care of stray animals."

"*Elle suce leur sang!*"

"Uncle," Liliana screamed.

Sade caught his breath and calmed himself.

"*Je suis vraiment navré.*"

"In English, Uncle."

"I apologize for my ghastly behavior, but that dog reminds me of another."

"Sir, originally the dog belonged to one of my downstairs neighbors, Mrs. MacManus. They found her dead just today."

"*Quelle tragédie!*"

"Yes, it was, Mr. Sade. She wasn't always pleasant, but still she came to a sad end. Seems she must have fallen and broken her neck."

"Enough! Why don't we go back into the living room? Uncle?"

"Yes, of course." Sade shook out his blousy silk sleeves and led the group into the living room. "Tell me, David, how did you manage to inherit *la chienne*?"

"Excuse me?"

"The dog. He wants to know how you came by Ginger."

"Picked her up in our apartment building hall a while ago. Thought it strange when the days went by and no Mrs. MacManus appeared to claim her dog. I had stuck a note under her door telling her that I had Ginger."

"That was very nice of you, David," Liliana commented.

"*Oui*. A saint for taking in that ragamuffin."

"I really can't give Ginger a permanent home. I've had a dog before, and I don't think my current work schedule could include caring for a pet. That's why I thought Liliana could help."

"*Ma petite*, you have suddenly become an adoption agency. I'm not sure you will be able to find a home for the animal."

"I'm keeping Ginger," she said with determination.

"Where?"

"In my room, if necessary."

Sade poured out a chilled glass of Tío Pepe and offered the same to his niece and David. They refused the offer, and both proceeded to sit on the couch. Sade lifted his glass and began pacing the room.

"If the dog is going to cause a problem here, I can certainly take her back. I'm sure I can find another home. Somewhere."

"She'll be fine here, David. Won't she, Uncle?"

"If the scent of it in your bedroom does not disturb your sleep," Sade hinted.

"I bathed Ginger before I brought her here. She didn't like it much, but we managed. Right, girl?" David scratched Ginger behind an ear and smiled. "In a way, I'll miss her."

"Take her home with you, *monsieur*."

"Uncle, David's not home nearly enough to care for a pet. There's usually someone here, either one of us or Matilda. It might even tempt Cecelia into coming back."

Sade slugged back the entire glass of sherry. Shame, the high just wasn't the same as when he was alive.

Liliana stood and walked over to her uncle.

"How about making peace?" Liliana leaned Ginger toward Sade's body. A throaty growl forced her to pull the dog back. "See, you've hurt her feelings, and now she doesn't like you."

"There may come a time, *ma petite*, when she learns not to like you," Sade whispered.

He saw his niece's hands tremble. *The hunger had overcome her today.* Her complexion held a deep hue, and she filled the room with a warmth that came only from satisfying the blood hunger. She squeezed the dog too tightly, and it yelped.

"Oh God, I'm so sorry. Perhaps my uncle is right, David." She turned to the young man still seated on the couch. "I may not be the right person to care for Ginger."

David laughed. "You hugged her too hard. Sometimes love hurts."

"Worn-out cliché," muttered Sade. "But now that I think about it . . . How about your grandmother? She's all alone and could certainly use a companion." Sade reached out to pet the dog, which snarled and snapped at his hand. "I guess we got off on the wrong foot." He smiled at David.

"Sometimes her disposition can be quite sour, Mr. Sade. I really don't believe it's anything personal."

"Grandmother?" Liliana was trying to digest the

thought. "She wouldn't want a pet. Her furnishings would be ruined."

"Ginger is house-trained, *n'est-ce pas*, David?"

"She's up in age and occasionally has an accident."

"Just like your grandmother, *ma petite*."

"I can't keep her, David. It wouldn't be fair. She'd be in too much danger. I mean, I couldn't follow her around our property, and I hate penning up animals."

"She's a house dog. Never saw greenery except for the neighborhood park down the block from our apartment house. I wouldn't advise letting her out," said David.

"Fine! Then the little . . ."

"Dog, Uncle."

"Yes, the word would have come to me, I'm sure. *La chienne*," he obstinately said, "returns to her park in Manhattan. I'm glad I came home to settle this before it became too complicated." Sade reached out for the dog. Ginger caught the tip of his right thumb. "*Le monstre* goes back to David, *ma fille*."

Sadly Liliana handed the dog back to David, who refused to take it.

"You've become so attached to Ginger that I feel awful taking her away so quickly."

"She's safer with you." Again she proffered the dog.

"Take the damn *chienne* back!"

"Uncle!"

David lifted the dog out of Liliana's arms.

"Perhaps I should be going," David said.

"At least *la chienne* should be."

David shrugged at Liliana, and they both headed for the front door.

Sade leaned slightly to the right, enabling him to see the pair share a parting kiss.

Superbe.

By the time Liliana returned to the room, Sade sat on the window bench watching David's car drive away.

"Have you taken him yet?"

"I'm not going to."

"Something set off a wild hunger in you today. Have you and he mated?"

"Mated?"

"Fucked."

"Thank you, Uncle, for the clarification."

"And I receive no answer. That has to mean you two have *made love*. You cannot possibly continue without feeding. Animal blood is not going to be the answer. Only his warm blood will relieve the tension inside your body." He turned toward her.

"Your hands tremble, *ma fille*. Your eyes are misted with the sweetness of the love play. The color of your cheeks have deepened. And your breath reeks of fur, flesh, and blood. Oh *non, ma fille*, don't look so worried. David could not catch the scent, but I know it well."

"I will not take his blood."

"Will you continue making love with him? I see by your expression that loving him is a great temptation. Remember, though, he is not the boy you loved many years ago. His features may be the same, but that is where the similarity stops. He does not have Stuart's grace, nor his naïveté. David is a man who has lived before he met you. I believe he has lived a full life, *ma fille*. A full life that includes the more perverse occupations."

"You don't know that."

"Let me say that I sense it."

"I will not kill him." She had moved close enough to Sade that the scent of her afternoon banquet made Sade's nose twitch.

"I am not asking you to kill him. I only want you to take of his blood, take of his life, and perhaps share an eternity with him."

"Our eternity is marred by sin, Uncle."

"Sin! It is a sin to pass on a gift?"

"Being made into a vampire is not a gift."

"Then don't make him a vampire and don't kill him, but at least taste of him."

"I tasted his skin, his hair, and his semen. I controlled myself through all."

"And then you rushed off to some place in the forest and feasted. Am I not right?"

"Yes." Liliana sat down on a leather hassock. "But I did not take his life, and I did not endanger his soul."

Sade laughed. He wanted so much to tell her of the prostitute who serviced not only himself but David. But if she were to hear that the woman was dead, she might run off to her grandmother, and Sade needed the girl's youth within his reach.

"It has, moreover, been proved that horror, nastiness, and the frightful are what give pleasure when one fornicates. Beauty is a simple thing; ugliness is the exceptional thing. And fiery imaginations, no doubt, always prefer the extraordinary thing to the simple thing."

The 120 Days of Sodom,
by the
Marquis de Sade

Chapter Forty-seven

Her arms dripped with a tattered cream-colored lace from another era. The lace continued across Marie's shoulders and swept down across her bosom, revealing a hint of the curve of her breasts and the dusky shade of her nipples. A silky faded blue skirt blended into the blouse. The waist was cinched too tightly, and the hem rippled in uneven strands of material.

Wil watched Marie move slowly, almost cautiously, around the darkened room. Apparently searching, looking, planning all in one wave of thought.

Her makeup looked almost casual. A faint tinge of color highlighted her lips. He could not determine the color. A burnt amber? A clay red? The color played tricks in the varying shades of the room. A light dusting of face powder allowed her pale flesh to glow. Natural eyelashes hovered over two delicately outlined eyes. And the hair fell in soft waves around her face. The fingernails had been recently trimmed and painted a soft vanilla. The toenails duplicated the trimming and coloring of the fingernails.

"I am so sorry, love. I cannot allow you into my bedroom as yet. I know you wish the relationship to go beyond this dreary dungeon, but there are things you must learn and understand first."

Marie stopped in front of a wall covered with whips, crops, and switches. The background made her look delicate. Vulnerable.

Wil smirked.

"I see you don't believe what I say. I told you that a death took place here . . ." Marie hesitated. "And somehow my name is linked with the deceased. I know who killed him, but I have no proof. I need your assistance in seeing that the murderer is punished without my name again being mentioned. Therefore, I am asking you to meet with my son-in-law, the murderer, and to try to gain his trust. I can barely see my granddaughter due to the rage he holds for me. However, do not tarry with Liliana, for she will do anything to protect her uncle."

"Have you told her that he killed someone?"

"It would not shock her. The concept of making him pay for the death would certainly escape her."

Wil attempted to reposition his body, but it proved impossible because of the bindings that held him to the table. Marie had tied the ropes too tight. She no longer worried about leaving wounds or scars. She owned him. The only person she need answer to was herself.

"The man died in this room, didn't he?"

Marie pointed to a bench across the room.

"Louis killed him before my eyes. And I could not stop him."

"How did he kill him?"

"Drained him of all desire to live. Broke the man's spirit into pieces and left them for me to puzzle together. I could not, you see."

"The man lay beyond medical help."

"Almost beyond God's help."

"Why did he kill the man?"

"To get even with me." Marie's eyes turned to look at Wil. "I was obsessed and careless. Obsessed with you and too lenient with my clients. I disappointed one client in particular."

"He turned to your son-in-law for punishment."

"Yes. The man had a family, children. I think he may have been jealous of you."

"Did I ever meet him?"

"No, but he met you in my eyes, and he watched you in the slide show of my mind."

"What is your son-in-law's name?"

"Louis Sade."

Wil laughed.

"This is a game, isn't it? Am I supposed to be petrified that you may bring *Sade* here to beat me?"

Marie's features hardened; the soft matron had disappeared. In her place stood a crazed witch contemplating how to cook her prey.

"Don't fear him." Her voice turned low. "Destroy him."

"I can't kill a man."

"He's already dead. Dead to virtue, to sanity, to love, and to contriteness. Most of all, he's dead to me."

"Kill him yourself."

"I am weak in comparison to him. He would

272

sense my hovering about him. He'd destroy me the next time."

"You've already had a confrontation with him."

Marie's fingers kneaded the silk skirt.

"I no longer know why he allows me to exist."

"Perhaps he, too, is afraid of what Liliana would think."

"No. He is egocentric enough to believe that she would forgive him. And I believe that too."

"I think you are wrong about your granddaughter."

Marie shook her head.

"You must see them together. Yes, they argue, but there's a magnetism between them from which neither can withdraw. He needs her youth. She is a kind of talisman for him. A good-luck charm that he keeps near."

"And what is he to her?"

"Her father . . ."

"Then he's not her uncle?"

"He's uncle, father. They share a deeper bonding of blood than you can understand *now*."

"She's your blood relation also."

The worrying of the material of her dress intensified.

"No, we both share his blood. It gives him a power over us. I do not even know whether I could destroy him." Marie raised her hand. "I touch his body and I feel the hardness of gold. The softness of down. He protects and punishes. His smell is sometimes with me even when he is not present. His voice wakes me from my sleep.

"I don't know how to free myself from him. I need your help, Wil." Marie moved closer to the table on which Wil lay. "He has no hold over you." Marie reached out her hands and touched Wil's body. "*He* has no hold over you." Her hands followed the curves of his pectorals, smoothed over his abdomen, and gently touched his penis, gliding her palm up and down the tender skin.

Wil's breathing increased. The muscles in his thighs twitched, calming only for a moment. Her lips kissed the tip of his penis as her fingers played the flesh.

"You'll help me, Wil, won't you?" Her tongue rounded the tip of his organ before she took him fully into her mouth.

His abdominal muscles pumped. He caught his breath in fragments, gulping down the air that had been sucked into his mouth.

Her right hand stretched across his body, fingers grabbing at the jewelry piercing his nipples.

When the throbbing started, she freed him from her mouth and nipped at his thigh, finally taking a bite, sucking the open wound.

Chapter Forty-eight

Daisies sprinkled the front lawn of Sade's house, daisies and some pretty yellow weeds that Cecelia couldn't name. She remembered loving their colorful show every year since she had been a child of five. Before Sade, another family had lived in the house. A big family, she recalled, one with many pets and several rather wild children. Cecelia's mother had worked for that family, and when they sold the house, they recommended her mother to Sade as a housekeeper.

Cecelia followed her mother to the front door of Sade's house. The door was made of wormy wood on which hung a green-tinged brass knocker in the shape of a large bird. She had never been able to guess what kind of bird, but as she drew closer, the detail of the bill, the brassy feathers ruffling the head, and the spread of the wings hinted that perhaps it was not just one species of bird but a composite of several.

She sniffed the air. Something had died recently; not a large animal, perhaps a bird or maybe a baby rabbit. Cecelia looked over her shoulder at the expanse of green, white, and yellow lawn and saw a speck of brownish gray at the foot of an old tree. Sniffing the air, she knew that speck caused the stink. From where she stood next to her mother, the speck seemed to be a baby bird, one that a nasty sibling had displaced. Cecelia had no siblings and had never wanted any, else she too might have had to find a way to eject the intruder from their home.

Her mother fingered the ring of keys she carried, searching for the correct key to open Sade's door. The tinkle of the keys hitting each other hurt Cecelia's ears, and the mélange of odors emitted from the keys made her wriggle her nose. Mingled with the keys' own metallic odor were the smell of soiled diapers, lasagna, bleach, newsprint, and her mother's own sweaty palms; all swam through the air. But above all was the odor of clay and dirt—the unusual odors that emanated from Sade. The closer she became to him, the more she noticed the odors. Soil never marred his fingernails or stained his white skin, but the suffocating stink of the earth encased his body. She had never asked why, even though she knew he did not work the soil as a laborer or a hobbyist.

The click of the lock pulled Cecelia away from her thoughts. Her mother opened the door wide and preceded her daughter into the house. As Cecelia crossed the threshold, she noted Sade's earthy perfume, but it was faint, left from earlier in the day. The air didn't quiver in excitement; instead a calm shimmered lackadaisically in the air, taking advantage of the pause Sade's absence allowed.

Just as well he isn't here, she thought. He hadn't wanted her to come to the house anymore, probably because he feared that anyone seeing them together would immediately suspect the relationship. But she secretly liked being back, even though she had whined all the way here. Today her mother needed her help washing the rugs. She had been happy to comply, but didn't want Sade to know, so she grumbled at her mother and insisted that she'd rather be with Joey. Ugh! Joey! A child, a clumsy child smelling of licorice and soda. A vision of Joey chewing like a cow on one of his licorice sticks made her sneer.

"Try to put on a better face. You wouldn't want Liliana to be offended, child," her mother warned.

Sade's niece offended Cecelia. The closeness Liliana shared with her uncle, the measured spans of time Liliana spent in her uncle's presence. Most irritating of all was the secret uncle and niece kept. Cecelia didn't know the secret yet, but hoped that she would someday. Confidently Cecelia believed that she could replace Liliana. Someday in a crowd he would step aside with Cecelia and whisper and speak in covert language as he now did with Liliana.

"Cecelia, I'm so glad you're back," said Liliana.

"Answer her," Matilda softly urged.

"Where's your uncle?"

"What kind of a question is that? I'm sorry, Ms. Plissay. Cecelia has been acting rather strange for the past month. She needs to spend more time at home and less running around with her friends."

"At Cecelia's age friends are very important." Liliana smiled as she excused Cecelia's behavior.

"Certainly not more important than spending

277

time with her family," Matilda said. "Come, we'll start with the rug in the living room."

"Oh, no. Please don't lift that. We can have a professional clean it," Liliana pleaded.

"Been doing rugs for years. I can assure you I'll do a better job than some stranger."

"Besides, Louis doesn't like having strangers in the house," Cecelia interrupted.

"How dare you get so personal, young lady? That's Mr. Sade. Do you understand?"

Cecelia nodded her head at her mother.

"I'm very sorry, Ms. Plissay. This is the first time I ever heard her use your uncle's first name."

Cecelia felt Liliana's eyes peering at her, memorizing something. She turned her face away and hurried her mother into the living room.

She hadn't remembered how ornate the room appeared. The stone fireplace mantel was covered with seventeenth-century bisque figurines interspersed with silver-framed daguerreotypes of beautiful women dressed in period clothing.

"First of all, you'll have to help me move the furniture. Cecelia. Cecelia, are you paying attention?"

"Who do you suppose these women are, Mom?" Cecelia fingered a filigreed frame.

"Unless you're going to dust them, don't touch them. Come over here and help me move this chair."

The arms of the chair were made of unupholstered wood. Cecelia walked over to the chair to run the palm of her hand across the polished wood. The rest of the chair was upholstered in gold cloth, small purple fleurs-de-lis spotting the material.

"Do you suppose the chair's an antique?"

"What's wrong with you, Cecelia? You're acting

like this is the first time you've seen any of these things."

"First time up close," Cecelia answered.

"I've had you help me clean this room many times, dear. Just that your mind was always else-where. Here, lift, for heaven's sake."

Each took an arm of the chair and moved it off the Aubusson rug. The underside of the arm Cecelia touched had several nicks. She could feel how they had been smoothed over and waxed.

Cecelia brushed her shoe across a frayed portion of the tapestrylike rug. She was about to squat and study the colors of the rug, but her mother inter-rupted, asking for help with the love seat. Although upholstered in the same fabric as the chair, the love seat had a dingy, faded look, and as she drew closer, she noticed the heavy scent of soil. *Sade must spend many hours here*, she thought, while running the back of her hand across the seat. She smiled. The skin on her hand stung and almost sparked as the crackle caught her mother's attention.

"Are you all right?"

Cecelia nodded dreamily, preparing to seat her-self on the love seat.

"What are you doing? We just got here, and you want to take a rest. I'm going to take you to the doctor and find out why you're behaving so lethar-gically."

The house suddenly came alive. The air vibrated, the furnishings seemed to shiver, and the knick-knacks trembled; but nothing moved.

He is in the house, Cecelia reasoned, instantly looking toward the entrance of the room.

"Uncle, try to talk Matilda out of doing such heavy work."

Cecelia strained to hear his voice. Whispers, garbled whispers that hinted at annoyance. He knew. He had scented her without being told. The girl willed her mentor to come to her. Instead he seemed to draw away from her, separating himself into another dimension, one she had not yet entered.

"Ah! *Madame!* My niece told me of your plans. How silly. We do not expect you to do the heavy housework. We will call in several husky men to wash and hang the rugs."

He appeared as a vision haloed by the musk of the outdoors.

"But you don't like having strangers in the house," said Cecelia.

Had she truly spoken? She could not be sure, since Sade did not deign to reply or even look at her. Her breathing stopped momentarily as she leaned the top half of her body toward him. Should she wave her arms? Should she rip off her clothes? Should she lie prostrate before him awaiting his wishes?

"But, Mr. Sade, I'm paid to clean the house and run errands. Lord knows I really don't have much in the way to clean here. You and your niece are quite tidy. Wish I could say that about my own family." Cecelia felt her mother's eyes fix on her.

Sade took her mother's hands in his and kissed the back of each.

"*Madame,* you are too delicate to ruin your dainty *doigts.*" Sade brushed his lips across her mother's fingers. Her mother's face flushed a deeper red than Cecelia had ever seen before. "Take the afternoon off, *madame,* and enjoy the *après-midi.*"

"Yes, my uncle is right. You've been working too hard, Matilda. You and your daughter should do something together."

Cecelia wanted to speak but found her mouth to be parched; her throat felt closed, knotted. An attempt to clear her throat brought on a raging bout of coughing. Her mother hurried the girl into the kitchen for a glass of water that the girl, racked by the hacking cough, spilled on herself.

"I think we should go home. Perhaps a nap would help."

"Cecelia," called Liliana. "Cecelia, are you all right?" Liliana entered the kitchen. Immediately she pulled out a stool and forced Cecelia to sit. "Go home," Liliana whispered in the girl's ear. "Go home and don't come back. Don't allow my uncle to win."

Matilda could not hear the words, because they were said privately in a voice only sensitive hears could hear.

I will win, Cecelia kept repeating inside her head. *I will win over you, Liliana. I will have your uncle.*

The coughing stopped, but Cecelia's voice did not return immediately. He had silenced her, she knew, and probably would not allow her to speak again until she left his home, a home she intended to make her own.

Chapter Forty-nine

"Release her, Uncle."

"Who, *ma chère*?"

"Cecelia. You are stealing her life like you did mine."

"*Mais non*; I made a terrible mistake with you by taking you all at once instead of having you slowly get used to the changes."

"You offer nothing to her except isolation."

"*Mais*, she would be with us. Never alone. Always desired."

"Until you tire of her."

"I have never tired of you, *ma chère*, even though you can be quite a tiresome bore."

"Uncle, I've been to the local cemetery."

"Visiting some neighbors?"

"They do exist."

"Neighbors?"

"The malformed. The mindless vampires who are more ghoulish than we are."

"*Des goules? Nous? Enfant*, you haven't looked in the mirror; there is nothing *de goule* about us."

"The way we live is ghoulish. Drinking blood to survive is ghoulish."

"And what about eating meat? What about the *merveilleux* steak tartare served in the best of restaurants? Thin ribbons of succulent beef lying raw on some sophisticate's plate. Or the blood puddings you used to delight in as a child? Ah! *Mais* a better analogy may be small babies suckling at their mothers' breasts. Gaining life by taking from the mother. Just as a fetus does. We are born predators, *mon enfant*, born to diminish the already living so that we may grow."

"Stop it!" Liliana screamed. "How could you compare us to the innocents?"

"Innocents? Those mewling, wet, whining, writhing, spitting savages that grow into repulsive teens and abusive adults?" Sade dusted a fleck from his black linen shirt. "Besides, we give far more forethought to our food than either the *enfants* or the poor wretches in the cemetery."

"What if Cecelia should end up like those things in the cemetery?"

"She will if I abandon her now." Sade sat on the love seat and pulled off his biker boots to rest his feet on the rug.

"You mean those creatures were never taken completely through the changes?"

"A guess on my part. However, she is already highly sensitive to the world around her. I feed her need for blood from my very own veins." He unbuttoned the cuffs of his shirt and rolled up his sleeves to show her his arms. No marks. There

283

would be none. He would heal quickly. All she saw were the bulging veins running up the inside of both his arms. No doubt he had recently fed. "I share like a nursing mother, suffering the twinges of pain for the tiny young one."

"Dammit, Uncle. You're no martyr. How much pain must she suffer until you're satisfied? What wounds does she carry with her from day to day? What scars from your hand?"

"*Mon enfant*, I hate scars. *Non, non,* that kind of play must wait until she is immortal like us." He smiled. "Then she will heal quickly and be able to endure far more . . . playtime."

"Stop what you're doing to this girl."

"I've already told you. It has gone too far too turn back. Her *mort* is assured." He reached out to grab Liliana's left wrist, but she pulled away. "Ah! Don't be jealous, *mon enfant,* you will always be the special one."

"Jealous of a girl who is dying? You don't know me, Uncle. I don't envy anyone who must live as I do."

Sade bit down on his right wrist. Blood spurted from the full veins. He stood and walked toward Liliana.

She felt herself cowering, moving back from the advancing steps he took, but she couldn't prevent her retreat. He reached out his right arm, and the smell of his blood fogged her mind until she realized he held her fast in the vise of his hand. She could feel the warm blood stain her scalp.

"Remember the taste, *ma chère.* Have you forgotten the sweetness of my blood? The strength my blood once gave to you? *Mais non,* I see the memory in your eyes. Replenish that memory now." Sade loosened his grip on her hair and brought his wrist to her mouth, spreading the crimson across her lips.

He had practically drained her while he had held her in his arms. His soft voice spoke of eternal life, of the exhilaration of intensified senses. The colors sounded beautiful. The sounds seemed so intense. His touch had soothed her fear, and the taste of his blood had been a salvation.

Liliana again found herself enveloped in her uncle's arms, sucking at the blood that dribbled from his wrist. She lapped at the rivulets running up his arm; the color, deeper in hue than the animal blood she survived on, caused myriad dreams to rush through her alert mind.

Stuart's arm again stretched out above the water. The veins pulsed wildly, excited by her presence. Her hand smoothed over his flesh, testing the depth of the purple network feeding his arm. She moved closer to him. The water cooled her feet and drenched the bottom of her dress so that the material hugged her legs. Her lips kissed his flesh before her fangs bit down.

A slap across her cheek laid her on the floor, Sade standing over her, rebuking her for her hunger.

"It's what you want. You've always wanted to share our blood like the first time." Liliana ripped away the collar from her blouse. "Take my blood and allow me to feed from you."

Sade stood over his niece. His face remained placid, unmoved by her pain.

"I want more than that, Liliana. I want you as a woman."

He squeezed his wrist, and she watched as the blood dripped down upon her face. A drop touched her upper lip, another smeared her cheek, another she caught with her tongue.

Frenzied, she tore at her clothes, shredded the

silk and lace that had lain close against her body. Instead she would invite her uncle to lie upon her skin.

The outer world had disappeared, or perhaps it never had existed, only the image of her uncle stripping slowly, leisurely, aware of the famine that drove her.

He knelt next to her and she grabbed at his bloodied wrist, but he held her face just above the wound. She smelled his blood and tasted the remnants on her tongue.

"Tell me I'm the one you want. Only me and no one else," he demanded.

Liliana started to say the name "Stuart," but Sade stopped her.

"There is no other man, only *moi, ma* . . . Liliana. And I will see to it that the child in you is at last gone." He moved his wrist, watching her gaze shift with each of his moves. Sade reached behind him and drew his thick studded belt from the loops on his jeans. "I have never truly shown you the extent of my love for you as a woman. I have not bled you in the fashion that most pleases me. Liliana, I have spoiled you."

His hand carrying the belt flashed upward, and Liliana's breath halted just before the pain echoed through her body.

Chapter Fifty

"Uncle is turning Cecelia."

Marie turned from the rosebush and stared at her granddaughter.

"I can't stop him."

Her granddaughter looked tired but healthy. A bloom swelled her cheeks with a dusty pink. Faint, but she could see that Liliana had finally fed from a mobile human, not one who lay on a metal table awaiting her granddaughter's ministrations.

"He's stealing her youth."

"As he did to you." Marie kept her voice soft and filled with empathy.

"He did it to both of us."

"My youth had passed many years before he turned me." A sad fact that always irked her days, she thought. "Is there any suspicion on the part of the parents?"

"They think their daughter is going through a

stage. Matilda has spoken of taking Cecelia to a doctor, but the child refuses to go. And since Cecelia does not really look ill, her parents haven't forced her to seek medical attention."

Marie turned back to her rosebush and snipped a pinkish flower in full bloom. She carried the rose to her granddaughter and offered it to her.

"A doctor will never be able to diagnose what is wrong with the child." Marie still held the flower, waiting for Liliana to come out of her lethargic fog.

Gradually Liliana spied the proffered rose and took it.

"Grandmother, I feel so helpless. I know what her life will be like, but I can't explain it to her."

"He must be stopped from ever turning anyone again."

"He'll never stop."

Marie rubbed Liliana's knee with her ungloved hand. "You remember all those children who went missing in Paris around the time we thought you had died?"

Liliana's hands began to tremble, and Marie placed her own hands around her granddaughter's.

"This is something we must talk about. We cannot continue to ignore his savage behavior." Receiving no response from Liliana, Marie persisted. "The general consensus of the people at the time and in history books, as far as I can tell, was that the children were kidnapped by the government in order to populate the new world.

"None of those children made it to the colonies. They were all killed, and Sade paid to have it covered up. I know because several people came to me and asked what to do. Of course, I was terrified of Sade and advised the people to accept the money.

I've been so ashamed. Obviously Sade bled those children and buried, burned, or in some way disposed of the bodies. I wouldn't be surprised to learn that many of the children are living wild as vampires."

"No," Liliana softly said.

"Why else would he pay to have the rumor spread about the government? He tortured those children and then drained their blood."

Liliana kept shaking her head.

"You can't continue to ignore the truth about your uncle. He's a fiend, and we are the only ones who can stop him."

"Grandmother, you don't understand."

"Evil." She squeezed her granddaughter's hands tightly. "Insane evil. Children as young as four and five being raped and murdered by that fiend."

"He didn't do it."

"Liliana, give up the denial. I've enlisted Wil's help in destroying Sade. He'll pound the stake in and cut off Sade's head, but we need to know when he is vulnerable. You live with Sade. He trusts you.

"Damn, stop shaking your head and pay attention to what I'm saying."

"He didn't kill those children," Liliana screamed.

"You believe that the government would send children just out of babyhood to colonize land?"

"No," Liliana whispered.

"Then help us, Liliana. Tell us when he is most vulnerable, for Wil means to destroy the fiend."

Liliana jumped up from the step on which she had been sitting and ran to her car, pulling the door open and throwing herself into the seat behind the steering wheel.

The car choked but finally started, and she drove away at high speed.

"Oh dear, Liliana, I tell you a little lie and you run away." Marie had always accepted the idea that the children were kidnapped by government agents; after all, it had happened several other times. She even knew people who had made a considerable amount of money delivering children. However, Marie had decided to use the incidents to enrage her granddaughter.

What if Liliana reported their conversation to Sade? Shit! She hadn't wanted to inform him of her plans. Perhaps the girl would be smart enough to keep the conversation to herself. If not, Marie was in big trouble.

Liliana undid the few buttons on the back of her dress and let the blue linen slide down her naked body. She slipped out of her sandals easily.

Before her stood the off-white coffin that her parents had selected for her. She opened the lid, and the smell of earth hit her nostrils. The yellowed satin had begun to gray and fray. The threadbare pillow lay crooked. The pretty lace dress her mother had selected for her lay to the side of the coffin. Bits and pieces of the convoluted lace spiked out from the dress. The light layer of dirt scattered across the bottom of the coffin clumped where her fingers had dug into the soil.

"Mama," she said, clutching the tattered lace in one hand. "Mama, I never meant to do any of it."

The feeding frenzy had gripped her tightly in its spell. Her uncle had allowed her body to be underground too long. She had awakened famished, clawing at the satin surrounding her. At first she had thought that she still lived, that she had to reach the surface or die. After two days lying conscious in the coffin, she realized she couldn't be

alive. No gasping for air. Sleep did not come to reprieve her from the insanity of being enclosed in a
small space. She had to be dead, and this was possibly her eternity.

When Sade finally pulled her up from the grave,
a ravenous hunger seized her body. He offered her
a young child. The other children she had hunted
and slaughtered on her own, until Sade instructed
her in how to be satisfied with a taste and not gorge
on blood.

Yes, there were times, many, she knew, when he
killed while drinking, but he loved the hunt and always felt the prey belonged to him to dispose of as
he wished.

He taught her caution and managed to rid Paris
of the small empty hulks she left behind. He paid
people to spread false rumors about the children
being kidnapped.

"No, Grandmother, you are blaming the wrong
fiend."

Liliana reached up to feel her fangs. Sharp,
pointy, only slightly larger than her other teeth.
Large enough to pierce flesh down to crimson
blood. She pulled at the fangs until her mouth
ached, but they stayed in place, waiting for the next
meal.

All those children coming to her, trusting her,
giving themselves over to her spells. Early on one
or two had fought before she understood the mes-
merizing control she could exercise over the tiny
minds. They had played games with her, shared
their sweets, and smelled of the dreadful hovels
from which they had come, hovels no worse than
the final resting places Sade had found for them.

One girl had felt so warm that Liliana had
stripped the child's body in order to touch the warm

flesh while savoring the freshness of the child's blood. The little girl's eyelids had closed over the dreamily shiny blue eyes while Liliana sang a soft lullaby. Eventually the gentle sleepy breaths slowed, then suddenly stopped.

Liliana pulled the lace dress from the coffin and rent the material, scattering the tatters onto the wood floor.

"Mama," she said, kneeling down to gather the threads into her hands. "Mama."

Lifting the remains of the dress, she stood.

"Mama," she said again and spread the ruined lace across the bottom of the coffin, mingling her mother's gift with her homeland's soil.

Her long legs stepped into the coffin. Immediately she felt the decay begin. Her skin would shrivel inside the coffin. The body would finally rest, at least for a few hours, never for eternity.

Cautiously she laid her body down. Shame, repulsion, and fear swept through her as the overworked skeleton eased into the centuries of abuse and pain.

Her uncle had raped her, but she had found a perverted joy in his taste, smell, and touch.

She yanked on the lid and let the coffin slam shut.

"Mama, come and save your little girl."

"And indeed what creature is more precious, more appealing in the eyes of men than the person who has cherished, respected, and cultivated the virtues of the earth and, at each step of the way, has found naught but misfortune and grief?"

Eugénie de Franval,
by the
Marquis de Sade

Chapter Fifty-one

Bubbles wet the flakes of skin on Keith's lips. The stale breath blew an occasional bubble away. He projected a hiss and a gurgle into the room. His stubby beard hid the slackness of his skin underneath. Hairs grew from his nostrils and snot clogged the air passages. The open eyes stared at the ceiling. Occasionally Wil thought he caught his father glancing at him. The furrows hemmed in between Keith's eyebrows seemed to have deepened since the accident. A pulsing vein caused the lines on his forehead to quiver. Keith's hair, swept back off his face, shined with an oily sheen.

Wil had been sponge-bathing his father, noticing the shrunken chest, the stretch marks covering the lean abdomen, and the wilted hood of his father's penis.

"Old man, how did this happen to you?"

Keith's legs shook in a trembling spasm, the right

foot kicking upward from the ankle twice. The son rested his hands on Keith's legs and waited for the spasm to quit.

"You know, Dad, I miss that wizened voice of yours. The throaty bark of your cough in the morning is something else that I miss. I never thought I'd ever miss those sounds, but yeah, I do." The spasm had ended, and Wil returned to sponging down his father. "Sometimes I imagine I hear you spitting up a gob of sputum. God, you were so disgusting. I wish you could do it again so I don't have to worry about pneumonia setting into your chest.

"One thing you got me to do, though, and that's stay here in this house. Can't put you away in a home, Dad. Can't go back to the city, either. May as well stay here with you. This is our one last chance to become buddies, and there you are, stricken dumb." Will shook his head and dropped the sponge back into the tepid water. "You're as clean as you'll ever be. Your skin, that is. Your soul is another matter."

Keith's fingertips pattered against the towel covering the sheeted mattress. He emitted a hoarse breath from his mouth. His lips trembled.

"I wonder whether anything is going on inside your head. Major thoughts of how to save the world? Or curses damning me? Maybe a whole lot of nothing."

Wil easily lifted his father and brought him into the living room.

"Have to leave you on the sofa for a few minutes while I change the bed. Here, let me wrap you up in this throw." Wil grabbed the hand-knitted blanket his mother had knitted while pregnant with him. "Has a few moth holes, but it will keep you warm until I get back." Wil looked around the room. "Want some television?" Wil shrugged his shoulders and used the remote to turn on the screen. He clicked between several stations before settling on a televised stock-car race.

When Wil returned to the bedroom, the stink suddenly hit him. *Stay in a room long enough and you start getting used to piss and shit.* He dumped the washbasin out in the sink in the bathroom. Another room he needed to clean, he thought, wiping shaving cream off the medicine chest.

In the bedroom, the distant roar of the televised car race seemed like white noise. He went through the mechanics of tossing the towels and used sheets on the floor. Down to one more clean set of sheets—then he'd have to do the dreaded laundry. He picked up the soiled bedclothes and carried them into the bathroom to fling on top of the rest of the laundry stacking up in the tub. *Thank God Dad had thought of putting in a shower stall*.

The dark wooden sleigh bed, a wedding gift to his parents, looked pristine covered in clean sheets, but he knew the sheets would soon be soiled again. He plumped up the pillows and took a deep breath, preparing himself for the return to the living room.

A red race car was spinning off the track when he entered the living room. His father's blanket-wrapped body lay on the couch, shaking.

"Hey, hey, old man. The excitement too much for you?" Wil shut the television off and hurried over to hold his father. "It's okay. How the hell did you get into this shape? How could anyone do this to you? I confronted Marie, and she denied having anything to do with this. Hell, she's strong, but not strong enough to break a man like this.

"You'd really be pissed now if you knew what she wants me to do. Kill her son-in-law. Says he's already dead. I'd just be disposing of the body." Keith laughed. "The worst part is that I agreed. Shit, I don't know how I got myself into this. Wants me to flee to Paris with her, but I can't leave you." Keith kissed his father's forehead.

Keith's hands began to claw at his son's shirt-sleeve. Saliva dribbled down his chin.

"Hey, don't worry, I'm not going to kill anyone for that bitch. Look at me. I'm talking to you as if you understood." Wil looked closely at his father's face. Tears welled in his father's eyes. Wil couldn't tell whether the eyes looked at him or through him. A knock on the front door distracted Wil. "Listen, Dad, I'm going to put you back in bed and see who that is." His father's seizure seemed to be almost over, but Wil lifted his still-trembling father with difficulty. Another knock. Wil cursed. Carefully he carried his father back to bed. Wil had laid out his father's pajamas at the foot of the bed, thinking that he would dress the old man before tucking him in.

Another knock.

"I'll be back in a few minutes, Dad." He left his father on the bed, bundled in the blanket.

"I hate waiting. You know that."

"Keep your voice down, Marie. Dad's recovering from a seizure."

"He piss himself again?" Marie walked into the house and directly toward the father's bedroom.

"No, no. You can't go in there," Will said, grabbing Marie's right elbow.

"I've seen him only once since the accident. Mind if I go in and give my regrets? Tell him how we're all praying for him?"

"Stop it, Marie."

"You are still talking to him, aren't you, as hopeless as it is?"

"The doctor said I should act as I did before the accident."

"Oh my God, you're not picking on him again."

"Marie, what do you want?"

"To take you for a drive."

"I can't go right now. There's no one to watch Dad."

"Call someone. What about that visiting nurse? Is this a visiting day?"

"She'll be coming over tomorrow."

"How about I get Liliana to come over and sit? You trust her, right?"

"I don't need to take a damn car ride right now."

Marie walked over to the side table where the phone sat, lifted the receiver, and started dialing a number.

"Shit, didn't you hear what I just said?" Wil moved forward to set his hand down on the cradle. Marie grabbed his wrist and held it, making it impossible for him to reach the phone.

"Liliana, hi. I have a favor to ask."

Wil felt Marie's fingers digging into his skin. Where her fingernails met flesh, blood seeped. Could she have savagely attacked his father? he wondered.

Marie had opened all the windows of the car. Her short hair barely moved. From the corner of her eye she could see that Will fought a losing battle to keep his hair off his face.

"Where the hell are we going?"

"A special surprise." She turned her head slightly to wink at Wil.

"I've had plenty of surprises."

"But this one is a treat."

Marie pulled into Sade's driveway. Liliana had

said that he would be at home. Out of his coffin, but still at home.

She turned off the ignition and invited Wil to follow her.

"Who lives here?" Wil asked.

"You'll see." Marie smiled and reached for the elaborate door knocker. The door opened before she had a chance to knock.

"Marie!"

"Hello, Louis."

"Liliana is not at home."

"That's okay. We're here to visit with you."

"I thought we were not even on speaking terms."

"By now you should know that I never stay angry with you." She brushed past Sade and crooked a finger in invitation to Wil.

"Monsieur?"

"I'm . . ." Wil looked at Marie as if he didn't know who the hell he was.

"Come in. Come in."

Sade stepped back and invited Wil into the house. Marie walked into the living room and settled herself on the striped sofa.

"Wil is my . . . new friend."

Sade walked a circle around Wil. Marie instantly recognized the predatory movements Sade made. *He's interested.* She had made Wil slip on a clean shirt. The poor boy had become as uncivilized as his father, hanging around in dirty T-shirts and worn-out shorts. The white cotton shirt emphasized Wil's tan.

"Isn't he beautiful?" She noted how Wil flinched when she had spoken. "You are beautiful, you know."

Sade began to laugh. He turned his back on the

guests and settled in a distant chair and spread his legs.

"A charming pose, Louis. I believe I can see the outline of your privates very clearly under those tight silk pants."

"Enjoy, Marie, for this is the closest you'll ever come to seeing them."

"Maybe I should go back home and take care of my father," Wil said.

"You can't. I drove." Marie reached out and patted the cushion next to her. "Sit down."

Wil continued to stand.

"Not very well trained, *ma* Marie."

"That's why I'm here, Louis."

"Ah! You've come to the *maître* for assistance."

"Yes, the master. You've proven that."

"You want this one broken like the other?"

"I'd rather you not be so enthusiastic."

She watched Sade's sly blue eyes study Wil. Sade had left his silk shirt unbuttoned. The white hair on his chest blended almost perfectly with the color of his flesh.

"I don't want scars," she said.

"Wait a second. I feel like I'm up for sale," Wil said.

"Certainly not." She turned to Sade. "He's a gift."

Immediately Wil spun around and headed for the front door.

"It is locked, *monsieur*. I am very careful about that."

Wil walked back to the doorway of the living room.

"Open the damn door!"

"You see what I have had to put up with."

Sade's lean, hungry face seemed tense. He could barely contain himself, she thought. His cock strained against the black silk. *Ooh, that must be uncomfortable*.

"I'm not submitting to anything."

"Once he does, he thoroughly enjoys it. Isn't that true, Wil?"

"I'll break the damn door down if I have to."

"*Monsieur*, the door is metal. I had it specially made. The windows are one-inch-thick polycarbonate. And the keys, *monsieur*, are in the pocket of my slacks." Sade stood and offered a hip to Will.

Wil's expression remained fearless. Marie knew that Louis's height and slight build would make Wil feel brave.

"I don't want to hurt anyone."

"Oh, *mais, monsieur*, I do."

"Who the hell is this guy?" Wil asked Marie.

"My son-in-law." Now he would understand, she thought. *Yes, this is the man I want you to kill*. He turned toward Sade.

"Sir, I have no argument with you. She's just causing trouble. She wants you dead."

"I already am *mort*."

"I told you." Marie's voice rang out as a soft bell.

"I'm not staying here with two nut jobs."

"Then come, *monsieur*, take the key."

Wil shook his head and walked over to Sade, hand extended to reach inside the pocket.

"I have deep pockets, *monsieur*; you may have to reach down deep."

"I'm not in the mood to play." Wil touched the silk and slipped his hand inside the pocket and found no key. When he tried to withdraw, Sade took hold of his wrist and forced Wil's hand deeper into the pocket, deep enough so that Wil's fingertips brushed against Sade's balls.

"I've heard rumors that he is rather large. Is that true, Wil?" Marie asked.

A light sweat had beaded on Wil's forehead.

"And very firm, *monsieur*."

Marie approached Wil, slowly undoing the buttons running down the front of her dress.

Wil's Adam's apple bobbed several times.

She allowed the dress to fall to the floor. She had purposely put on a leather corset with thigh-high silk stockings.

"I need a taste of you, Wil," she said.

"What the hell does he have to do with this?" Wil's eyes remained fixed on Sade's hand.

"You're a peace offering. The best of my slaves. I demand you satisfy the whims of my enemy."

"It is difficult to satisfy me, *monsieur*, but we can spend hours trying."

"I did not think myself in a position to hesitate;
by accepting this cruel condition I exposed myself to further dangers, to be sure. . . ."

Justine,
by the
Marquis de Sade

Chapter Fifty-two

"A tattoo right about here." Marie grabbed the inside of Wil's naked thigh far enough up to brush the back of her hand against his penis. "That would be nice, wouldn't it, Wil?"

Drenched in sweat, Wil gave a low groan.

The small room had a very different decor from Marie's dungeon. Here Wil experienced not only a sense of claustrophobia but the dizzily weird sensation of being in a wonderland of torture that needed only a few instruments to bring a profusion of pain.

The room went beyond sparse: the blank walls, the barren floor, the simple wood board on which he knelt, supported only by three wooden sawhorses that were tied together so that they would not move.

Sade and Marie had played his unfettered body for some time. He didn't know how long. He had accepted the probing and lashings as a penance. Forever he would be pleading for forgiveness; and with his father now mute and dumb, grace would never be granted.

Marie had stripped naked in order to feel his damp sticky flesh against her own. Once or twice she had reached out to touch Sade's privates, which were still tucked away inside the silk pants. However, Sade rebuked her silently each time with a swat or simply a stare. She did not dare disobey him. Was this man her master?

Sade's untucked shirt slipped off his left shoulder, the silk immediately creased because of the fall. The white skin made the shoulder blade look like bone. Sade's breathing never seemed labored, no matter how hard he struck a blow.

The only sweat stinking the room seemed to be Wil's own. The other two remained dry, although their passion ran hot. Sade and Marie moved with great speed and agility. Sade seemed almost to forget Marie's presence, but Marie remained quite aware of him. Instead of working in unison, Marie assisted Sade as a nurse would in an operating room, attempting to think one step ahead in order to have the appropriate utensil available.

"Sit," Marie commanded.

Wil turned and painfully lifted each knee off the board.

"Hurry, fool." She lashed out cruelly with her tongue, using words that stung by their own torrid heat, but she did not lay a whip on him. "Shall we tie him for the tattoo?"

"Tattoos. I am bored with *monsieur*'s tattoos. He already looks ridiculous with the cartoons decorating his legs. Besides, he's used to that kind of pain and probably would like something far more stimulating.

"What is it, *monsieur*, that would spark a fire that could combust you into flying free far from this earth?" Sade leaned against a drab pale wall. "You no longer scream in true pain. The piercings, the scars have numbed you." He smiled. "Certain scars are missing, *monsieur*. Ones that tingle the skin even when at peace. A smile, a laugh, a brooding sigh, or a touch of anger can cause a raging train of pain up and down the nerves.

"Marie, there is rope on the back porch. Fetch it *pour moi*."

"Shouldn't we gag him?" Marie asked.

"Why? The room is soundproofed, and I shall not indulge myself until you return."

Marie hesitated a moment before leaving the room.

A throaty chuckle followed the closing of the door.

"Ah, *monsieur*, it is not only you that I torture, but my despicable mother-in-law also." Sade leaned in close to Wil's face. "*Pourquoi* did she bring you to me? Why?"

"Just as she said, I guess," Wil answered. "I didn't expect to come here."

"*Non, monsieur*, nothing is as she says. She has taken your blood, *n'est-ce pas?*"

Wil swallowed. Did this strange man want blood also? So far they hadn't broken his skin, hadn't attempted to mar his skin. The pain had been subtle. Whipping, twisting of piercings, penetration. Nothing that drew his blood. Carefully it seemed that had been avoided.

"*Monsieur*, it will take her a while to find the rope,

306

but not forever. Tell me, have you shared blood with her?"

"What do you care?"

"She needs to feed, but I have forbidden her to share."

"What the hell are you to her?"

"Her master."

"You taught her all the tricks of the trade."

"Not all. Besides, she can be very imaginative." Sade took hold of Wil's hair and pulled his head back. "Answer me, *monsieur*, has she shared?"

The door opened.

"The rope wasn't on the porch. I found it in the garage, awfully greasy and frayed, though. Must get used a lot."

A powerful pull and Will's head hit the board. His body lay prone and vulnerable.

"Raise your arms, *monsieur*."

"Marie . . ." Wil's voice faltered slightly.

"Do as he says, pet. Do not embarrass me."

Wil raised his arms, and Marie quickly circled his wrists with the filthy rope. She pulled tight, making the frayed rope dig into Wil's flesh, pulling even tighter when she looped the rope through the fastener under the board.

"*Ici*," Sade said.

Marie threw the long end of the rope to Sade, who stood at the foot of the board. He then attached Wil's ankles to the board. The rope running across the front of his body scratched the skin and put enough pressure on recent bruises to cause constant pain.

"I left a tin of lighter fluid on the kitchen counter. Retrieve it, Marie."

Wil watched Marie's chest heave. This definitely was torture for her. Why the hell was she doing this? This man she wanted destroyed. Why feign respect for him and scurry as a trained pet for him?

Again she left the room.

"This time she will return faster, *monsieur*. I really did leave the lighter fluid on the kitchen counter. You always look so pained when she leaves. Can you be that dependent on her?" Sade leaned over and whispered in Wil's ear. "Has she shared her blood with you?"

Sade's voice chilled Wil's body. The shiver brought deeper pain. *This is her secret from this man.*

Sade yanked Wil's earlobe so hard, his neck spasmed in pain.

"*Monsieur*, do you wonder why I have sent her for lighter fluid? Think about it. Think of the precious parts of your body that could be blistered and peeled into a blackened stump." Sade's hand wavered over Wil's cock. Instead of heat, the hand seemed to emanate cold. Sade pulled out a gold, garnet-studded lighter. "I could just fill up my lighter."

The door opened.

"Too late, *monsieur*."

Sade had kept his voice low, but Wil could tell that she had heard. She seemed relieved, as if she had guessed that a failed inquisition had been taking place in her absence.

Sade took the fluid from Marie and shook the can.

"We are in luck, *monsieur*. The tin is almost full." Sade plucked the lid from the can and threw it to the floor. "The fluid will refresh your sweaty skin." He began to pour the fluid lightly over Wil's chest, moving down to the stomach and abdomen.

Wil felt his penis stretch and swell. *Shit, how*

much of a masochist am I? The fluid ran through his pubic hair, dribbling down between his thighs.

"Just enough, *monsieur*."

Sade dropped the last of the fluid on the tip of Will's penis. Wil knew that a bit of his semen mingled with the drippings that rolled down his organ.

A flick of Sade's finger lit the ornate lighter. He carried it to the head of the board.

Wil felt the cold of Sade's hand brush his cheek. The smell of burning hair forced him to jerk his head.

"Only a few strands, *monsieur*. Your hair is so dark, long, and thick, I envy you."

"Don't, please. Marie, stop him. I don't want this."

"Finally, *ma* Marie, something that frightens *votre chouchou*."

The man just needed to scare him, Wil thought. If he showed enough fear, this dead man would back off. This dead man that needed to be destroyed. *Oh, Marie, you were so right.* But Wil needed to take out more than this sadist. He turned his head and looked at Marie. She stared back. A flicker of emotion never disturbed her features as she allowed Sade's hand to move down closer to his chest.

"She shared her blood with me," Wil yelled.

His chest flashed in waves of flame that progressed down to the lower half of his trunk.

Screams. His own. Marie's, as he saw the man sweep his fist into her mouth.

The ceiling light stayed lit after they left, but Sade had turned up the dimmer. Wil felt spotlighted. His burned body flinched under the glow of the high-wattage bulb that seemed to heat his stinging skin even more.

They had left him tied, but he still could tuck his chin in and see the blisters forming on his chest. He could not see the lower half of his body, but pain informed him of the damage that had been done.

"Bastard." His voice quivered. His anger passed a stream of pain through his body, rippling down as a tide. "I'll destroy you," he screamed, and the pain intensified, swelling into a new wave. Tears blurred his eyes and spilled down the side of his face. He inhaled, attempting to gain control over his emotions; instead, the smell of burnt meat turned his stomach. A dry heave contorted the pain into an unbearable trap that couldn't be escaped. He tasted blood and realized he had bitten down on his bottom lip. His tongue lapped at the blood. A fierce thirst overpowered him. Saliva wouldn't come. He kept sucking on the lip, but it didn't satisfy.

The door opened, then the light dimmed as the door shut again. He heard the rustle of clothing, the squeak of a floorboard, a cold hand wrapping around his left ankle, and the smell of paraffin.

God, have they not done enough?

Warm wax was dribbled onto his left foot. The heat seemed minor in comparison to the flame that still withered and blistered his skin.

The heat of wax, the cold of a frigid hand faded. The savage moved closer to his head. The smell of Marie focused his mind. She stood where he could see her and blew out the candle. She brought her face close to his.

"I forgive you," she said.

"Forgive?"

"For telling Louis that I had shared my blood with you. He is afraid to do any real harm to me, since Liliana knows that I am here. A frown." She rubbed a thumb across his forehead. "Yes, I had told her I would come here when she and I had stepped aside for a minute. He loves her, you know. A sick love, but still a controlling emotion she has over him. He would never destroy me, because her wrath would break his . . . dare I say, heart. But you were a bad boy." Marie leaned forward to kiss his lips.

Wil spat the congealing blood into her face. Marie raised her fingers to the blood and slowly wiped her face, licking each finger clean between each of her strokes. When finished, she lowered a finger to his cut lip and wiped away blood that she ran across her own lips. She used her tongue to mop the blood from her lipsticked mouth.

"I had to show you how much of an animal he is. I didn't think you completely trusted what I said. Did you?"

Silence pitted the two against each other.

"I didn't think so. Louis is hard to imagine. I'm here to rejuvenate you, my poor pet. It will take time, but your body will heal. I promise not a scar will settle into your skin."

Wil's body began to shiver.

"I had best hurry." She almost laid a hand upon his chest, but stopped when he took a quick intake of air.

Too late, Wil thought, as his action ignited his flesh all over again. Through the haze of his distant world he saw Marie rip apart the flesh on her right hand. Blood. His thirst seemed beyond containment. Blood. The metallic, sweet smell almost drowned out the odor of singed meat.

"I forgive you, Wil," she whispered. "I've come to heal, my savior." She brought her cut wrist to his mouth. "Drink, Wil. Quench that thirst that dis-

311

tracts your mind. Drink. When you get stronger, you will be able to get even."

Staring into Marie's brown eyes, Wil suckled at her wrist. He sucked so strongly that he saw her face crimp in pain.

Bitch, he thought, while tasting her on his tongue, allowing her to glide down his gullet, to seep into the pores of his body.

Chapter Fifty-three

Dressed in a black cassock with a purple stole crossing his chest, the priest unlatched the gates of the cemetery. He swept the gates open and led the mourners down the path to the family plot. Liliana stood far back in the line, not wanting to intrude on the family's privacy. Her uncle walked close to Matilda, whispering, comforting, lying, offering condolences that were empty. Offering his condolences when he took pleasure in the mourner's sorrow.

The hymns at the church had been solemn, emphasizing the hysteria of the mother when she called out for her baby. The screams resounded in the hollowness of the church as the choir continued to sing. Matilda had to be held back, else she would have lunged for the white coffin, which, covered with a full bed of white and red roses, seemed to float in the midst of the pallbearers. The priest's ser-

313

mon had dwelled on the shortness of Cecelia's life, the potential that had vanished with her, the love she had for her family, and the peace she would find with her Lord.

Not with her *lord*, Liliana thought. Never would Cecelia find the kind of peace the priest had promised. Cecelia would know a never-ending hunger.

Liliana closed her eyes and remembered awakening inside her coffin, the days-long confinement, the hopeless cries that were smothered by the earth. Had her uncle prepared Cecelia? He had not prepared Liliana. Perhaps after seeing Liliana's famished, gaunt face, her bloodied fingers, and the rigidity of her frightened body, he had learned a lesson.

The last of the mourners brushed past her, and when she opened her eyes, she realized that most of the entourage had already assembled at the grave. Quickly she fell into step with those who preceded her.

At the grave site the coffin already hovered over the gaping maw of the earth. The priest, book in hand, waited for the crowd to still. Liliana looked for her uncle and found him standing next to the parents, his hands folded in prayer and his head bowed to the Creator. *Such blasphemy.*

Dressed in a black custom-made designer suit, her uncle looked striking. No, she corrected herself, he looked ethereal, with his white, jaggedly cut hair dipping down on his forehead and his somber but confident face of chiseled features.

He must have sensed her watching, for he looked at her and barely broke a smile to acknowledge her. Liliana looked away quickly, unable to accept the familial recognition. She and he were the same. Cecelia would join the family. He couldn't remain here with Cecelia. Where would he suggest going? Liliana didn't want to move on. She wanted to lie in David's arms, peaceful, loving him too much to unleash her taste for blood on him.

She and her uncle were the only ones of their kind here, except for the others, the mutated vampires that merely existed in the cemetery.

My God, what of Cecelia? They'd certainly smell the fresh body and come for her. Quickly she looked back at her uncle. Matilda leaned on his arm, dabbing tears from her eyes. Her uncle offered her his clean linen handkerchief, and she sobbed at the thoughtfulness of the gift.

Liliana reached for Sade's mind and finally knew she had captured his attention when Sade kissed Matilda's hand and encouraged her to stand nearer the priest as the final words were being said. He dropped back from the family, disappearing for several minutes until he whispered behind Liliana.

"Something disturbs you, *ma chère.*"

Liliana moved out of the mourners' circle and walked to a distant tombstone. Not until they stood next to the headstone did she realize it belonged to Wil's mother.

"The mutants I told you about are going to smell her body. She'll be too confused to protect herself, Uncle."

"I will linger among the trees. They will not have the opportunity to suck her flesh." His fingers brushed her cheeks. He looked at his own hands, remembering something. He reached for the crested ring on his left hand and removed it from his finger. "I shall always love you, *ma petite fille.* Always you will be first in my life." He took Liliana's left hand and slipped the weighty ring on the middle finger. Raising her hand to his lips, he kissed

315

the ring and turned her hand over to kiss her palm. "Cecelia quenches a hunger that merely satisfies my fantasies. But she will never have my love."

Snuggled in David's arms, she played with the fine hairs of his chest.

"That tickles." Playfully he pushed away her hand. Like the legs of a spider, her fingers started moving up the trunk of his body. "Uh-uh. Wrong direction." He drew her hand down between his legs. "That's the right spot. Can't you tell?"

"But what if I want to tease you?"

"I like where you're teasing me now."

"But this isn't teasing. This is foreplay. Next thing you know, you'll set me atop your hips, and we'll be way beyond the teasing stage."

"What sort of coquettish game do you want to play?"

Liliana slipped the peach-colored silk sheet back off their bodies and kneeled.

"I want to take turns driving each other crazy."

David took the down pillow from her side of the bed and placed it under his head along with his own pillow. "That will require thought and a filthy imagination."

She watched David's eyes scan the bedroom.

"This is so neat for a lady's boudoir. I expected to see black lace teddies hanging off dressers, makeup scattered around the bathroom sink, dresses left out from the arduous morning selection of what to wear . . . But wait, if I lean over the side of this mattress, will I find nylons scattered beneath the bed?"

Liliana sighed.

"Don't look so depressed because you're not a slob." He chucked her under the chin.

"I dress in another room."

"Ah! And you take your lovers to the bedroom, but never the dressing room. Oh, Liliana, I thought I had found the perfect housewife."

"We have . . . we had help."

"I'm sorry about the death of the housekeeper's daughter. I didn't mean to ruin—"

She pressed two fingers to his lips.

"Let's talk about our sexy romantic fantasies."

"Who starts?"

"You seem eager. Why don't you go first?" Liliana smiled, and shifted her weight to her right buttock.

"Actually, some of my fantasies I'd like to live again."

"Then these aren't just fantasies."

"Even used fantasies are new with different lovers."

Strange how the thought of other women made her stomach sink. He knew she was no virgin when they first made love. Each had had experiences with others that amplified their ability to satiate the other.

"I'd like to sweep you away." He grabbed her wrists and brought her back down on the mattress. "And I'd indulge myself in whatever manner I wanted. I could tie you down and give you orgasm after orgasm until your sleepy eyes told me you were intoxicated with the smell of our sex and the warmth of my breath on your skin."

His hot breath chilled Liliana as much as the kisses with which he liberally moistened her flesh.

"Orgasm after orgasm," she repeated.

He looked at her and smiled.

"Tempted? I know how to take you on a high beyond anything alcohol or a narcotic could give you."

"That easily?"

"Takes lots of sweat and ingenuity on my part." He released her wrists and ran his hands down her arms and across her breasts, squeezing and plucking until sexual excitement forced her to push his hands away. "I can't bring you to peak after peak . . ." he tapped her nose lightly with an index finger, "after peak, if you keep pushing me away."

"But my breasts are so . . ."

"Sensitive. That's the point, so to speak." He tweaked one of her nipples. "To have multiple orgasms you have to stay on the edge of torment and ecstasy."

His wet mouth covered hers, his tongue gliding against the roof of her mouth. He took hold of her wrists and brought her arms over her head. The cold brass and iron headboard felt refreshingly cool in contrast to David's burning flesh. Holding her wrists with one hand, David reached for something. The shifting of skin against skin increased the sexual tension between them. When he moved back onto her body, she raised her hips into him. He began to loop cloth around her wrists, tying her to one of the brass posts.

She pulled her mouth away from his.

"What the hell are you doing?"

David's soft voice hushed her.

"I want to pleasure you the way no one else has. Let me cater to your needs this time."

Her body relaxed, and David kneaded the flesh on her arms. He moved down to delicately caress the sides of her breasts, kissing each nipple and using his tongue to cause the nipple to swell. Liliana rested her head back on the mattress and allowed him to massage her thoroughly. He fingered each hidden crevice and inflamed the nerves running through her white skin. Her body drew up to his hands, wanting more and loving the control he had taken. Her moans drove away all thoughts of her uncle's actions and settled her spirit into lustful self-indulgence.

He used the belts from their jeans to secure her ankles to the foot of the bed and placed one of the down pillows under her buttocks. She watched him stand back to admire her pose.

"You're beautiful, Liliana. Almost too delicate-looking, with the paleness of your skin and the sharp curve of your bones. Hell, I bet you don't save yourself just for me. Men must flatter and seduce you all the time. What's it feel like with the other men? Can they fuck for as long and hard as I do?"

He shook his head and walked over to the closet. She saw him turn back to her in surprise.

"There's no clothes in here. A couple of hangers and some fresh towels. Oh wait, there's a hairbrush on the floor and a riding switch?"

"I used to ride," she answered.

"Baby, I'm going to ride you now."

He walked back over to the bed, carrying all the items that had been in the closet.

"My bedroom's better equipped, but I know how to improvise."

The air around Liliana quivered and thinned. A sweaty chill rumbled through her body.

"Don't, please, David."

He leaned over her.

"Don't you trust me, baby?"

"Liliana."

"Go with the fantasy," he whispered back to her. "I'm going to find out who gave my little slut that ring on her finger."

"My uncle gave it to me today at the cemetery."

319

"Your uncle didn't give you shit."

"David, I don't like this game."

She studied David's moves. He had changed. His shoulders hunched, his palms sweated, his breaths increased, his whole body moved like a predator. Even the smell of him had altered from a sexy musk to a raging sweat.

"David, I can't play out this fantasy."

"You'll do what I tell you and you'll tell me what I want to know. First, who gave you that damn ring? Didn't you think I'd notice? I could feel the touch of metal when you caressed my cock. I know you never wore a ring before. Why do you wear that one now?"

"Please, my uncle gave me the ring. Believe me."

"Why should I fuckin' believe you?"

His voice sounded raspy and tormented.

He twisted a bath towel in his hands while he spoke. "You're going to tell me all sorts of secrets about the men you lay. How about women? You go for them too?" David swung the towel hard across her abdomen.

Choking with rage, Liliana tried to hold herself in check, tried to think of a way to convince him that she didn't want to partake in this kind of fantasy. The towel stung her abdomen again. She had stopped hearing his words. His face barked out questions, and she repressed the violence building inside her.

"I'm going to cut that damn finger off if you don't tell me everything I want to know."

His voice sounded in her head again, but somehow at a distance. The sound couldn't be part of David. The harshness and accusations had to be coming from someone else. A stranger, a demon who had stolen his body.

After several more blows, he clutched her hips in his hands and ate her out, causing her to writhe and almost snap free of the bonds, bonds that couldn't hold her except as she allowed them.

David dropped the towel on the floor. Liliana relaxed until she spied him reaching for the switch that lay by her right foot.

"Please, David. This is upsetting me." She attempted to keep her voice level. Hysteria would only drive him and herself harder. "I want to make love to you, David, but I don't want to be hurt, and I don't want to hurt you. Please."

David smiled.

"Look at you. How could you possibly hurt me?" He played the switch across his left palm. "Only way you could is by refusing to play the scene out with me. And on that you don't have much of a choice, baby."

"Liliana." If she kept repeating her own name, perhaps he would become bored and realize the game was no fun unless she cooperated.

"Baby, don't upset me. I'm on a roll now. Haven't been here in a long time, and it feels good." He hit the foot of the bed with the switch. The smack echoed in the room.

"Please, I beg you. Stop."

"Hey, now, that's better, more in keeping with the mood I'm trying to set."

His swift movement appeared to her as slow motion, with only the sting of the switch on her upper right thigh drawing her back into reality.

"What, no scream? You'll be yelling eventually, begging me to back off."

This time the switch made contact with her left thigh.

"Stuart." Her voice softly spoke the single word.

"Shit! Who the hell is this Stuart?" The switch came down hard on her thighs.

David looked like Stuart, but he didn't have the softness, the gentleness, the caring of the dead man. *Yes*, she said to herself, *Stuart is dead and will never come back to me.*

The switch kept stinging her thighs.

The man in the room with her was a cruel similacrum of the one she loved. This man knew none of the loving, soft words or actions that had made Liliana give up drinking warm human blood. She looked at David and saw perspiration forming on his forehead. The muscles of his striking arm were tense; he did not hold back on her punishment. And yet a numbness had spread through her body. He took a deep breath and struck her again and again. Her thighs burned. A spot of blood appeared on the switch. Blood, and still he struck.

"Bitch, I'll show you what I think of women who fuck around on me."

David reversed the switch and drove the handle into her vagina. Excruciating pain lit her body. Her wrist sprang forward, breaking the bonds, allowing her to spring at David, wrapping her hands around his throat and dragging him down onto the mattress.

"What the fuck . . ."

The belts around her ankles snapped free from the foot of the bed, giving her enough leverage to set herself on top of David. Her powerful legs held David in place while he sputtered and fought. Her hands held him fast, and she bit into his neck, drawing blood from his carotid.

"It was only a game. Only a game" were the last words she heard him speak.

Chapter Fifty-four

The mourners hurried back to their cars; only the immediate family lingered by the grave. The priest attempted to give comfort, but quickly realized the mother would not be calmed by words of an afterlife. The father shook the priest's hand, and Sade thought he saw an exchange of money. Matilda whimpered, and the priest slowly paced out of the cemetery.

"Why?" It seemed to be the only word Matilda knew. "Why? Why?" Matilda spied Sade leaning against a mausoleum. Sade lowered his head to avoid eye contact, but the silly woman came to him.

"You've been so generous, Mr. Sade. The coffin, even the plot . . . I don't know how to repay such . . ." A sob in her throat prevented Matilda from completing the sentence. "I'm so sorry, Mr. Sade, that I . . ."

"*Toutes mes condoléances*. It is you, madam, who

323

suffers the greatest loss. A child starting to blossom into a woman, suddenly taken in the dead of night."

"They still do not know what killed her. The doctors, the autopsy, but all they say is she died from a loss of blood. She was menstruating. Their guess is that she hemorrhaged and didn't tell anyone. She had faded bruises on her body. They think she was into self-mutilation."

"I think that boyfriend of hers, Joey, beat her up a few times," said the father.

"Why wouldn't she tell me, Mr. Sade?" the mother pleaded.

"Because she was a frightened child, madam."

Matilda shook her head. Her husband guided her away from Sade and toward the cemetery gates. Sade followed them beyond the gates and watched as they pulled away in the chauffeured limousine he had rented for the family. The darkened windows hid Matilda's tearful face.

A Latin hymn sparked a memory, and he began singing the hymn as he walked back into the cemetery:

"Miserere mei, Deus, secundum magnam misericordiam tuam:
Et secundum multitudinem miserationum tuarum, dele iniquitatem meam.
Amplius lava me ab iniquitate mea.
Et a peccato meo munda me.
Quoniam iniquitatem meam ego cognosco,
Et peccatum meum contra me est semper."

Magically two workmen had gathered at the gravesite, ready to bury the coffin six feet deep.

"Messieurs," Sade called.

The workmen seemed startled and slunk to the side, embarrassed that they hadn't waited longer to make sure all the mourners were gone.

"*Messieurs*, it will not be necessary to bury the coffin."

The men looked at each other. One man, short, thin, with a mustache and a nervous twitch of his upper lip, started to speak, but his partner touched his shoulder and the man fell silent.

"*Messieurs*, if I allow you to bury my maiden, you will just be making work for me."

The taller of the grave diggers spoke. "Sir, are you a member of the immediate family?"

"I am now."

The taller man shuffled his boot-covered feet and sighed.

"Listen, man, we got a job to do here. If you're not the father or brother of the deceased, we have to ask you to leave so we can finish our job."

"Ah, *monsieur*, but your job is *fini*. You may leave. Now!" Sade's voice rose in a stern demanding tone, causing the taller of the two men to stand taller still.

"Why do we get the nut jobs?" the shorter man said out loud, but seemingly to himself.

"We don't want any problems here, mister. Just get into your car and spin away."

"*Des problèmes!* It is not I who insist on burying a coffin that doesn't need to be buried." Sade walked to the coffin and laid a hand on the rich wood. "Leave me, *messieurs*. Go home to your families." Sade bowed his head.

"Rob here isn't going anywhere," said the tall man, thumbing toward the shorter man.

"Huh?" Rob looked up at his partner.

"You stay here while I go get the police."

"Me?"

"*Messieurs*, you do not understand. This is a matter of saving your own lives."

"Hell, he's threatening us, Rob."

"I'll get the police," said Rob. He took a single step backward, and his partner grabbed the gray work shirt Rob was wearing.

"There's two of us, in our prime. This guy's up in age. What are you, in your fifties, sixties? You don't want to threaten us with anything."

"Maybe he just wants some time alone with the coffin, Ed."

"Did you see how arrogant this guy has been with us?" Ed turned back to Sade. "Yeah, I wanta go home, mister. That's why we're going to bury this box now, not later."

"I will fill in the hole *pour vous*."

Rob nudged his partner off to the side. They mumbled for two long minutes and then they both looked at Sade.

"We're sorry about your loss, but we have a job to do. Ed and I will go off to get some coffee, then come back in about twenty minutes. Okay?"

"It is up to you, *monsieurs*, for she will not be here."

"Shit, man, we try to give the guy a break, and now he's talking about stealing the body," said Ed.

"Sounds better than doing bodily harm to us." Rob shrugged.

"Listen, we have a responsibility to see to it that the box is safely buried."

Sade sighed. "But she will need the . . . coffin," Sade corrected.

"That's right. You're getting it now. Whoever's in that box will need it for eternity."

"Well, at least for the ride over to Europe, *monsieur*."

"We can't have nobody stealing bodies we're responsible for. We'd lose our jobs."

"Yeah," added Rob. "If you want to dig her up later when we're not around, we don't care. We just want to complete our job."

Sade lifted his hand off the coffin and tapped his index finger on his lips. They could serve a purpose. He had expected to present her with smaller prey, but . . .

Sade spun around toward the grave diggers and rushed at them with both arms outstretched.

"Holy shit!"

Sade couldn't tell which of them had spoken, but he did see both men take on a stance to down him before he grabbed each by the neck and tumbled both to the ground. He kicked one in the head and rapped the other man's head against a tombstone.

Sade checked their pulses. Neither man was dead, simply unconscious. He needed them alive and warm.

Sade flung the flowers onto the ground and drew up the lid of the coffin in a swift heave that broke the seal. Cecelia's head lay quiet and still on a lace and satin pillow. Her hair, spun in ringlets, lay spread out like a halo. Sade had suggested that the parents not allow her to be marked in any further way and recommended a sealed coffin with immediate burial. The family had agreed; otherwise, he would have been pulling out stitches, barbed wire, and all sorts of paraphernalia used in this modern day to preserve the beauty of the dead for the short duration of a wake.

Cecelia had on a frilly, lacy high-collared dress that her mother had insisted on, a dress that supposedly duplicated the child's First Communion dress. Had not the mother noticed that her daughter had grown into a woman? Sade wondered. Wrapped around Cecelia's fingers was a rosary, light blue crystal beads that glinted under the movement of the day's clouds. Her body appeared to be drowned in lacy fussy folds. Her feet were naked; even the dark red polish that her mother had hated had been removed from the toenails.

Sade turned back to the two men lying on the ground, the smell of blood rousing his passions. The one whose head he had knocked against the tombstone was bleeding. Sade drew near to the man and swept his fingers against the wound. The blood glistened and ran down Sade's fingers. Tempted to lap up the spillage, Sade immediately returned to the coffin and spread the blood across Cecelia's lips. He did this once more before he noticed the corpse pick up the scent. Her nose twitched, her tongue slipped across her lips, and gradually she came alive. Seeing Sade, she burst into laughter.

"*Mon enfant*, they did not get the chance to bury you. I stayed with you." He smiled and pushed her back down when she attempted to rise. "First you must feed."

Sade went back to the two men, lifted the bleeding man in his arms, and carried the unconscious gravedigger to Cecelia. When she saw the bleeding man, she swallowed hard.

"Move over, *mon enfant*." Awkwardly Sade laid the man next to Cecelia. The thin, short man took up little room next to her. She reached out to touch his wound, but pulled back before her fingers made contact.

"Do not be afraid, Cecelia. Touch it," Sade encouraged.

Slowly she reached out her hand again. This time she did touch the blood, but withdrew her fingers immediately as if burned.

"Must not be queasy, *mon enfant*. This is your dinner." He watched her again take a hard swallow. "Smell him. Smell the blood. Do you not hunger?"

She nodded.

"Did you not drink of me?"

For a moment she thought. "But he isn't you. He's a stranger."

"So are the roast beef and chicken you've been eating for years."

Cecelia reached a hand up to Sade, begging him to share his blood with her.

"No, *mon enfant*. Occasionally in passion we will take from each other, but true nutriment will come from those who are not driven to suck human blood."

Cecelia looked at the man.

"He may not be pretty, *mon enfant*, but he is rich in the blood that mars your dainty pillow."

She lifted herself slightly so that she could view the spreading stain. Sade allowed her to chew on the lace and satin for a few minutes. He knew that would enliven her hunger and force her to turn to the source. She began licking the gravedigger's wound, but Sade forced her head down until her lips touched the man's neck.

"Feel the pulse, *enfant*."

She nuzzled into the neck. When joy lighted her features, Sade knew she had located the carotid.

"Now, *enfant*, take what you need. Bite down and take what you need."

Cecelia bit down.

"No, *fille!* Gnash down upon his flesh with all the power you contain."

She bit harder but still did not crack the skin.

"Grip his flesh in your fangs and tear, *mon enfant.*"

Her chest heaved in desperation. Finally she screamed, grabbed the man's head between her palms, and furiously bit down.

The blood spurted onto her nose and mouth, and the man's head seemed to cave in on both sides.

"Does not matter. He will not be needing what little brains he had, *mon enfant.*"

Chapter Fifty-five

Liliana watched her uncle feed his new protégé. She wondered whether he would suck dry the other man or leave him for the mutants.

Dressed only in an oversized sweatshirt and panties, Liliana hid behind a bulbous trunk that belonged to an old maple tree. She could hear the sopping sounds of lips worrying flesh, the noise made by a novice that unnecessarily rips and tears.

As the girl gained strength, she rose to hover over her meal. She began shredding the man's clothes with her fingers in search of his sex, needing to feed all the hungers of her body. Sade allowed her to explore. He obviously relished the frantic exhibition. Liliana watched his eyes shimmer with delight. Watched his own mouth work in unison with Cecelia's. Watched his hands fold into tight fists. Watched his body stiffen with his own sexual arousal.

Liliana reached down between her legs and through the cotton she fingered herself, her blood hunger rising again at the sight and smell of the unconscious men.

But the man on the ground moved. So engrossed in watching his charge, Sade did not notice. In a squat position Liliana bounced up and down, ready to spring, ready to kill.

A moan came from the man. This Sade heard, and he turned to catch the eye of the doomed man. Moving in a flash, Sade grabbed hold of the man before the man could gain his footing. Partly kneeling, partly cowering, the man fussed as a baby in his father's arms. She knew Sade enjoyed the scramble, enjoyed finding fear in his prey's eyes, enjoyed the slow kill.

The man opened his mouth to scream, but Sade held him so tightly by the throat that he could not. Grinning, Sade hissed and brought his fangs down on the man's carotid. Blood poured from the wound, and Liliana could barely keep herself from running toward her uncle to share or, better, to steal the meal.

She looked back at the coffin, hoping to quell the terrible thirst. Cecelia sat atop her victim, her skirt raised up around her waist as she bounced herself on his body. Had he really died with a hard-on, or did Cecelia make do with simpler contact?

Liliana pulled herself to her feet and ran toward the old section of the cemetery, David's bloodstains tightening her skin as she moved.

Once surrounded by the decrepit tombstones and crosses, she fell face forward into the dirt. Her hands clawed at the earth. *This is where I belong. This should be my home.* She rubbed her face into the dirt, cleansing herself of the complex world her uncle had taken her into.

An animal. Just like the other animals that dominated this section of the cemetery.

She turned over and stared at the sky. Dusk would be here soon. Their time of night, she thought. The mutants would scurry around the cemetery looking for dregs, the same as she herself did when she imbibed of the bodies she embalmed.

She no longer heard her uncle and Cecelia, but she did still smell the blood flowing down mouths, sliding down fingers, staining clothes. The breeze carried the scent across the cemetery, spinning and swirling through the air, a hint of the scent settling over the cemetery.

Feeling the stickiness of the dry blood on her legs, Liliana began clawing up clots of soil to rub across the stains. She kept rubbing until her own skin was abraded, the sting sharpening her senses. The sound of a wispy movement came from the right. She stopped rubbing her skin and sat silent for several moments, attention dedicated to her surroundings. Another soft sound confirmed what she knew. The mutants had come out early, awakened by the smell of blood. Slowly she rose to her feet. Looking around, she caught sight of a moving body. Male? Female? She couldn't tell, not until she saw the pendulous breasts swing in movement with the mutant's gait.

"Sister," Liliana called and reached out her arms to embrace what she was.

"Sister," she called again, but the shadow slipped beyond sight.

Trees grew densely in the farther part of the cemetery. Liliana guessed that the movements of leafy limbs were not from any breeze. She envisioned the

333

mutants shuffling up trees to have a bird's-eye view of the funerals. Not only could they smell the deceased, but they could watch as the body was interred. Under cover of darkness, they would know exactly where to find the remains. Two of their finds tonight would be dry. After the scent in the air, how would they deal with dried husks?

Slowly Liliana walked toward the densely packed trees. Evolution reversed, she thought, searching for another clue to where the mutants hid.

When she had almost reached the trees, a frantic wave of movement shook the branches.

"Sister," she called once again and moved in among the trees.

She heard the tread of feet, the sliding caused by the fallen leaves, the hissing of frightened, mindless beings.

"I'm one of you." She spoke slowly and clearly. "I, like you, feed on blood. I belong here with you." Not among the living, she thought, a flash of David's mangled body forcing her to rub her closed eyelids, hoping to erase the reality. Taking her hands away from her face, she forced herself to focus on why she was here. "This is all I deserve. Not even this. Less. You steal from the dead. I have caused death. Children. Lovers. Strangers. And those whom I have judged."

Liliana looked around her and spied a frail mutant peering down at her from the branches of a close-by tree. The mutant's blue ice eyes remained fixed on Liliana as she moved closer.

"I want to join you. I want to make peace with you."

Liliana noted that the limbs of the mutant's tree spread out over the spiked fence of the cemetery, but the mutant did not seem to possess any fear of falling. Instead it jiggled the limb it knelt on like an excitable chimp. However, this mutant did not try to escape Liliana. Instead it watched and sniffed the air hovering over her. *David's blood*, she thought. Liliana picked up dead leaves and rubbed them over most of her body, hoping to at least lessen the odor with the smell of decay.

"May I join you?"

The mutant scratched its head and scratched its crotch. But the blue ice eyes maintained their fascination with Liliana.

"Those eyes must have been beautiful when you were alive. They still hold some beauty." What was she doing here, trying to communicate with something that could no longer understand? She had to know these creatures before she could know herself. Hadn't she lost control? Hadn't she almost attacked her own uncle for blood? Were the mutants as mindless as they seemed? They obviously experienced fear and the need for self-preservation. Were they vampires who had given up the killing? Did they cluster and take on animal-like qualities as a penance? Had they been driven mad by the knowledge of their own brutality?

"I'm one of you," she said softly. Liliana scrambled up the tree in which the mutant knelt, stopping only once or twice to make sure the mutant hadn't moved. It sat and watched her, its head held at an angle, its body still.

Once she attained the same level as the mutant, she tried to slide closer to it. It didn't move. A bit closer, and it leaped to another limb. Liliana took its place on the narrow limb.

"I'm not here to harm you. I want to know if this is how it ends. Does this curse drive one eventually mad? Can you comprehend anything I'm saying?"

The mutant seemed to sigh, its body relaxed, and it reached out a stubby hand toward Liliana.

Smiling but not showing her teeth, she put her hand out to take the mutant's hand. A tongue slipped out between the lips of the mutant. The tip had been bitten off the rust-brown tongue. No sheen of moisture shimmered on the tongue; instead a crust coated the surface.

Stretching to her limit, Liliana barely touched the thing's finger stubs.

"Teach me about myself," she pleaded.

The mutant leaned farther out over the space separating them. It made a lunge for her hand, throwing her off balance and out of the tree.

For a brief moment she saw the spikes, then they were in her, piercing her breast, penetrating her abdomen, catching her jaw from below, preventing her from turning her head. Any movement drove the spikes deeper. Her shock came out in a jumble of syllables that could no longer be formed into clear words.

When she tried to lift her head, her body sank deeper onto the spikes. She drew her arms in toward the spikes, hoping to use her hands to leverage herself. Vibrations passed through the metal into her body.

God, no. She knew they were climbing, reaching up to feed on her. The first bony spidery hand touched her left thigh. A simple awkward cry from her throat drove the hand away. She glimpsed arms outstretched between the bars, attempting to attack her from the other side. A tug on her shirt. A clawlike hand gripping her upper left arm. Spindly fingers weaving in her hair, trying to press down on her right shoulder.

The pain ripped at her insides and flashed a

bright light before her eyes. Blood clogged her throat and ran from her mouth.

The mutants tugged, and she felt the spike break through the skin of her back, tenting the sweatshirt she still wore. The material ripped. Pain dove into the depths of her soul.

" 'Tis but folly in our parents when they foretell the disasters of a libertine career; there are thorns everywhere, but along the path of vice roses bloom above them; Nature causes none to smile along virtue's muddy track."

Philosophy in the Bedroom,
by the
Marquis de Sade

Chapter Fifty-six

"Hello, Keith." Marie closed the bedroom door behind her. "You can hear and understand me, can't you?" She walked to the bed and took hold of Keith's chin, turning his head toward her. "Yes, I see the fear. Your quivery eyeballs tell me lots. They tell me that you fear not only for yourself but also for your son. I'm here today to end the tension for you. Relieve you of any sense of responsibility for a son you didn't want."

Keith's hands shook against the sheet-covered mattress, the rapid movements causing a muffled incessant shuffling noise. His eyes blinked, and she saw a tear run down his left cheek.

"Oh so touching. I wish I could feel for you. Unfortunately for you, that tear means nothing to me. You're just an old man who's in the way of my sweeping your son off to Paris with me." Marie's fingers tightened on Keith's jaw.

Keith issued a gurgle, and saliva began running out the side of his mouth, streaking down his chin to fall lightly on Marie's index finger.

"Hurt, does it?" Marie squeezed harder, and the pop of collapsing bone filled the room. Marie took her hand away, noting the prints of her fingers and the caving-in of flesh. "Tell me, Keith, what makes you hold on to life? Fear of oblivion? Fear of retribution? You are scared to die; I can see it in those misty old eyes. I can hear it when you take a breath. You scratch at the sheets, hoping to recapture the old freedoms you once had. Walking. Standing. Talking." She brushed back a few strands of gray hair from Keith's forehead. "I bet you were a handsome man once. But that had to be long ago. Long ago when your pretty wife wanted to make a baby with you." Marie swept back the blankets that covered Keith's body. "You been losing weight? The gut seems flatter. I bet these old muscles are turning to gristle," she said while kneading his arms.

Slowly Marie started to undo the buttons on Keith's pajama top. The pajamas were new, the sizing still stiffening the cotton material.

"White is not your color, Keith. You're way too pale for white."

Marie leaned down to whisper in Keith's ear. "In what color do you want to be laid out? Has Wil been through your closet yet to select an appropriate suit? He probably doesn't have the money to buy you a new one. But it doesn't matter, because it won't be Wil's problem. We'll leave you for the mailman to find. When the smell becomes overwhelming, I'm sure he'll either investigate or call in the police. I guess by then there won't be enough solid flesh to fit into a suit."

Marie kissed his cheek.

"Goodbye, you old bastard."

She lowered her lips and rested on the carotid drumming in his neck. The thrumming aroused her. She sensed a slight smell of Wil, either left from his touch or owing to the genes both men shared. Closing her eyes, she visualized Wil, the last time she had fed him, the ashen odor of his flesh drifting in and out of her memory. When she touched Keith's chest, she touched the hideous blisters that had percolated across Wil's flesh. Her scratching nails caught hold of Keith's chest hair, different from the crisp edges of Wil's wounded flesh, but still something to claw at while she prepared not to give of her own blood, but to take Keith's.

Her wet tongue slid along the pulsing beat of his heart. Another mournful gurgle. The brushing of his fingers against the sheet sent a vibration reaching out to the knee that Marie rested on the bed.

"Wil," she uttered, and with force she bit down on inviting flesh.

Wil sat under the shade of an old willow tree. As a boy he would sit here and do his homework or dream. There weren't any dreams left in him. He stared vacantly before him, a mind blanked by pain and loss.

The flesh on his chest was healing miraculously fast. Hardly a splotch stained his chest. The pain had eased quickly after Marie had given him her blood. He bit down on his own tongue for a taste of blood. Lately he had been doing such things as licking a wound on his finger. When he nicked his father while shaving the old man, Wil had almost drunk of his father. The temptation had shaken Wil enough that he had left the house and had come out here near the stream and the tired old willows.

Blood leaked slowly into his mouth. The taste was metallic and sweeter than it was when he was a child. "Gross out," children would scream when one caught another sucking his own blood. "Gross out." Not anymore. Now he found pleasure in blood, pleasure in the taste, smell, texture, color.

His father needed him. The old man had stared up into his son's eyes after being nicked by the blade. Stared, attempting to communicate something, and all Wil could do was flee from the house. Unlock their eye contact and flee. He hadn't even seen to the nick on his father's face.

Wil pulled away from the trunk of the tree, sparking feathery sensations across his healing flesh. With some amount of pain he stood. His bare feet began striding through the grass, heading back to the house. Had his father fallen asleep? Perhaps he should allow his old man to grow a full bushy beard, become a Rip Van Winkle.

As he came around from the back of the house, he noticed Marie's car. His pace quickened. He picked the lightweight white cotton shirt off the porch's railing and put it on while exhaling a sigh. He buttoned merely two buttons so that his father, if he could understand, would not see the healing burns.

Opening the door, Wil staggered under the spell of blood. His mouth watered, his skin came alive with pain and pleasure. The scent filled the room, but was not of the room.

"Oh, my God!" His legs stumbled toward his father's bedroom, reaching his hands out to push open the closed door.

Marie looked up at Wil from his father's bed, her mouth smeared with blood, her fingers streaked with the browning stain, her teeth shining under the tinting. Giddy as if drunk on champagne, Marie giggled and beckoned to Wil.

His father lay still, the blue eyes staring up at the ceiling, the mouth agape.

"What the hell have you done?"

Wil rushed to the bed, roughly took hold of Marie's shoulders, and pushed her to the floor.

He checked his father for a pulse. None. Hardly any blood leaked from the wound; she had almost drained his father dry. His stomach roiled at his own instincts. He wanted to taste his father. Taste the blood. Taste the salty sick flesh.

"Damn you," he yelled, turning away from his father to look for Marie.

She had managed to lift herself off the floor and was rounding the bed to leave, he had no doubt.

"Bitch!"

He rushed her, swinging out his right fist to catch her right jaw in a powerful sweep.

Marie fell to the floor. Her head lay lopsided on her neck. Her attempts to move her head only showed how little control she had. Wil realized he must have broken her neck. He watched her arms and legs flounder, heard her whisper his name, saw the pleading in her eyes as he backed away from her and returned to his father.

Chapter Fifty-seven

Sade stiffened in pain. His innards were being ripped apart. His skin lay open, exposed to the mangling hands that twisted his intestines.

He dropped the man from whom he had been drinking to look down at his chest and abdomen. They were still whole. He saw only the matte black of his suit.

"Liliana," he whispered. "Liliana," he called. "Liliana!" he shouted. "Liliana!" he shouted again and his mouth twisted into a scream and he ran toward the old section of the cemetery.

He sensed her odor, her life.

"Ma petite chérie!"

"Mon enfant!"

Her life shimmered in the air, wavering in and out of existence.

A block of trees before him weaved with the

movement of beings scurrying, lapping, and teasing his sight.

"Mon enfant," he mumbled, falling to his knees at the edge of the cluster of trees. His sight had momentarily been blinded. Dead meat, rotted meat scented the air. Animal sounds screeched in his ears.

"Liliana," he whispered, smelling the air for her life.

Too weak to stand, he crawled forward, feeling the spongy, soggy moss beneath his hands. Twigs bruised his skin and leaves became glued to his hands.

"S'il te plaît, Liliana."

He did not feel the life of the little girl who had grown into a beautiful woman. The one who had driven his sleepless nights, the one of whom he had dreamed while locked in the Bastille.

Vague forms hustled out of his way, but he ignored them.

"Liliana, *mon enfant."*

The forms began to disappear, except for a solitary shade who sat in a tree, writhing among the branches and leaves. Clawing and sucking at flesh, it did not seem to notice Sade.

"Donnez-moi ma fille!"

The shade trembled, allowing the meat to slide from its skeletal hands.

The lower part of an arm fell to the ground, brushing the side of Sade's left cheek. The chill of blood wet his cheek. A single drop rolled down his quivering flesh. Deadweight falling on leaves. Deadweight indenting the earthen layer before him.

Sade looked down to see the lower portion of a slender feminine arm. The jagged flesh had been ripped at the elbow, the arm white, sticky waves of faded blood marring the freshness of the skin.

"Mon enfant."

Seconds spoiled the air about him, informing him slowly of her destruction.

"Liliana."

His stomach roiled.

"Ma petite chérie."

He threw himself back on his haunches and reached his hands out to touch the remains before him. Icy as his flesh, but an empty cold that does not preserve the flesh, instead allows the flesh to decay.

His niece, his child, his woman, his lover. Gone. A life taken by loveless husks intent on feeding their own appetites.

A shiver of leaves and twigs behind him. Sade turned in fury with Liliana's appendage raised high above his head as if to signal the *casus belli*. In a single leap he was on his feet and standing before Cecelia. Her eyes wide, she took the opportunity of his frozen tableau to take a step backward.

"Louis?"

His eyes focused on his newly born lover. Her clothes, rent and bloodstained, flapped in a breeze. Her mouth was smudged with shed life. He watched her lips form his name. How many times? He could not hear, for the rush inside his head sent waves of pain resounding through his thoughts.

His fingers intertwined with his niece's, her fingers becoming unyielding while he felt his own flesh turned into a lover's touch.

Sade turned his back on Cecelia and faced the wood. Falling to his knees, he wished he could pray to Liliana and beg her forgiveness, beg her to return once more to him.

Sade lowered her hand to his lips and kissed her

palm. He turned the hand over and saw the ring he had given her. A marriage only briefly consummated. He slid the ring off her finger and laid the arm on a bed of leaves. Raising the ring skyward, he saw the quarter moon peaking between the limbs of the trees.

With whom could he share his love?

"Are you going to bay at the moon now?" Cecelia's question shattered the quietness of his thoughts.

Sade returned the ring to his own finger and stood, knowing that there was no longer any reason to tolerate La Maîtresse.

"And the villain leaves peacefully! And divine lightning strikes him not!"

Justine,
by the
Marquis de Sade

Chapter Fifty-eight

"Who was she?"

Sade felt Cecelia's eyes staring at him.

"It was Liliana's arm, wasn't it?"

He knew this child reveled in her rival's death, but he could not fault her for the jealousy. Now Cecelia and he belonged to each other. There existed no third party to dampen his passion for his newest . . . He could not allow the word *love* to be spoken, even in his thoughts. His newest what? Passion. Yes. His newest passion.

"She's dead, isn't she?"

Sade drove faster, heading for La Maîtresse's house. Headlights flashed on passing objects. Occasionally he noticed a broken fence, a ramshackle barn, a signpost that simply blurred by.

"Are we going back to your house?"

The Jaguar held the road, taking turns with ease, turns that he had memorized late at night in fits of passion when he decided to bring a victim to the dungeon. Innuendo had encouraged the drive, small talk had filled the air in the car, small talk and nervous hand movements covering the victim's anticipation.

"You said we would leave for Europe right away."

Right after his visit to his mother-in-law.

A house came into view on the left side of the road. Sade glanced casually, taking in the tired porch, the old Cadillac parked to the side of the house, and Marie's car at the foot of the driveway.

Sade stomped the brakes, and the car spun several times. He heard a high-pitched scream sound from the passenger seat. He regained control of the car and parked it immediately behind his mother-in-law's car.

"Why are we stopping here, for Christ's sake?"

"Stay in the car, Cecelia. Wait for me. Don't leave the car. You don't want to be seen." Sade looked over at the girl and immediately swept her off the seat and onto the floor. "Stay out of sight."

If she protested, he didn't hear. Instead his mind reached out to the house, seeking the existence he meant to destroy. He slammed the car door behind him. Inside the house a weakened Marie waited in fear. He sensed the sickening odor of decaying flesh, wounded, fighting, scrambling about wanting escape, but trapped.

Sade laughed, allowing his presence to be announced in the vibrations of the air that separated him from Marie.

"I'm closing in," he whispered, knowing that night breathed his words inside her head.

"Stay still. What the hell's wrong that you can't be still until I can check your condition?" Wil approached Marie and she struck out, ravishing the air with her nails, missing Wil completely. "Damn, I'm not trying to hurt you anymore."

Marie rasped. Trying to speak? He could not tell for sure. Dragging her body in short spurts, Marie headed away from the entrance to the bedroom and closer to the farthest window.

"Marie, I want you dead, but not by my own hand."

The words seemed to strike terror in Marie's eyes. Without moving her head, her eyes searched the room. While attempting to stand, Marie crashed her head against the wooden leg of the bed.

Like an animal, he thought. Like an animal hit by a car on a lonely road. No understanding in the eyes, only fear.

The front door opened and closed. He always forgot to lock the door; this had often caused arguments between him and his father.

"Shit," he cursed. How could he explain what had happened in this room? Would anyone believe him? "Shit!"

Sade kicked aside a fallen book. The room to his right filled his heart with glee. She was there. Waiting. Unable to escape him.

He touched the knob of the door and hesitated. Slowly he rubbed the faceted glass. His chill already permeated the room, he knew. While holding the knob, he lightly tapped an index finger against the wood panel of the door. Hardly audible by most, but meant to echo inside Marie's head.

Suddenly the door was pulled open and Marie's favorite slave stood in the doorway.

"What the hell are you doing here?"

Sade reached out and touched Wil's healing chest.

"She is sharing her blood with you." He *tsk*ed.

Wil went to push his hand away, but Sade grabbed Wil's hand and squeezed, squeezed until Wil on his knees begged him to stop. Sade pulled back his own hand and kicked Wil to the side.

A dead man lay on the bed: Marie's last meal. Beyond the body he sensed La Maîtresse on the floor. Quiet now, she lay in a crooked ball, her neck out of kilter, her mind racing, her time decreasing in seconds, moments.

"Liliana has been destroyed."

"What?" Wil's mouth hung open.

Marie made no sound.

"At the cemetery *mon enfant* was torn apart by raging, demented husks called vampires."

"Vampires? What the hell are you talking about?" asked Wil.

But Marie was still.

"*Une belle enfant, une belle femme* lost to me forever."

"She's dead?"

"*Elle a eu une existence misérable* between an uncle too enchanted to free a lovely *jeune femme* and a grandmother wrapped in her own hedonism. We were wrong, Marie. We should have let her go long ago." Sade walked around the bed to confront his mother-in-law. "*Vouz allez cruellement souffrir.*"

"What in hell are you talking about?" asked Wil, on his feet, looking lost.

Sade looked at Wil. "*Monsieur,* you are one of us, or perhaps almost one of us." Sade looked over at Marie. "You always liked the slow, excruciating way. Now you will not be able to complete your creation. A creation you swore you never would consider making. I know you can't help but lie. I was to be freed from the Bastille, only I didn't know that I would immediately be taken to an insane asylum. But I grew in strength there, Marie. A strength you cannot imagine in a puny body like yours.

"*Monsieur*, I noticed you have a fireplace. Does it work?"

"Hell, on a hot day like this, what does it matter?"

"Does it work, *monsieur*?" Sade stared directly into Wil's eyes.

"Yes."

"Firewood is outside?"

"Yes. Needs to be chopped, but it's there for winter."

"*C'est l'hiver, ma petite amie.*"

Sade turned away from Marie and strode out of the room. He hesitated at the threshold and looked over his shoulder to see Wil moving closer to Marie.

"*Monsieur*, you must show me where the ax and firewood are."

"I'm not helping, you bastard."

Sade sighed. "*Monsieur*, do you know why you are healing so quickly?"

"I know why I have these scars."

"No, no, *monsieur*, that is not the point. It was a test to see how quickly you could recuperate. You see, she is turning you into one of us."

"God help me, I'll never be like either of you."

"True, since she will not have the opportunity of completing her *vicieux* work. I'm not sure what you will become, *monsieur*, and I don't really care. But you will find yourself with a strange thirst, and you will need to feed just as she has on this poor old man."

"My father."

"Ah! *La vengeance est douce, monsieur.*" Sade saw

the blank look in Wil's eyes. "Revenge, *monsieur*. Do you not seek to avenge the death of your father?"

"I don't want any more killing."

"*Monsieur*, that is the philosophy that caused my poor Liliana's demise. If you wish to survive, you will learn to enjoy the stalking, the smell of fear, and the golden feel of prey pressed between your palms."

Wil shook his head.

"I hope you will at least not try to stop me."

Wil backed away from Marie and walked over to kneel by the side of his father's bed.

Holding his father's hand, Wil silently asked his father for forgiveness. If he had never come home, his old man would still be living his grouchy hermit life, grumbling at neighbors, refusing Wil's calls. Caring for his mother's grave. Now Wil would have to care for both parents. He knew that his mother had been buried deep enough so that his father could eventually join her. It would only be a matter of opening the grave, inserting Keith's coffin, and adding Dad's date of death to the tombstone.

The house belonged to Wil now. His father had never prepared a will, unable to leave his possessions to an ungrateful son and unable to disinherit his wife's only child.

His throat felt parched. The skin on his chest itched. He looked down at himself. Initially the top layer had swollen into something that looked like the crust of a freshly baked pie. That layer had fallen off in a solid piece, and he had stomped on it until all the scum had gone down the shower drain. Layers had continued to rapidly peel away, until now there were only splotches left of the old burn.

Gurgling sounds interrupted his thoughts, and he looked up at his father's mouth. Lips still agape, the old man had not uttered any sound. The gurgling persisted, and he remembered Marie. He turned to his right side and saw how she hissed and heaved trying to speak, reaching out to touch his dirty faded jeans, dragging herself across the rough wood floor. A splinter of wood protruded from her right palm, big enough so that he could see it plainly catch on the woven cotton blanket that got in her way.

"Kill me." Her words had come out distorted, but she was not requesting to be killed, he knew, for she repeated the sentence more slowly, attempting to enunciate where her voice box failed.

"Don't . . . let . . . him . . . kill . . . me."

"Why should I stop him, my mistress?" The words were spoken coldly and sarcastically.

Her hand waved at his chest, and again she reached, but couldn't touch him.

"You'-re . . . life," she wheezed.

"I don't think he wants to kill me, my mistress." "Mistress" came out with tawdry disgust.

"Bl-ood." She made a leap and fell against his body.

"Get away from me," he said, pushing her back, watching her head fall uselessly against the leg of the bed.

Wil stood to look at his father's body. Finding a penknife on the nightstand, he used the point to jab his father's arm.

"Damn you! You sucked my father dry!" he yelled.

"*Oui, monsieur*, Marie is a *sangsue*. What you would call a vampire. Now help me start a fire. You must have newspaper or something I could use."

"Lighter fluid." Wil stared darkly at Sade.

Sade smiled. "Good to retain a sense of humor, *monsieur*. You will be needing it. Meanwhile, you torture my poor Marie with this lingering wait. Even she would prefer it over, *oui*, Marie? Ah, no! I am afraid Marie has a grip on her existence that she refuses to unlock.

"Paper, *monsieur*, lighter fluid, anything. I must be gone by morning *quand nous serons dans la merde*. A translation for you, *monsieur*: when the shit hits the fan."

Wil did not assist Sade; instead, he checked the wounds on his chest. He healed much faster than normal. His strength had increased to the point where he no longer could gauge the power behind his moves.

A vampire, he thought. A humorless chuckle caught his breath when he thought of his friends in Greenwich Village who had pretended at vampirism. How they would envy him.

He smelled smoke and rushed to the living room, where he found Sade adjusting the fireplace damper.

"*Monsieur*, a good cleaning certainly is in order here. My . . . former housekeeper can recommended a reliable chimney sweep. She always saw to that.

"Marie, come view the fire." Sade started toward the bedroom.

Wil assumed that Sade was mad, with talk of vampires and setting a fire in midsummer. He watched as Sade carried Marie to the living room.

"Come, sit before the fire, Marie." Upon setting her down on the oval rug in front of the fire, Sade lifted an oil lamp in his hands.

"Better than lighter fluid, *monsieur*." He dumped

the full contents of the lamp onto Marie's head, rubbing the oil into the fine fibers of her hair.

Marie twitched and wrinkled her face horribly. The oil seemed to run into her eyes and mouth. She attempted to spit the oil out, and Sade scooped the oil from her chin to press between her lips.

Wil's body felt tired. His arms ached, his legs wobbled unsteadily, and his heart beat so faintly that he couldn't be sure he still lived.

"I am sorry for the mess, *monsieur*, but there is a shortness of time." Sade reached for the ax that he had carried in with the wood. "I cannot tarry with you any longer, Marie. I have someone waiting to begin her new life, and she is eager." Sade swung back the ax and lowered the sharp edge quickly on Marie's neck. The head rolled away from the body, stopping short of the flagstones leading to the fireplace.

"She, too, is eager, *monsieur*." He smiled at Wil and shrugged when he received no response.

Blood soaked the oval rug and had splattered the old Barcalounger his father had used every night.

Wil looked down at his right hand and found that blood had marred his skin, round red dots blotching the blue and white of his veins and skin. The smell of his mistress's blood caused his breath to catch. By the time he noticed the odor of burning flesh, he found himself standing on the oval rug, lapping at his right hand.

"Feel free, *monsieur*. Don't be embarrassed. I will certainly not fight you for that crone's stale hostile blood." Sade made a magnanimous hand motion toward the headless body dripping its contents. "If you do not hurry, it will be wasted in the fibers of that disgusting cheap rug." Sade continued to poke at Marie's burning head, which melted in the fireplace.

The blackened flesh shriveled and layered itself onto the burning wood.

"I will take the skull bones with me, *monsieur,* and dispose of them when I am sure that they are ground into unformable ashes. You, *monsieur,* are wasting time." Briefly he used the poker to indicate Marie's headless corpse. "You will need the nourishment. I suspect it will take you a while to understand certain aspects of your new life, but here, allow me to guide you this once." Sade walked over to Wil and pressed the hot poker on Wil's left shoulder, driving him down onto his knees directly in front of the spilling blood. Sade left Wil there to drink his full.

Wil realized he was alone when the stickiness of Marie's blood made him feel dirty. Blood no longer flowed from between the body's shoulders. The staleness of blood, wool, and dirt emitted by the oval rug turned his stomach, and he lifted himself to his feet and returned to his father's bedroom to curl up next to the cold body.

"Profit from the fairest period in your life; these golden years of our pleasure are only too few and too brief. If we are so fortunate as to have enjoyed them, delicious memories console and amuse us in our old age. These years lost . . . and we are racked by bitterest regrets, gnawing remorse conjoins with sufferings of age and the fatal onset of the grave is all tears and brambles . . . But have you the madness to hope for immortality?

Philosophy in the Bedroom,
by the
Marquis de Sade

DOUGLAS

HALLOWEEN
THE
MAN
CLEGG

The New England coastal town of Stonehaven has a history of nightmares—and dark secrets. When Stony Crawford becomes a pawn in a game of horror and darkness, he finds that he alone holds the key to the mystery of Stonehaven, and to the power of the unspeakable creature trapped within a summer mansion.

___4439-0 $5.50 US/$6.50 CAN

Dorchester Publishing Co., Inc.
P.O. Box 6640
Wayne, PA 19087-8640

Please add $1.75 for shipping and handling for the first book and $.50 for each book thereafter. NY, NYC, and PA residents, please add appropriate sales tax. No cash, stamps, or C.O.D.s. All orders shipped within 6 weeks via postal service book rate. Canadian orders require $2.00 extra postage and must be paid in U.S. dollars through a U.S. banking facility.

Name_____
Address_____
City_____State_____Zip_____
I have enclosed $_____ in payment for the checked book(s).
Payment <u>must</u> accompany all orders. ☐ Please send a free catalog.
          CHECK OUT OUR WEBSITE! www.dorchesterpub.com

THE TAKING

DONALD BEMAN

What could Sean McDonald possibly have done to deserve what is happening to him? He was a happy man with a beautiful family, a fine job, good friends and dreams of becoming a writer. Now bit by bit, his life is crumbling. Everything and everyone he values is disappearing. Or is it being taken from him? Someone or something is determined to break Sean, to crush his mind and spirit. A malicious, evil force is driving him to the very brink of insanity. But why him?

_4202-9 $4.99 US/$5.99 CAN

Cold Blue Midnight

Ed Gorman

In Indiana the condemned die at midnight—killers like Peter Tapley, a twisted man who lives in his mother's shadow and takes his hatred out on trusting young women. Six years after Tapley's execution, his ex-wife Jill is trying to live down his crimes. But somewhere in the chilly nights someone won't let her forget. Someone who still blames her for her husband's hideous deeds. Someone who plans to make her pay . . . in blood.

___4417-X $4.99 US/$5.99 CAN

DRAWN TO THE GRAVE — MARY ANN MITCHELL

"A tight, taut dark fantasy with surprising plot twists and a lot of spooky atmosphere."
—Ed Gorman

Beverly thinks that she has found something special with Carl, until she realizes that he has stolen from her. But he doesn't just steal her money and her property—he steals her very life. Suddenly she is helpless and alone, able only to watch in growing despair as her flesh begins to decay and each day transforms her more and more into a corpse—a corpse without the release of death.

But Beverly is not truly alone, for Carl is always nearby, watching her and waiting. He knows that soon he will need another unknowing victim, another beautiful woman he can seduce...and destroy. And when lovely young Megan walks into his web, he knows he has found his next lover. For what can possibly go wrong with his plan, a plan he has practiced to perfection so many times before?

___4290-8 $4.99 US/$5.99 CAN

Dorchester Publishing Co., Inc.
P.O. Box 6640
Wayne, PA 19087-8640

Please add $1.75 for shipping and handling for the first book and $.50 for each book thereafter. NY, NYC, and PA residents, please add appropriate sales tax. No cash, stamps, or C.O.D.s. All orders shipped within 6 weeks via postal service book rate.
Canadian orders require $2.00 extra postage and must be paid in U.S. dollars through a U.S. banking facility.

Name_____
Address_____
City_____ State_____ Zip_____
I have enclosed $_____ in payment for the checked book(s).
Payment <u>must</u> accompany all orders. ☐ Please send a free catalog.

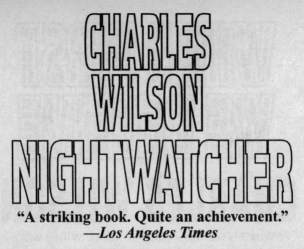

CHARLES WILSON

NIGHTWATCHER

"A striking book. Quite an achievement."
—Los Angeles Times

The staff of the state hospital for the criminally insane in Davis County, Mississippi, has seen a lot in their time—but nothing like the savage killing of Judith Salter, one of their nurses. And with three escaped inmates on the loose, there is no telling which of them is the butcher—or who the next victim will be. Even worse, as the danger and terror grow apace, the only eyewitness to the nurse's death—a psychopathic mass murderer—begins to reveal a fearsome agenda of his own.

___4275-4 $4.99 US/$5.99 CAN